BROKEN ALLIANCE

MARC DANIEL

Text copyright © 2020 Marc Daniel

All Rights Reserved

To my readers

Acknowledgements

Once again Amy and Katherine deserve my first thanks for their much-appreciated help as beta readers and their valuable feedback.
My next thank you goes to Sarah who provided the professional editing touch the manuscript required and for which my readers will no doubt be grateful.
Katherine hunted down the last remaining typos and deserves a round of applause for conducting this painstaking exercise with her usual dedication and professionalism.
My last thanks are for my wife, Jasmin, who once again put up with me through the writing of another book.

Cover Design: Ivan Zanchetta (bookcoversart.com)

Also by Marc Daniel

MICHAEL BIORN SERIES
Michael Biörn

Shadow Pack

Unholy Trinity

Close Enemies

Twisted Love

Broken Alliance

ETHAN ARCHER SERIES
The Girl Who Went Nowhere

OTHER
Into the Woods

Prologue

The prisoner heard the sound of heavy bolts sliding on the other side of the wall an instant before the cell door swung open to reveal the loathed silhouette of the warden.

"I hope you slept well, because you're going to need all your strength today," announced the warden.

What kind of twisted training program had the sadistic asshole come up with this time? In the grand scheme of things, it really didn't matter, yet the prisoner was curious.

His cellmate placed her hand on his cheek, a gentle caress he hadn't expected from the cute brunette. "Whatever it is, you can do this," she said, her eyes sinking into his. She looked worried.

He'd grown fond of her over the past few days, and he, too, worried for her. She wasn't defenseless, she'd proven it on more than one occasion, but in a place such as this one, it took more than decent fighting skills to survive.

"We don't have all day. Your public awaits," said the warden, tapping an imaginary watch on his wrist.

The prisoner walked out of his cell to find four guards waiting for him on the outside. One held the easily-recognizable remote controlling the collar around the prisoner's neck. The three others had their assault rifles trained on his chest.

"You'll be wearing a different kind of jewelry today." The warden was dangling an object the prisoner recognized immediately. It was one of those mind-control devices the bastards used to impose their will upon the praeternatural captives. They'd never made him wear one before, but he knew all about them.

"Don't worry, these things aren't nearly as bad as you imagine." The warden winked at him before sliding the diadem behind his head.

An instant later, the prisoner felt two needles penetrating his skin and burrowing deep into his flesh.

"Let's get moving. It's show time!"

The prisoner had no idea what that was supposed to mean, but the warden's enthusiasm didn't bode well.

After a short walk along the cell block's reinforced concrete walls, they exited the building through a door the prisoner had never used before. They then took a path through the woods that was closer to a deer trail than to anything man-made and soon arrived at their destination.

"So? What do you think of our arena?" The warden was beaming.

The arena in question looked nothing like the circuses of ancient Rome or their more modern version where butchers dressed like puppets tortured bulls for the delight of a cruel audience. There was no sand covering the ground, no bleachers surrounding the stage, just a twenty-foot-tall cage the size of a tennis court in the middle of a clearing. Sitting on cheap patio chairs five feet from the cage's iron bars were a dozen or so guards salivating in expectation of the spectacle to come. A woman sat alone beside an empty chair a few feet from them

The warden grabbed the prisoner by the arm and walked him to the door located on one end of the cage. "We found you a worthy opponent, so don't disappoint us. Who knows... a youngster such as yourself might even survive the fight." He punctuated his statement with a wink and shoved the prisoner inside the cage before slamming the door shut. "I almost forgot... Hand me your collar," he added as the metallic contraption slid open around the prisoner's neck.

The prisoner ripped the device from his neck and threw it to the ground.

"And now, all you have left to do is fight for me, Michael Biörn." The warden's smile spread from ear to ear.

It had been meant as an order and soon the diadem at the base of his neck would make sure Michael obeyed, but for now his eyes were trained on the opposite end of the cage where three guards were ushering in a mountain of a man.

The giant was nearly seven-foot-tall, and that wasn't even the troublesome part. The wind had covered his opponent's scent up to this point, but the man was now close enough for Michael to smell him. And his scent was all wrong.

When the mountain morphed into his beast an instant later, Michael realized how wrong he'd been.

Chapter 1

Three weeks earlier

Michael Biörn stood at the window of the elvish dwelling that had been his home for nearly three months. Despite the breathtaking beauty of *I-Naur-Tal,* the elvish city hidden in the heart of Montana's Gallatin National Forest, Michael felt restless. Aside from the daily walks he took with Sheila—and sometimes Olivia and Daka who lived three doors down—there was little to keep him busy. That left him with way too much time on his hands, time he spent brooding over the events of the past few months.

The third fragment from the Eye of the Phoenix was still safely kept by the faes in Lord Vaalt's castle, but that was just about the only positive thing to say about the current situation. Those responsible for the death of his friend, Bob Spencer, were still at large and continued abducting praeternaturals left and right. And according to Leka, the master and his followers had started wreaking havoc among the magical community.

Leka... the elf was almost the only contact the four refugees had with the external world, and the lack of action was seriously starting to weigh on Michael's mood.

Today was different, though. Today, he had something to look forward to. Ezekiel had announced his visit, and the wizard's presence would no doubt break the monotony of their painfully relaxing existence among the elves.

Michael turned away from the window as he heard Sheila stirring from the nap she'd been taking in a ludicrously comfortable armchair made of woven fronds expertly assembled onto a live sapling. He walked to the journalist and sat down beside her on the oversized armchair. Taking her in his arms, he buried his face in the crook of her neck, breathing in her enticing scent, just as he'd done every day for the past three months.

For this he was grateful. Before being forced to hide from their enemies, the longest stretch of time he'd been able to spend consecutively with Sheila had been a mere two weeks. But now the two of them had spent three entire months in each other's company, and going back to living fifteen hundred miles apart was likely to prove difficult. It wasn't something they needed to worry about at the moment, though; it wouldn't be safe for either one of them to return to their normal lives anytime soon.

They heard a knock on the door and an instant later found Ezekiel standing in the middle of their living room. The room looked nothing like a typical *living room*, but the term was fitting nonetheless. The walls made of breathing trees and the stream running at their feet literally made the place alive.

"Good afternoon, my dear. It's been too long," said Ezekiel, kissing Sheila's hand like a knight of old. "Michael," he added with a nod.

"Oh, I see. *I* don't get a kiss on the hand…"

The wizard's dark look quickly wavered, and he broke into a smile. "Are the two of you alone?"

"As alone as we get these days," said Michael, nodding towards the closed door at the end of the hallway.

"I take it Jason Parrish is still your guest?"

"He sure is…" Sheila sounded slightly frustrated.

"I don't know what to do with the guy," said Michael. "He's told us everything he knew—which wasn't a whole lot—but I can neither bring myself to *dispatch* him nor let him go," he added in a lower voice.

"He was just following orders, and technically he didn't harm anyone," explained Sheila. "He doesn't even know the actual location of the detention center where they keep the kidnapped praeternaturals."

"What does he know?" asked Ez, settling down in a seat made from the finest silk and which looked halfway between a hammock and a settee.

"He knows that his employer is a secret branch of the US government called Department of Supernatural Affairs, or DSA for short," said Michael. "It's been around for nearly two decades, according to him, but nobody he knows has worked there for more than a few months."

"Interesting... and doubtful." The wizard appeared contemplative.

"My thoughts exactly," agreed Michael. "The department is run by a woman Jason refers to as *The Director*. He's never met her in person, though; he's only talked to her on the phone or by video conference."

"You think this is relevant? Could that director be a front for someone higher profile in the government?"

"I suppose it's possible," replied Michael thoughtfully. "That would explain her anonymity."

"Maybe the woman Jason has seen in video conferences doesn't even exist. She could be computer-generated. You never know nowadays," chimed in Sheila. "At any rate, that doesn't put us any closer to figuring out who we need to go after to stop the witch hunt. Which means it's not safe for us to roam around in the outside world. In short, we're stuck in here." She hadn't complained directly to Michael about their current situation, but it was clear from her statement that she, too, was ready to get out of *I-Naur-Tal* and regain her freedom of movement.

"This forced retreat of yours may be a blessing in disguise, my child. Believe me, there are worse things than the DSA out there. The situation is getting pretty tense."

"Tenser than it was three months ago?" asked Michael, remembering the three-way battle they'd fought alongside the Eastern Covenant against the master's warlocks and a group of rogue vampires trying to overthrow Vulpe Zamfir.

"I'd have to say yes..." Ezekiel looked tired. "The master has been busy recruiting among magical folks, among wizards, even..."

"And he's been successful?" asked Sheila.

"In some instances. In others he hasn't, but he doesn't take no for an answer. Several wizards have mysteriously disappeared while others have been found murdered in their homes."

"Is the dark mage getting personally involved or does he still use warlocks to do his dirty work?" asked Michael.

"He has yet to show his face. I'm not too sure what he's waiting for to be honest. He's plenty powerful enough to take on anyone already. And let's not forget about these warlocks of his... another question mark."

"What do you mean?"

"What I mean, my young friend, is that warlocks don't grow on trees. He's apparently recruited a number of them already, and I'd like to know where he finds them."

"What about the dark mage himself? Where does he come from?"

"If we knew that, Michael, we'd be in a far better position."

"Why?" asked Sheila. "How would that help us?"

"If we understood where he comes from, we may have a better idea how to defeat him, my child. Because you see, there's something very wrong with this picture. If the master is truly a dark mage, as we suspect he is, he should still be a child. We only started sensing his presence a mere six months ago… As a matter of fact, he should be an infant!"

"Except that he clearly isn't," said Michael.

"Precisely! The master is a full-grown mage, and mages aren't born as adults. So where does he come from?"

"Could he come from another dimension? Another planet?" As a good journalist, Sheila had always been openminded, and the world she'd discovered since she'd met Michael had only encouraged this trait.

"I can't categorically rule it out, but I doubt it very much. This isn't the way things work. I've never heard of a wizard able to move through time or dimensions. Wizards are born in a specific location, usually with some vague recollection of their past existences, but nothing definite."

"But you've never encountered a dark mage before," replied Sheila, and even Ez was forced to admit that she had a point.

Chapter 2

Michael was still with Ezekiel when the werewolf scent reached his nostrils, a scent that was getting stronger by the second. He wasn't especially alarmed, though; he'd grown accustomed to this particular odor over the years.

An instant later the front door was pushed opened and Olivia entered the dwelling with Daka in tow. "Look who we found in front of the house!" she said, as Leka followed them in.

The high-born elf greeted Sheila and Michael before turning towards the wizard. "The council's meeting will begin in a few minutes, Ancient One."

"Thank you, Leka," replied Ezekiel.

"Do you have time for a quick drink?" Sheila asked the elf.

"I'll have a glass of your lemonade, if you have some ready."

Sheila smiled and walked to the small kitchen to fetch the elf's refreshment. Other than accompanying Michael on walks around the city and its surrounding woods, there wasn't a whole lot for the journalist to do in *I-Naur-Tal,* and she had turned to juicing as a new hobby. She'd experimented with a variety of exotic fruits, herbs and vegetables, but her hibiscus-infused lemonade remained everybody's favorite.

"What's this council about?" asked Michael.

"Some matter that needs to be discussed," replied the wizard.

"Would you care to elaborate?" askedMichael, watching Sheila return from the kitchen with Leka's lemonade.

Ezekiel hesitated a moment before answering. "I suppose I can expand on the topic a bit. I'm meeting with the elves to discuss how we intend to protect some magical artifacts we wouldn't like the dark mage to put his hands on."

"How many artifacts are we talking about?" asked Michael.

"Just a few. There are thousands of magical artifacts, but we only worry about the most powerful ones. Since the warlocks already tried to put their hands on the Eye of the Phoenix, it's likely they'll go after the others next. We therefore decided it might be a good idea to proactively protect these artifacts."

The Eye of the Phoenix was a fae artifact that had been broken into three fragments to prevent anyone from usurping its power. The three fragments had nearly been stolen by the warlocks, but thanks to Michael and Ezekiel's intervention, their enemies had only been able to steal two of the three pieces required for the artifact to display its full power. Even in two pieces, the artifact was already quite powerful since it bestowed the powers of any nearby fae upon the bearer, but such power was still a far cry from the artifact's full potential. With all three fragments reunited, the bearer could emulate the magic of any fae on the planet, regardless of where they stood. Fortunately for everyone, the third piece of the artifact was at the moment safely kept by the fae themselves.

"What other artifacts are you worried about?" said Michael.

Ezekiel scratched his chin before replying. "In addition to the Eye of the Phoenix, there are three artifacts worthy of concern."

"What do they do?" asked Sheila, clearly interested by this revelation.

"The Cloak of Amariel is a very unique garment. Its maker was a brilliant wizard of the second circle who lived thousands of years ago. The cloak shields whoever wears it from any magical attack or influence. It's a sort of *magical invincibility* cloak, if you will."

"So what you're saying," said Michael, "is that if the dark mage were to find this artifact, he would essentially be unkillable?"

Ezekiel smiled. "Unkillable by magic, yes, but there is a flip side to this coin. The shielding works both ways. The cloak also prevents the bearer from using magic on others. The wearer can still use magic on themselves but not on anyone else, which means they would be unable to cast spells on anyone."

"And where is that cloak at the moment?" asked Michael, who wasn't certain why the dark mage would have any use for an artifact inhibiting his own powers.

"No one knows… The cloak has been lost for over four millennia."

"That's reassuring…" Sheila looked anything but reassured.

"What are the two other artifacts we need to worry about?" asked Michael.

"One of them is an elvish artifact called the Healing Stone."

"Let me guess," said Michael. "It provides healing powers to its bearer?"

"Bingo," answered the wizard. "Whoever has the stone in their possession will enjoy healing abilities not unlike your own, Michael. It wouldn't bring someone back to life, but the bearer would heal from any wound in a matter of seconds."

"And do we know where *that* wonderful stone is, or is it lost, too?" asked Michael.

"It will soon be here," said Leka. "Its safekeeping has been entrusted to the elves of the Frozen Kingdom for the past thousand years, but given the gravity of the situation, the High Kings decided it would be safer here in *I-Naur-Tal*. In exactly four days from now, I'm to take custody of the stone at the entrance of the forest. We're confident that the stone will be safe until it enters the woods, but past that point my men will escort it all the way to *I-Naur-Tal*, just in case the city is being watched."

"What about the third artifact?" asked Olivia, who was leaning against a column made of braided vines beside Daka.

"The third one is called the Soul Catcher, and just like the Cloak of Amariel, it's a wizard artifact. The Soul Catcher's function is precisely described by its name. At the time of the bearer's death, his or her soul is captured by the artifact. The body dies, but the soul remains trapped within the magical object."

"That sounds horrible!" said Olivia.

"Yes and no," answered Ezekiel. "A learned practitioner can then use that stone to essentially resurrect the dead wizard. All they need to do is reinsert the soul into the dead body... or into a different body, for that matter."

"And do we know its location?" asked Michael.

Ezekiel seemed to hesitate an instant before answering. "Let's just say it's in safe hands."

Michael didn't press the issue; it was pretty clear the wizard wouldn't reveal any more about the stone's location. Ezekiel no doubt had his reasons—he always did.

Chapter 3

A dozen people were already sitting around the gigantic table by the time Ezekiel entered the room. With the exception of Tabitha, all were elves.

In addition to Leka, High King Dariel and High Queen Leanna, the elvish delegation was composed of representatives from the other four kingdoms. Just as Ezekiel had been expecting. What he hadn't expected, however, was the presence of Maya, Dariel and Leanna's daughter. The princess wasn't sitting next to her parents, though, but on the opposite end of the table beside the representative of the Frozen Kingdom.

Maya had been exiled to the Frozen Kingdom some years earlier after her association with a disreputable lot of vampires that had nearly forfeited both Ezekiel's and her father's life. This was the first time the wizard had seen her since her exile, and he couldn't help but wonder what her presence signified. Was she being pardoned? Was Dariel contemplating bringing her back home? Ezekiel felt uneasy at the idea. Maya held a strong grudge against Michael and having the two of them living within the walls of the same city seemed like a terrible idea.

"Welcome Ezekiel," said Dariel. "We were about to start."

The wizard sat down next to Tabitha, who was wearing a gorgeous pink sari for the occasion. Wizards could adopt whichever form they wished, but they typically chose to maintain a single physical appearance the majority of the time. While Ezekiel had adopted that of an elderly Caucasian man, Tabitha favored the looks of a woman of Indian descent in her mid-thirties. Since the death of Methuselah at the hands of the dark mage, Tabitha and Ezekiel were all that was left of the Second Circle.

Tabitha winked at Ez as Dariel started.

"Thank you for coming, my friends. As you know, we are living in dangerous times. The powers of the dark mage are unmatched, and his forces are growing. Our wizard friends present at this table informed us that the dark mage, who has previously found his followers among witches and sorcerers, recently started recruiting wizards of the Fourth and Third Circles."

The announcement was received with surprise and concern by the assembly.

"I think we can all agree that the growing threat represented by the dark mage is of great concern to any living being on this planet," resumed Dariel. "I've asked all of you to travel here today at Ezekiel's request, and I will now let him speak for himself."

"Thank you, Dariel," said the wizard. "And thank you to all of you for traveling long distances to be here today. As Dariel already mentioned, we're facing an unprecedented threat. One that requires extraordinary measures. Tabitha and I are in the process of unifying the wizards of the Third and Fourth Circles in a single front to oppose the enemy, but even if we succeed, it won't be enough. The dark mage is simply too powerful for us wizards to defeat him alone. That's why we're here today; the elves must join the battle if we want a chance to beat the dark mage." The elves were looking at each other intently but remained silent.

"Ezekiel isn't overstating the problem," interjected Tabitha. "The dark mage has already killed Methuselah, one of the most powerful wizards on this planet."

The revelation generated awe and consternation around the table as most of the elves had been unaware of the famed wizard's demise.

"Methuselah was every bit as strong as Ezekiel and me," continued Tabitha. "And yet he wasn't strong enough. The dark mage is the most serious threat the Second Circle has faced in recorded history." She had turned towards Ezekiel to pronounce those last words, and he nodded his agreement. "The dark mage is now at war with the wizards, but it's unlikely he'll be willing to share this planet with the elves once he is done dealing with us."

Ezekiel saw heads nodding, but no words were pronounced until Dariel himself intervened. "The Burning Kingdom has already rallied to the wizard's cause, but I cannot speak in your names, my friends. Each one of you will need to decide for themselves whether your kingdom will stand and fight beside us or remain neutral in the war that is about to fall upon this world. I know you'll probably need some time to think things over and we're not asking you for an answer today. But I beg you to consider the matter carefully, for it is of the utmost importance to the survival of our people."

"We've heard that the dark mage has found the three pieces of the Eye of the Phoenix. Are the rumors correct?" Ezekiel recognized the woman who'd asked the question as the High Queen of the Emerald Kingdom which extended across all of Central and South America.

"The rumors are partially correct," he replied. "The warlocks did, very briefly, seize the artifact, but we were able to retrieve one of the fragments. The dark mage only has two of the three pieces in his possession. The third one is held in safekeeping by Lord Vaalt."

"Isn't it likely the dark mage will go after other major artifacts next?" asked the same woman.

"We're already taking measures to prevent this," replied Dariel. "The Healing Stone will be moved from its current location and brought to this very city in the coming days. My daughter Maya will be in charge of assuring the transfer."

Dariel's last comment raised quite a few eyebrows. Tabitha gave a questioning look to her fellow wizard, but Ezekiel was as surprised as she was; he hadn't been informed of the decision. The reason Maya would be entrusted with such a crucial mission after her betrayal was far from obvious.

Ezekiel's eyes went to the young princess sitting at the end of the table, and the lovely blonde smiled at him in return. It was a friendly smile, but he disliked it all the same.

Chapter 4

Cameahwait had assembled the pack at his house. The old man knew he was near the end of his life, but it had been a long and fulfilling life. As a skinwalker, he'd spent it protecting humans from vampires, a job he and his pack were especially well equipped to tackle. Skinwalkers were immune to vampire magic and could therefore fight the undead plague on a more equal basis than most shifters. Unlike werebears, werewolves or any other type of werecreatures, skinwalkers were pretty easy to kill and didn't heal from mortal wounds the way their cousins did, but centuries spent fighting the bloodsuckers had made well-honed weapons out of them when it came to vampire control.

The party had been going on for well over an hour, and most of the ribs, hot dogs and other grilled delicacies had already vanished into his packmates' stomachs by the time Cameahwait raised his voice to request the attention of his audience. "My sons, my daughters, you all know that Daka has been living in hiding for the past few months because of the threat posed by those we now know as the Department of Supernatural Affairs."

The name provoked a few boos from the younger members of the crowd who'd already drunk more than their fair share of the beer kept in ice-filled coolers in the kitchen. But the silence quickly returned as Cameahwait resumed. "At first, we believed that the DSA's interest in Daka was due to his friendship with Olivia, a werewolf they had in their sights, but over the past few weeks there has been an increasing number of sightings of strangers within the borders of our reservation."

Cameahwait saw a few heads nodding in agreement. "I don't believe in coincidences and I'm more and more convinced these strangers are spies. Whether they're still after Daka and Olivia or are up to something else entirely, I do not know, but we must remain on our guard at all times."

In addition to the thirteen shifters that still lived in the reservation and could transform into their wolf alter-ego at a moment's notice, the audience counted numerous friends and spouses to the pack: thirty odd people all in all.

"We'll be ready if they come," yelled a young pup in his early twenties. The statement was received with encouraging cheers by a couple of his friends.

The kid had no idea what he was talking about, but Cameahwait gave him a benevolent smile. "I hope so, my young friend. I truly do."

And then the howl came, a warning from one of the sentries posted outside. A single howl couldn't communicate the nature of the threat, but a threat it was, there was no doubt about it.

In a split moment Cameahwait took the decision to move his forces outdoors where they would stand a better chance to escape if need be. At any rate, the darkness of the night would at least give his wolves, who benefitted from superior night vision, an advantage over their enemies, since the elder doubted they were dealing with vampires; the threat was most likely of a human nature. He had no evidence to support his guess, but he could feel it in the pit of his stomach and knew he was right.

An instant later fourteen wolves erupted out of the house, shortly followed by humans equipped with various makeshift weapons. Only three of them wielded firearms, guns that belonged to Cameahwait.

The elder saw nothing at first, but he could smell the enemy: humans, and a lot of them. A gas canister came flying from the darkness and landed at Cameahwait's feet, the irritating smoke filling the air around the wolves.

When the sounds of gunshots replaced the silence of the night, Cameahwait watched, powerless, as his brothers fell one after the other. The rifles that a moment earlier had been locked up in his gun safe were now lying on the ground beside the bodies of those who'd held them.

The wolves started running for the incoming line of men in black military fatigues but none of them reached their objectives. Strong nets, shot out of bazooka-looking devices, wrapped around their bodies, stopping them dead in their tracks.

Cameahwait was still standing, but he was one of the few; at least two thirds of his wolves had already been snared by the military-grade webs. He ran back to the house, hoping his remaining pups would follow him, and saw from the corner of his eye that a couple of them did. They needed to escape through a different route. This was the last thought that crossed his mind before the bullet entered the back of his head.

After a two-hour trek through the woods, Michael and Daka reached the trailhead parking lot to find it deserted.

"They aren't here yet," said Daka, looking worried. The skinwalker had knocked on Michael's door a little after one in the morning, and Michael had immediately known something terrible had happened.

The details were sparse at this point, but one thing was clear: the Shoshone pack had been attacked while gathering at Cameahwait's. Only two of Daka's packmates had managed to escape, and they'd immediately called Daka, who had in turn warned Michael. Olivia had insisted on coming with them, but Michael hadn't budged. He needed Olivia to stay with Sheila in the elvish city. He didn't want the journalist alone in the house with Jason Parrish. It was unlikely the man would be able to untie himself, but Michael wasn't willing to take the risk.

"Give them some time," said Michael. "It's a long drive from the reservation. They'll be here soon."

He found a knee-high boulder and sat down to rest his legs, but Daka was too restless to do the same. For over an hour Michael watched the skinwalker pace back and forth from the trailhead to the road leading to the parking lot.

They finally heard the sound of an approaching engine a little after five in the morning. A moment later, the headlights of a beat-up pickup illuminated the parking lot as the vehicle stumbled to a halt beside Daka. Two Shoshones jumped out of the truck and Michael recognized them immediately. The man was Nayati, a tall, lanky twenty-something. The woman, who was named Kimama if Michael's memory was correct, was roughly the same age. The two might even have been dating the last time he'd met them, but Michael could never be certain about that sort of thing.

Michael approached the three skinwalkers who were already in the midst of an animated discussion.

"What happened, exactly?" asked Daka.

"We were ambushed at Cameahwait's," answered the man.

"By whom?"

"They looked like military, they wore black fatigues. They were armed with assault rifles and bazooka-propelled webbings."

"Bazooka-propelled webbings?" repeated Michael

The man and the woman nodded in agreement.

That was new... The DSA didn't typically rely on nets for their kidnappings as far as Michael knew. They used collars to control their prisoners and weren't afraid to shoot them dead in order to safely place the devices around their victims' necks. So why were they switching their modus operandi? It was highly unlikely they were dealing with yet another outfit; the coincidence would be far too great. The only logical explanation was that the DSA knew the difference between a skinwalker and a werewolf. They'd known Cameahwait's pack wouldn't have survived being shot with assault rifles, hence the nets.

"Could you start from the beginning?" asked Michael.

The natives described how they'd been listening to Cameahwait's talk when the sentry posted outside the cabin had alerted them of the danger. They'd all rushed out to meet the enemy in the open and that's when things had gone south.

"I think they even had werewolves with them," said Kimama.

"Werewolves?" repeated Michael, uncertain he'd heard correctly.

"Yeah. We could definitely detect wolf scents that didn't belong to our pack. And since there is no other pack on the reservation, I'm pretty sure these were werewolves."

"So the whole pack has been captured?" asked Daka.

The man and the woman looked at each other a long moment before answering. "We're the only ones who managed to escape as far as we know... Most of our brothers were captured." They pronounced the last words uneasily, looking at Daka.

"Most?" asked Michael.

They nodded in unison.

"Most," repeated the woman, the look on her face clearly indicating she had more to say but was reluctant to do so.

"What's going on, Kimama?" asked Daka. "What aren't you guys telling me?"

"Cameahwait wasn't captured, Daka. They shot him in the head. Cameahwait is dead."

In the beam of the headlights, Michael saw the color drain from Daka's face. The young skinwalker took a few unsteady steps before sitting down on the ground in the middle of the parking lot. Michael knew there was nothing he could say that would ease the pain, and he decided to give the man a minute to absorb the shock. Cameahwait was like a father to the pack, but he was also one of Michael's dearest friends. And Michael had very few friends. Someone was going to pay for this.

"Were the wolves the only targets? Did they capture any of your human mates?"

"I don't think so," replied Nayati. "They shot a few, but I think they only targeted those who were armed. Two or three of our brothers had guns and they were the first ones to go down."

"How did you manage to escape?" asked Michael. He wasn't suspicious, just curious.

"We were keeping close to Cameahwait and when he suddenly retreated, we followed him. He must have decided that the battle was lost and meant to lead us around the house and take off from the north, but the bullet brought him down before he could complete the maneuver. We followed up on his idea and managed to slip into the night. They had the house surrounded, but their net wasn't tight enough and in the confusion of the battle I don't think they noticed us."

Michael remained silent a moment, thinking things over. "The two of you need a place to hide," he said finally. "I'll talk to the elves on your behalf and ask Dariel to give you sanctuary."

Nayati and Kimama thanked him as Daka rejoined the group. The shock had passed, and now he just looked incredibly pissed off. Michael knew exactly how he felt. The bastards were going to pay for this, the time for hiding was over. Now it was time to kick some ass.

There wasn't a whole lot Michael could do against the dark mage and his warlocks, but a bunch of humans wielding guns and nets were definitely not above his paygrade.

Of course, before Cameahwait could be avenged, they would need to locate the enemy… But Michael had an idea to draw the assholes into the open. An idea that just might work.

Chapter 5

Ezekiel materialized in the middle of the gardens surrounding Lord Vaalt's castle located two hours south of Paris. The faes had built an exact copy of the famous Chateau de Chambord thirty miles from the original and that's where Vaalt lived, surrounded by his court. The wizard could have materialized directly inside the castle, but it was difficult to arrive precisely in the middle of a room from a distance as great as the one he was traveling. He didn't want to surprise the fae leader too much, either. The last thing he needed was for the fae to perceive his visit as a threat or an offense.

As he walked the hundred yards separating him from the closest doors leading inside the building, he saw a woman of ample proportions running towards him. She looked to be at least three hundred pounds and was more round than tall, but that's what the fae wanted humans to see, the glamour she was projecting to mask her true form. But her magic wasn't strong enough to deceive Ezekiel who could see both the human form and the troll hiding behind it. He was surprised to see, however, that the troll was indeed a female. He hadn't encountered too many of those before.

"I'm here to meet with Lord Vaalt," said Ezekiel as the troll was ten yards from him, but the announcement didn't slow her down.

She held a large club in her hand which she began swinging at the wizard as soon as she got within range. Ezekiel dodged the blow with grace and a speed that looked perfectly implausible coming from a frail old man wearing a pointy hat and a gray cloak. The troll appeared surprised but quickly recovered and swung the club once again. Ezekiel grew tired of this game and neutralized his attacker with a spell that bound her to the ground. It was a harmless spell that would buy him enough time to get away and reach his destination.

A few more guards came towards him but, having learned from the troll's misfortune, they remained at a distance.

Ezekiel was met at the door by a high fae he'd met before and explained the purpose of his visit. This was the third time he'd come to see Lord Vaalt in the past four months, and it was getting easier to meet the ruler with every visit. This time it only took twenty minutes for Ezekiel to be shown inside the lounge where Lord Vaalt was having coffee.

"My respects, Lord Vaalt," said the wizard, bowing slightly. The fae responded with a slight nod. Through the open doors, Ezekiel could see the remnants of a copious lunch being cleared away by servants in an adjacent room.

"To what do I owe the honor of your visit?" asked Vaalt.

The statement was no doubt sarcastic, but it wasn't obvious based on his host's tone of voice.

"I came to check on the Eye of the Phoenix. Is it still safe?"

The fae gave him a toothy smile before taking a long sip of coffee. "It is safe," he said finally. "No one will come and get it here."

Ezekiel couldn't help but think that it was in this very castle that one of the fragments had disappeared not so long ago... He knew the fae had taken extraordinary precautions to prevent such a thing from happening again, though. Short of a full-on attack from the dark mage's forces, the artifact was indeed safe in Lord Vaalt's hands, which was the only reason the wizard had entrusted the fragment to the fae in the first place.

"That's good to hear," said Ezekiel, smiling lightly. "As you no doubt already know, our enemy is growing stronger by the day and seems to be amassing an army of supernaturals and praeternaturals."

"Praeternaturals?" asked Lord Vaalt, looking surprised.

"I'm talking about witches and sorcerers. We don't believe he's recruiting shifters at this time."

Lord Vaalt nodded. "Sorcerers and witches are something we can handle."

Ezekiel knew that the faes' magic was more than a match for second-grade witches and most sorcerers, but he was amused that Lord Vaalt seemed more concerned with shifters. He suspected Michael's last visit to the castle—a visit during which he'd killed the high fae's pet hydra—

probably had a lot to do with the newfound respect the fae appeared to have for werebeings.

"I come straight to you from a council where I met with the leaders of the five elvish kingdoms. All of them have allied with us, and we'll be fighting side by side against our enemies. I have come here today to make the same request of you. Will the faes join forces with us?"

Lord Vaalt gestured to one of his servants for more coffee. As two sprites lifted the kettle and carefully poured the steaming liquid into his cup, he turned a dark look towards Ezekiel. "This is the second time you come and ask for our help this year, wizard. We weren't interested in helping you the first time; what makes you think this time will be different? I haven't forgotten your treachery. I haven't forgotten how you robbed me from my right to punish the vampire who'd stolen from me."

Ezekiel inhaled deeply. "Lucy hadn't stolen anything from you, but this is beside the point. You know joining forces with us is the best option for your people. You are a good leader. You will make the right choice."

The fae laughed out loud, a humorless laugh. "We're more than strong enough to survive this little war of yours. But even if you were right, even if we found ourselves forced to take sides in this conflict which doesn't concern us, what makes you think we would choose your side?"

Chapter 6

Wes Thortan completed his daily review with a smile on his face. The cells were nearly full, all of them. Soon they would need to expand the detention center.

He felt little compassion for the misfits trapped behind the thick walls of Plexiglas. Monsters, that's what they were, all of them. These animals represented a threat to humanity itself. A threat he was proud to help eradicate, although there wasn't nearly enough eradicating going on to satisfy his killer instinct.

In another life, Wes had been part of the Delta Force, a member of the special forces elite. An assignment that had given him plenty of opportunities to do what he enjoyed the most: killing. But that was all behind him. He'd caught a bullet in the leg on his last mission and it had been the end of his special forces career. He now walked with a slight limp and a fancy cane, although the cane was more for show than a real need.

Wes had been pushing paper in an army office when the director had approached him and offered him a job "worthy of his skills." That's the way she'd put it.

As warden of the supernatural detention center or *detention center for monsters*, as he liked to think of it, he had carte blanche to run the facility the way he pleased and could do whatever he wanted with his prisoners... almost. He couldn't choose which freaks lived and died, and this bothered him greatly.

His prisoners weren't technically human and didn't fall under any laws. Killing them was therefore not a crime, but nonetheless he'd been explicitly forbidden to do so. He could still shoot them to pieces, stab them, hang them or do anything else to them that would temporarily stop their lives... But beheading, the only thing that would stop the monsters from coming back to life, was off limits. The director alone held that right.

He'd only met the woman in person once, the day she'd offered him the job, but she'd left a lasting impression on him. The pretty brunette looked to be in her early forties and was exactly his type, but only on a physical level. He liked his women submissive, and that one was anything but submissive. There was no question she was in charge.

The precious few times she'd done him the honor of video conferencing with him had been enough to give Wes an idea of what the woman was about. Strong-willed was a nice way of putting it... She'd probably clawed her way to the top of the hierarchy.

In truth, he knew next to nothing about his boss. He had no idea where she spent her days—probably some god-awful office in the basement of the Pentagon—and was equally clueless about her reporting structure. Was she answering to some general... to a civilian? He had no idea. The program was so hush hush that she might be answering to the President himself.

On his way back to his office, Wes stopped a moment in front of the cell holding the latest batch of recruits. They were all wolves, but these had been placed in a separate enclosure, not with the general werewolf population. He had no idea why, though. Once again the orders had come directly from the director, and he hadn't been given any explanation.

The wolves looked fairly young. With the exception of a couple probably in their thirties, the rest appeared to be in their mid-twenties. Ten of them, an even number. There should have been more but one had died in the operation and a couple had managed to escape. Or so they thought... In truth they'd been allowed to escape. The whole operation had been an advertising campaign. And for an advertising campaign to work, one needed advertisers... Someone to spread the word...

Satisfied that everything was under control, the warden walked the three hundred yards of hallway that separated this particular cell block from his office and locked the door behind him. He opened a drawer of the massive mahogany desk that stood in the middle of the room and took out a flask of bourbon. It was only noon, but what the hell. He unscrewed the flask and took a long swallow just as his computer chimed on the desk. He hurriedly replaced the flask into the drawer and sat down in front of his screen to answer the call.

"Good morning, Ma'am," he said, as the face of the director filled the screen.

"I hear you have new guests."

"That's correct, Ma'am, they arrived only a couple hours ago. Ten wolves. All placed in a separate cell as you instructed. But we're starting to run out of space, this was the only cell left empty. The next lot will have to share space with others." He couldn't help but smile as he pronounced the words. Mixing freaks of different types generally led to bloody confrontations of a very entertaining nature. Sometimes, he placed the freaks in the wrong cell just for fun.

The guards always managed to stop the fight before somebody got *permanently* killed, but accidents did happen, and if one of these days a werewolf happened not to walk out of the lion's den... it probably wouldn't be the end of the world.

"Don't worry about space. You'll soon have all the real estate you can wish for," said the director.

This was the first time he'd heard of such news; what did she have in mind? Were they going to build more buildings? If that were the case it would be a while before new cell space became available; he had yet to see a single construction crew. He asked no questions, however. He'd learned that the director typically volunteered all she was willing to share. His follow-up questions typically remained unanswered. Still, he'd have liked to know why these wolves were to be kept separate from the other ones. What would happen if he added them to the general population?

As if reading his mind, the director asked, "You know that these wolves were captured with nets, correct?"

"Yes, Ma'am, I've been told."

"Do you know why that is?"

He shook his head.

"That's because if we'd used the usual technique of shooting them to place collars around their necks, these particular wolves wouldn't have survived."

Wouldn't have survived? What did she mean by that?

"These aren't werewolves," she continued. "These particular freaks are called skinwalkers. They aren't your garden variety supernaturals. They can shift into their animal form in the blink of an eye. Effortlessly and painlessly. But they're just as mortal as you and I. We can't use the same collars we use on the others, either; the devices wouldn't work on them. Bottom line, they cannot be shot! Is that understood?"

"Yes, Ma'am, very clear. May I ask why we brought them in?"

"You mean instead of just dispatching the threat?" the director asked.

He didn't reply but that was exactly what he'd meant.

"Because for our plan to work we need bait. If we want to draw the bear out of his lair, he needs to have something to come after. The bear is much more likely to show up for a rescue mission if there is something to rescue."

Wes wondered what was so special about that bear. He was a tough cookie for sure, but for the director it almost seemed personal. He could see where she was going with her bait idea, but he couldn't help thinking that killing those skinwalkers would have been just as efficient to get the bear's attention. Whether he came for vengeance or for rescuing his friends made little difference to them; all they needed was for Biörn to show his face.

Chapter 7

Dariel readily granted asylum to Kimama and Nayati, and the two had arrived at Michael and Sheila's late in the afternoon. The small elvish dwelling was a bit too cozy to comfortably accommodate their new guests, but this was only temporary. The elvish king was arranging for another house to be freed to put them up. A good thing, too, because Michael could tell that Sheila wasn't particularly pleased with the idea of sharing their home with two more strangers. Jason Parrish was clearly more than enough for the journalist's taste. She'd tactfully suggested to Michael that Daka's packmate might be more comfortable staying with Daka and Olivia, but Michael had pointed out that the couple's accommodation was even smaller than their own and Sheila had dropped the issue.

No one beside Michael could have guessed the journalist's true feelings, though. She acted as a perfect hostess, smiling and offering refreshments to their guests gathered in the living room. As Olivia and Daka had joined the party, every single seat was occupied.

Sheila had served their guests a snack of berry pie, which everyone had appreciated. Though a few more pies would have been necessary to satisfy the hunger pangs Michael felt in the pit of his stomach, for once he'd been smart enough not to voice his feelings.

Sheila served another round of lemonade and turned to Michael. "Should I offer some to our other guest?" she asked, nodding towards the closed door behind which Jason Parrish was kept prisoner.

Michael considered the question a moment before answering affirmatively.

As Sheila entered the prisoner's room, Daka asked, "And how many praeternaturals do you expect to be at that meeting?"

"Probably eight or nine," answered Michael.

"What kind are they?" asked Olivia.

"Most of them are mountain lions, but there will be a couple of eagles, too."

"I didn't realize you had so many friends," teased Oliva.

Michael gave her a look. "There are many things you don't know about me, young lady. You don't get as old as I am without making a few acquaintances."

"So is the meeting confirmed for tomorrow?" asked Kimama.

"Yes, I already received replies from most of the attendees. I should hear back from the others later this evening."

"Where is the rendezvous point?"

"We'll meet at Lava Lake at nightfall," answered Michael.

"And you think you'll be able to convince them to join our cause?" asked Daka.

"I'm pretty sure they won't turn down an opportunity to go after the DSA. Jason Parrish and his friends believe they can use praeternaturals to hunt us down? Now it's time to show them the other side of the equation. My *friends* are some of the most dangerous praeternaturals on the continent."

As Michael pronounced the last sentence, Sheila walked out of the prisoner's room and closed the door behind her.

Jason was lying in bed, as he had for most of the past three months. The first week of his captivity had been the roughest, but to be honest his interrogation at the hands of Michael could have been a lot more painful. Luckily for him, his jailer didn't believe in torture, but Michael's questions had still left a few bruises on the prisoner's face.

Had Jason actually known the information Biörn was after, he would have probably spilled the beans. Fortunately for the DSA, Jason truly didn't have answers to his captor's questions. He simply wasn't privy to the director's secrets. He'd never been to the detention center hidden in the heart of Nevada and had absolutely no idea where the facility was.

The most painful part of his captivity was the boredom. Aside from a daily thirty-minute walk with Biörn as babysitter, Jason wasn't getting much exercise. His muscles hadn't atrophied too much yet and he could still move unassisted, but he'd lost at least ten pounds since his capture. In all fairness, the food he was given by his jailers was quite tasty, but the amount was often lacking.

He needed to get the hell out of there. He needed to rejoin the world he understood, the world where elves couldn't be seen walking the streets of a gorgeous but strange city. A world where journalists didn't date bears. He simply couldn't take it anymore and felt like he was going crazy.

Sheila, the bear's girlfriend, had been kind enough to bring him some lemonade a moment earlier, a very rare treat, and through the open door he'd plainly heard the discussion Biörn was having with his guests. This was information the director would pay good money to have. Unfortunately, there was no way for him to pass it on to anyone on the outside and no way to escape.

These people knew something about knots, he could barely move his fingers. Though on second thought… it seemed like Sheila hadn't tightened the knots as much as she usually did. His fingers could definitely move a lot more freely than usual. Maybe there was hope after all.

Chapter 8

There was no clock in the room that had been Jason's cell for the past three months, but he estimated the time to be nearing midnight. He could hear Biörn snoring loudly in the bedroom next door. Sheila was quiet but was most likely asleep as well.

He didn't know what the two had been celebrating with their friends, but based on the commotion, there had been a lot of drinking involved. Maybe his luck was finally turning…

After working tirelessly on his bonds for two hours, he'd finally managed to free his hands. Freeing his feet had been a triviality after that. Fearing his jailers might come to check on him before heading to bed, he'd kept the loose rope wrapped around his legs and feet, but the precaution had been in vain. They'd been so busy partying that they'd even forgotten to bring him his evening meal. He hadn't minded at all, though; the adrenaline pumping through his veins gave him all the strength he needed for the task at hand. This was his chance to escape—a better opportunity would never come.

He walked to the window and pulled it open. A moment later, he was carefully moving through the streets of *I-Naur-Tal*, a shadow among shadows. He'd been on enough supervised walks with Biörn to know his way around the city, but the precise location of the exit was unknown to him. How did one get outside the wall protecting the elvish town? He doubted there would be signs, so he had to pay close attention. Everything was strange in this city. Put together, his strolls along the city's streets amounted to a few dozen hours, but given the size of the place, that wasn't nearly enough to learn its secrets.

He ducked behind a building at the sounds of footsteps and watched two elves strolling by a moment later. They showed no sign of having noticed him and soon disappeared around a corner. He let out a sigh of relief.

He had to admit that the elves knew how to build; their architectural style was unique but breathtaking. Everywhere the constructions were in perfect harmony with the woods, as if the architects had built the houses around the constraints of Mother Nature instead of bulldozing their way to an easier solution. No tree had been chopped down; no stream of water had been rerouted. Everything had grown organically around nature.

After two hours of fruitless search for an exit he'd likely never find, Jason heard voices coming to his right. One of them was familiar to him. It belonged to the elf by the name of Leka, one of Biörn's few recurring visitors. He dropped flat to the ground behind a shrubbery of aromatic plants and watched Leka and two females walk right in front of him. They were heading towards two trees growing a foot apart from each other. Their trunks were massive, easily three-foot-wide and sixty-foot-tall. He saw the elves squeezing their way between the trees before suddenly disappearing. At that instant, Jason knew his search was over. This was the exit, or at least one of them, and he'd walked right past it a dozen times… Cautiously, he waited a few minutes, but the elves never came back, and he headed for the portal.

Jason estimated three hours had gone by since he'd exited the elvish city, but he still had no idea whether he was heading in the right direction or what the right direction was even supposed to be. He'd intended to carefully mark the location of the city in his mind, but he wasn't certain he could get back to it after this little midnight trek in the woods.

He heard the sound of running water and picked up the pace. He hadn't had anything to drink since Sheila's lemonade ten hours earlier and felt dehydrated to the core. Spring nights were rarely warm in Montana, but the constant movement kept him comfortable.

He stumbled upon a small mountain stream a moment later and washed his hands in the ice-cold water before cupping the deliciously clear liquid to his mouth. The water was so cold that it hurt as it went down to his stomach. He was careful to sip slowly the second time around.

It took him nearly five minutes to drink his fill at a pace that minimized the discomfort to his body. He then granted himself another five-minute break before getting back on his feet.

He followed the stream in the direction of the current as it moved down the mountain. Small streams run into bigger streams, and bigger streams eventually into rivers. So, by following the water, he was bound to get to a road at some point, and from there he'd find the nearest city.

The sun had been up for several hours by the time his plan finally bore fruit, and he stumbled upon a black-top road. It was another twenty minutes before one of the few passing cars stopped to pick him up.

"Where are you heading?" asked the driver, a man in his early fifties.

"To the nearest town."

"That would be Bozeman. What happened to you?"

"I got lost in the woods. I was planning to go on a couple-hour hike but that was two days ago…"

"Gee-whiz! Thank God you're alright!"

Jason Parrish smiled at the man, nodding agreeably though he doubted God had anything to do with it.

"Do you live in town?" asked the man.

"No, I'm just visiting the region. I'm staying at a motel on the edge of the city," he lied.

Thirty minutes later, the man dropped his passenger off in front of the hotel he'd indicated, and Jason walked right in.

The clerk behind the desk didn't look a day over nineteen. "How may I help you?" she asked, unable to hide her surprise at his unkempt appearance.

"May I please use your phone? Had a horrible day. I was hiking and lost my backpack with my phone, wallet, everything. I need to have a friend come and pick me up."

"Sure, go ahead," she said, placing the phone on the counter. He dialed a number he knew by heart as the clerk's cell phone started ringing on her desk. She picked it up and disappeared in the back office. This was an unexpected break. Now that he had no witness to worry about, the situation would be a lot easier to explain to the director.

She answered on the third ring. "Hello?"

"This is Parrish."

"Where have you been?"

Jason explained what had happened to him and the director listened patiently to his account.

"Do you think you'd be able to find that city again, Jason?" she asked, the eagerness clear in her voice.

"It's hard to say, but I believe I might."

Chapter 9

Demetra's invisibility spell was powerful enough to hide her from any vampire on the planet. That included Vulpe, who was fighting a werejaguar thirty feet in front of her in the gardens of the Eastern Covenant's Transylvanian castle. The night was dark, but she had no problem following the action. A dozen vampires surrounded the beast, cutting off any potential escape route, while the leader was fighting it one on one.

The warlock wondered where the vampires had stumbled upon this rare find; a werejaguar wasn't a common sight, especially in Romania... She had little doubt the vamps had imported the beast, but for what purpose? She knew vampires enjoyed using enthralled shifters as pets—or more precisely as bodyguards to keep watch during the day while the vamps slept—but this one didn't look enthralled to her.

The vampire elder and the cat were cautiously circling one another, staring each other down. The cat pounced, but Vulpe avoided the attack effortlessly and responded with a powerful jab to the animal's midsection. The cat groaned in pain before landing on his paws and immediately spinning around to face his enemy. He was on Vulpe in a flash, and once again the elder blocked his opponent's attack, albeit not as easily as the time before, and thrust his sharp nails into the beast's neck. Blood spurted from the open wound, but the jaguar immediately started healing. A few seconds later, the blood had slowed to a drip and it wasn't more than a minute before the wound had disappeared altogether.

The fight went on for another ten minutes before the vampire finally put an end to it by eviscerating the cat with his bare hands.

"This one has spirit," said Vulpe to the other vamps who'd been watching the fight from a distance. "It will make a great addition to our army. Put him in chains. Tomorrow we'll enthrall him."

Demetra chose that moment to drop her invisibility spell and reveal herself to the vamps. Three of them immediately rushed her but she blocked their attack with a flick of her wrist that sent a shock wave rushing towards the bloodsuckers. The invisible wall stopped them in their tracks and sent the three rolling to the ground.

"I'm not here to fight you, Vulpe. I'm here to talk," said Demetra.

Vulpe raised a hand to order his men to stand down, but by the look on his face, he clearly wasn't convinced.

"I know you, don't I?" The question was rhetorical; the elder had perfectly recognized her.

"We've met before," she answered. Only a few months had passed since Demetra and the now dead Lotar had fought Vulpe and his men inside the elder's winter quarters in southern France. Lotar had been killed by Ezekiel during the offensive and Demetra had managed to get away carrying two pieces of the Eye of the Phoenix, so she was pretty sure the vamps weren't about to forget her face.

"Did you come back to return what you stole from me?" asked Vulpe.

"From what I recall, it's your brother who stole from you. I just stole from him in turn... And, no. This isn't the object of my visit."

"Then what are you doing here?"

"I came to offer you a truce."

"A truce?"

"Well, maybe truce isn't the right word. How about an alliance?"

Vulpe laughed. It sounded forced but the intent was clear. "An alliance, and with whom do you want me to ally?"

"With my master, the most powerful warlock of all time."

"Is that so?"

"It is. Only a few months ago my master singlehandedly defeated a wizard of the Second Circle without breaking a sweat. And our forces have been growing day by day since. So the only question you should ask yourself is whether you want to fight on the winners' side or with the losers."

Vulpe seemed to consider the matter a moment before answering. "We don't need to pick sides. Your quarrel is of no concern to us. Whether your master or the wizards win in the end makes absolutely no difference. As long as you stay out of our business, we have no quarrel with you. But for future reference, the next time you plan on asking someone to ally with you, I'd suggest you refrain from robbing and trying to kill them first. Now, you have exactly ten seconds before I order my men to tear you to pieces."

The threat sounded authentic and maybe with enough time and sufficient reinforcements the vampires would have eventually defeated her, but the dozen individuals surrounding her presently posed no threat whatsoever to Demetra. Out of spite, she stared the elder down while slowly counting to ten, and then she stared at him a while longer, daring him to attack, before finally vanishing into thin air.

Chapter 10

Michael, Leka and the thirteen elves accompanying them made it to the rendezvous point around 9 AM. They were a bit early, a full day ahead of the supposed meeting as a matter of fact, but they couldn't afford to be late. On the contrary, they needed to be here well in advance to prepare the terrain for the ambush.

The gathering of lethal praeternaturals they'd discussed the night before at Michael's cabin had been pure fiction, a misinformation campaign targeting Jason Parrish. What Jason's friends would actually find when they'd show up to crash the party was an army of elves the DSA jerkoffs would be utterly unprepared for.

Leka gave orders and his men spread out around the area, climbing trees faster than Michael could have ever imagined. Within minutes the elves had completely disappeared, absorbed by the surrounding vegetation. Hidden in the high branches, they waited patiently, their bows ready for whatever would come. These were some of Leka's best marksmen. A regular sniper wouldn't know what to do in a heavily wooded area—too many trees for a bullet to find its target—but the elves didn't seem impaired by the evergreen giants. Michael hadn't seen them miss their mark. It was as if the elves' arrows curved around the trees in pursuit of their targets. The DSA men wouldn't know what hit them.

"Are you certain they will show?" asked Leka.

"I'd be surprised if they didn't," answered Michael. "We made sure Jason's door was wide open. There is no way he didn't overhear our conversation. The man's a trained spy, for God's sakes. This was a bonanza for him."

"You don't think he might smell a rat? The same day he gets this kind of information he manages to escape from his bonds…"

"He might," acknowledged Michael. "But that's a chance we have to take. It still took him a few hours to break loose from his bonds. It's not as if Sheila conveniently forgot to tie him back up. She was just a bit more careless with the knots than she should have been. That's all…"

"I hope you're right," said Leka.

They settled side by side behind a boulder, waiting for the enemy. They still had nearly ten hours before the advertised nightfall rendezvous. Michael expected Jason's friends to show up well ahead of the meeting, though. They needed time to prepare their own ambush, after all.

Two hours went by without anything happening.

"Are you certain that Jason was able to communicate with his hierarchy? They may not even know about this supposed meeting…" said Leka.

"Ezekiel confirmed Jason had relayed the info."

Leka looked at him with interest. "What do you mean? When?"

"I mean after Jason took his sweet time to exit the city, obviously…"

"Tell me about it!" interrupted Leka. "I'm the one who had to point the portal out to him. He'd still be walking around aimlessly if we hadn't shown him the way."

Michael smiled. "As I was saying, Ezekiel didn't only place a trace on Jason, he bewitched him to act as a spy for us."

Leka looked at Michael with surprise. "He did what?"

"Jason has no idea, but he is now spying for Ezekiel. Whatever he sees or hears, Ezekiel will too. As soon as Jason returns to the DSA's base, we'll know its location, and from there we'll take the fight to the enemy and rescue Daka's packmates."

Leka appeared shocked by the revelation. Michael himself had been very surprised when Ezekiel had told him about this specific curse. Up to that point, he'd had no idea a human could be bewitched that way. He'd asked the wizard if the same curse could be used on praeternaturals and Ez had answered that it depended on the praeternatural. That was spoken like a true politician.

"So, what are we doing here then? It sounds like we'll soon know where to find them no matter what?" said the elf.

"Well, for one thing it wouldn't hurt to take down a few of their men before we decide to launch an offensive on their main compound."

Leka nodded at the logic and Michael continued. "And we're going to need to consider the fact that if Jason hadn't been told about the location of the detention center up to now, he may not be brought out there at all… In which case we'll need to painstakingly follow his progress clue by clue until we have enough information to go up the chain of command and identify individuals higher up in the food chain."

Another two hours went by without the slightest sign of action, then four, then five.

"I'm starting to wonder if they're going to show up," said Leka.

Michael was wondering the same thing. As a matter of fact, he'd been wondering this for some time already. Ezekiel was gone, and at the moment they had no way to know where Jason Parrish was. This was a problem… They had no way of telling whether the enemy would actually show up.

"If Jason was able to talk to his boss and no one comes tonight, that means they didn't take the bait. They must have suspected a setup," said

Leka.

Michael was forced to agree with his friend. Dusk was still a few hours away and all wasn't lost yet, but things weren't looking good.

Chapter 11

Ezekiel had been walking through the Australian outback for nearly two hours. Having traveled all the way from France, the trip had taken a toll on his magical reserves, and he hadn't been able to teleport all the way to Tabitha's location.

It was far from his first visit to the continent, but the wild landscape of the outback never ceased to amaze him. The vegetation was sparse and few were the trees taller than a couple of feet, but the wild eucalyptus, acacias and desert oak trees towered as testimony of the existence of life on this otherwise bare land. Smaller but no less evident signs of life could be found in herds of wild camels roaming the steppes. The camels had been brought in from Afghanistan and India in the nineteenth century during the colonization of the continent, but with the arrival of automobiles the animals had been released into the wild, where, left to their own devices, they had thrived and prospered.

The wizard spotted a couple of kangaroos in the distance. The marsupials were common in the outback and these weren't the first specimens he'd seen today.

He finally reached his destination and found Tabitha standing, head bowed, under a large acacia. Ezekiel knew the wizard had detected his presence, but she showed no sign of interrupting her meditation. He went to stand beside her, and he, too, bowed his head in respect over Methuselah's grave.

They remained there in silence for a long moment.

"How was your trip?" asked Tabitha eventually.

"Uneventful."

"That's good to hear. Uneventful is a privilege these days."

Ezekiel didn't disagree; these were troubled times, to say the least. "So, where was he killed?"

"I'll show you," answered Tabitha, already leading the way. They walked a half mile to a small creek bordered with river red gums, a variety of eucalyptus endemic to Australia. "I found him under this tree," she said, pointing at a massive trunk.

"How long had he been dead?"

"I'd say about an hour."

Ezekiel nodded contemplatively.

"At least that's how long it took me to reach him after I received his distress signal," she added.

"I never received it," said Ezekiel.

"I know. I think he was too weak to send one to you, knowing you were so far away. He was probably too busy battling for his life as well…"

Ezekiel had no doubt on that point and the thought sent a shiver down his spine. A wizard of the Second Circle hadn't been defeated in battle for over two millennia and Methuselah was one of the most powerful wizards of the Second Circle Ezekiel had ever met.

Ezekiel wasn't afraid for his own life, but he feared for his friends and for the lives of the countless individuals who would perish if the dark mage wasn't stopped.

"It's a good thing he had enough strength to contact you. Otherwise, we may have never found his body and could have spent the rest of our days wondering what had happened to him."

It was Tabitha's turn to nod in agreement

"Did he leave a message?" asked Ezekiel.

Tabitha shook her head. "At least none that I found, but I was in shock and didn't look very hard. On second thought, I don't recall looking at all…"

Ezekiel understood the oversight. Finding Methuselah's dead body must have been such a shock, Tabitha couldn't have been thinking straight.

"Well, it's been a few months, but we could search the area."

They didn't waste any time looking for an obvious message, such as a tree bark carving or words traced on the riverbank. Instead they relied on magic to reveal any hidden message that Methuselah could have left behind. The two spread out, each whispering incantation spells along the riverbank.

The first ten minutes led to no discovery and Ezekiel was starting to despair when Tabitha called to him. He hurried to her side. There, on a boulder about two feet wide, was a message written in gold letters. There was little doubt the words had been left by Methuselah; the spell Tabitha had used to reveal it had been a creation of the deceased wizard himself. No one else could have hidden the message with this very spell.

"What does it mean?" asked Tabitha.

Ezekiel read the words for the third time, but he had no answer. Part of the message was a set of coordinates which, if he wasn't mistaken, corresponded to a location somewhere on the Australian continent, pretty close to where they were as a matter of fact. "I suppose he wants us to go there," he said, feeling like he was stating the obvious.

"What about this?" Tabitha pointed at the rest of the message which was composed of a single word: AMARIEL.

Tabitha had only been roaming this earth for a couple thousand years and was therefore too young to have known the woman, but Ezekiel remembered the wizard vividly. Amariel had been a wizard of the Second Circle whom Ezekiel had first met five thousand years ago in ancient Egypt. She'd been dead for nearly four millennia, though. Killed in a coward's ambush by two powerful warlocks. Ezekiel had hunted down those responsible for her death himself and had taken more pleasure than he should have in dispatching them.

No matter how hard he tried, Ezekiel couldn't understand what Amariel's name was doing written on this boulder. What was it supposed to mean? What had Methuselah been up to?

Ezekiel and Tabitha cautiously approached the shack. The wooden structure looked about to collapse. There was no magical energy coming from it, so they pushed the front door wide open.

Having no idea what to think of Methuselah's message, they'd decided to start by checking the set of coordinates he'd left them.

They stepped inside the cabin, Ezekiel's staff in hand ready for action. It only took the two a minute to convince themselves that the cabin was empty. At least empty of anyone living. The decomposed body in the corner of the room was definitely human, though.

"Do you know what this is?" asked Tabitha, pointing to the ground where glyphs had been drawn in blood.

Ezekiel nodded. "I recognize the language, but I've never practiced it."

"Can you read the glyphs?"

"Some of them... The whole thing looks like a localization spell. It would seem the dark mage was searching for something."

"Or someone..." said Tabitha.

"I don't think so. I believe this spell can only be cast for magical objects."

"So our assumption was correct. The dark mage is looking for other artifacts."

"Or maybe that's what he used to locate the Eye of the Phoenix in the first place; we don't know how long these glyphs have been here. Based on the state of the skeleton in the corner, it's probably been some time. I suspect it belonged to a witch or a sorcerer of some sort. The dark mage probably used the poor soul's blood to cast his spell."

"Can you feel this?" asked Tabitha.

"I can."

There was a very faint magical vibration in the air. Was the dark mage approaching? That wouldn't be good. Even the two of them together had little chance of defeating the dark mage. But the vibration didn't grow in intensity; it remained faint, almost lost in the background.

"Could it be residual magic?" asked Tabitha.

"It could be, in which case it only confirms what we already knew. To leave such a signature long after he's gone, the dark mage's powers must be..." Ezekiel didn't finish his sentence. The implication was obvious.

Chapter 12

Demetra was walking through the makeshift streets of the favela wondering why the master always picked the crummiest places to live in. She turned around a moment to take in the view of the city. All in all, Rio de Janeiro was a pretty decent place. The statue of El Christo Redentor stretched its arms over the city, the sugar loaves erupted out of the gorgeous blue water... But the city was surrounded with favelas—the local ghettos where the poorest fraction of society was forced to live due to the exorbitant price of local real estate—and so of course the master had decided to take up residence in one of them.

The houses lining the streets of the slum were made of all sorts of repurposed scrap materials. No two dwellings looked alike, but they were all eyesores.

The favelas had a reputation for violence, and tourists were strongly advised to keep out. Five minutes after Demetra had crossed the invisible border delineating the ghetto, a gang of six men in their late teens fell upon her. She smiled at them amiably. The master awaited her report; she had no time to waste with those humans. They spoke to her in Brazilian Portuguese, and although she understood the language perfectly, she didn't bother replying. They wanted her money, and since she had none, she had no reason to stop either.

She continued walking as two of them took out switch blade knives to which she paid no heed. When a third one slapped her on the cheek, she felt the blow but opted for a measure of patience towards the rude individual and kept going. But when the same man decided to punch her, his fist met a face that was as hard as concrete, and she heard his knuckles crack under the impact a split second before his scream of pain reached her ears. She then grabbed him by the throat and shoved him against the makeshift wall of a house hard enough that he went through it and landed in the middle of the wood pallets that passed for furniture. His friends got the message and took off in all directions.

Demetra reached the master's house a few minutes later, wondering once more what they were doing here. The master's need for secrecy and constant hiding was beyond her understanding.

She spoke the words to disarm the magical force field protecting the dwelling and stepped inside. She was surprised to see that the master had actually made some effort to redecorate. From the outside, the shack looked like every other one on the block—a pile of garbage—but the inside was spacious and tidy, with real furniture. Nothing fancy but actual wooden chairs, a table and a couple of comfortable-looking beds.

"Give me your report, Demetra. What news do you have?"

"Things are progressing, Master. Another thirty witches and seventeen sorcerers have joined our cause this week."

The master nodded, pleased. "What about the wizards, did you make any progress?"

Demetra shook her head. "Not really. Maybe one will turn this week, but I cannot guarantee it. So far we've only been able to turn five wizards of the Fourth Circle and one of the Third Circle."

"And how many did you kill?"

"About three times that number."

The answer appeared to satisfy the master.

"Shifters are also giving us some problems, they don't seem eager to join our cause," continued Demetra.

"It matters little. Whether they're willing or not, they'll join us."

"I'm actually returning from the Eastern Covenant—"

"Please do tell. How did that go?" interrupted the master, staring at the warlock with interest.

"Not well. Vulpe refuses to bow and says his vampires will remain neutral."

"The idiot! We can't allow bloodsuckers to remain neutral. They could join our enemies at the drop of a hat, and this isn't something we can tolerate."

"I understand, Master. I will take care of the problem, but I'll need reinforcement. The Eastern Covenant isn't without defense and Lotar won't be assisting me this time…"

"I'll give you more warlocks. Have no fear, Demetra. Enough to eradicate the Eastern Covenant's vermin."

Chapter 13

Michael and Leka were sitting on the bank of the small river that meandered through *I-Naur-Tal*, staring at the water. A topographic map was lying between them. Michael picked up a flat stone from the ground and threw it with a flick of the wrist across the surface of the water. The stone ricocheted five times before finally sinking into the crystal-clear liquid.

"Look who's here," said Leka, looking over his shoulder.

Michael turned around to see Ezekiel approaching at an unhurried pace. The wizard was using his staff as a walking stick, leaning heavily on it. His helpless elderly impersonation was so good it could have convinced even Michael… if he hadn't known better.

"Salutations, Ancient One," said Leka, bowing his head as a sign of respect.

"Good morning, youngsters."

"How was your trip?" asked Michael.

"The trip was alright, I guess. Although we did find something unexpected."

"What did you find?"

"A clue left by Methuselah. Coordinates that led us to a ramshackle cabin in the middle of the Australian outback. We believe this was where the dark mage had been hiding all these months, but we found the cabin deserted."

"That's it, that's your clue, an empty shack?"

"There was a bit more to it, but I'm still looking into the other part."

Michael didn't press the issue; Ezekiel didn't look like he was ready to reveal anything more at this time.

"Were you able to figure out why the dark mage isn't a mere infant despite having appeared on your radar so recently?"

"No, and the conundrum is haunting my nights… It simply makes no sense!"

"Could he have been hiding during his whole childhood to only reveal himself now?"

"No, he couldn't have. As I've told you before, I can feel his power wherever I go on the planet. His magical signature is so strong that he cannot hide. He would have had to bottle up his aura from birth and only release it recently…" The wizard pronounced the last words eyes on the horizon, lost in thoughts.

Michael suspected Ez had been thinking aloud more than talking to them. "What do you mean by 'bottled up his aura'?"

Ez cast a sudden glance at Michael, as if surprised to see him. "I didn't mean anything. I'm just rambling. An infant couldn't have done such a thing. Not even an infant mage."

"Done what? Bottle up his aura? How does that even work?" said Michael.

"Just like it sounds. Using a complicated spell. A powerful wizard can trap their magical aura into an object and release it back into their body at a time of their choosing."

"And if he'd bottled up his aura, you wouldn't be able to sense his presence?"

"Of course not. If he'd bottled up his aura he'd be without power, magicless."

"Maybe that's what he did then. He kept his aura bottled up for years and only released it recently," said Michael.

Leka was following the discussion closely but seemed reluctant to interrupt the two friends with his own questions.

"That's impossible, Michael. Nobody would do that. Why would such a powerful mage decide to become mortal when he has all this power at his fingertips? He'd have been the most powerful being on this earth from the time of his birth, so why would he go into hiding? From fear of what?"

Michael looked at Ez, bewildered. "*Become mortal?* Are you trying to tell me that if you bottled up your aura, you'd die of old age within a human lifespan?"

"First of all, I'd never do such a thing. No wizard in their right mind would! And second of all, not quite… I wouldn't age like a human. My metabolism and aging process wouldn't change, but I'd definitely die if I got... run over by a car for instance."

Michael took a few seconds to digest the information. "Okay, so the mage didn't bottle up his aura... Maybe he was simply hiding all those millennia then, slowly becoming more powerful with time, until finally he became so strong that he could no longer hide from you."

"That's an interesting theory. But in that case, I should have first detected a feeble magical signature. One that would have gradually grown over time. But that's not what happened. It was like flipping a switch; one day it wasn't there and the next it was."

Michael was out of ideas, and there was little doubt Ez had already thought of all possibilities anyway. If the wizard hadn't come up with a plausible answer, it was unlikely he would.

"So, you never encountered a magical signature of such intensity prior to the dark mage's arrival?" asked Leka.

"Never! The magical field isn't always stable. There have been fluctuations in the past. Surges, if you will... Some of them of equal intensity to what we're experiencing now, but they never last more than a few hours and are few and far between. They don't occur more than once every few years... This is different, though. The present distortion started a few months ago and never stopped. The previous ones could always be explained by variations in the magical field, but this is no variation. This is a constant. A dark mage's signature."

The crash course in magical field fluctuation left Michael more confused than enlightened.

"And how are things going on your side?" asked Ezekiel.

"Well, you won't be surprised to hear that Cameahwait's death motivated me to go back on the offensive against the DSA thugs."

Ezekiel was indeed not surprised. "Which is why you allowed your prisoner to escape, I suppose?"

"Obviously... And now that you're here, you can tell us where to find him. We set a trap with the intent of capturing a few of his friends yesterday, but the jerks never showed... And since I'm tired of trying to come up with explanations as to why that may be—"

"You want me to locate Jason for you so you can use him as bait for another trap," interrupted the wizard.

"Something like that."

"As I've told you before, Parrish indeed communicated to his hierarchy that you were to join a gathering of werebeings last night. I sensed no distrust in his voice, and he didn't state anything over the phone that would indicate he suspected a trap."

This was even more troublesome. Why hadn't the DSA showed up then? Could it be due to logistical reasons? Had their shock troops been busy with another mission and unable to reach the pretend meeting in time? Something in Michael's gut told him this wasn't the reason. "Would you mind telling us where we could find Jason at the moment?"

"Not at all! He happens to be back in the woods."

"He is?"

"Absolutely! About ten miles south of here."

"And he's alone?"

"He had some company a while back. But his friends left some time ago. He's been by himself a few hours now." Ezekiel's eyes were distant and unfocused. "Yep! He's alone as we speak."

Michael was utterly confused. What the hell was going on?

Sheila had been looking for Michael for some time when she finally found him sitting by the river with Leka. The two of them were staring at a weird map lying flat between them.

"Here you are! I've been looking for you," she said, bending down to kiss Michael on the cheek. She felt him twitch under her touch. Michael wasn't big on public displays of affection, but she didn't care. She needed it.

"Hi, Sheila. What's going on? Did something happen?" he asked, already sounding worried.

"Relax. I just wanted to get out of the house for a while." This was the truth. Her visit had no particular purpose. There was no urgent message to deliver… other than she was bored out of her mind and desperately needed company. Other than she would soon go nuts if she was forced to remain in this place much longer.

I-Naur-Tal was an idyllic place. Six months ago, she'd have killed for a chance to spend a two-week vacation with Michael in such a paradise. But they'd been stuck here for over three months now and the magic no longer had any effect on her. She missed her friends, her job and a million other things that came with living among humans. She'd come to see the gorgeous city as a golden prison, one from which there was no escape.

"Is everything okay?" Michael sounded concerned.

"Everything's great! What are you guys up to? Looking for a treasure?" she replied, staring at the map. With its colorful topographic lines, it truly reminded her of a treasure map.

"We're studying the best route to escort the Healing Stone back to the city." Leka traced a path across the paper with the tip of his finger.

For all that meant to her, he might as well have been pointing at the sky. Sheila had no idea how anyone could make sense of such a map. It was challenging enough to try and decipher a road atlas with clearly labeled highways and intersections… "I'd forgotten about the stone. It's arriving tomorrow, isn't it? Are you going with Leka to retrieve it, Michael?"

"No. Ez gave me Jason's current location, and I'll be heading there first thing in the morning. I need to go discreetly check what our old roommate's up to," he replied in a conspiratorial tone of voice.

"Oh, I see..." She forced a smile on her lips, hoping she didn't sound as disappointed as she felt. It looked like she'd be spending the day alone, again.

Chapter 14

Demetra was still in shock. The master had more than delivered on his promise to provide her with reinforcements to go after the Eastern Covenant. In addition to the fifty odd witches and sorcerers she typically had at her command, the master had also provided twenty-three werewolves and two warlocks. Two warlocks! This last point was by far the most mesmerizing to her. The master had pulled two full-fledged warlocks out of nowhere in under twenty-four hours. She had no idea where he had gone to get them. All she knew was that she'd ceased to feel the presence of the master's aura for an hour or so, which could only mean one thing... He had found these two warlocks on another dimensional plane. How such a thing was possible, Demetra had no idea.

What she did know was that the two had been placed under her command, just like the rest of the troops. She was the one in charge of the mission. An honor that came with responsibilities. If they failed, she'd be the one who answered for it.

Demetra had thought long and hard on the best way to carry out the attack, and she'd come up with a plan which, although not perfect, provided a high chance of success.

Military convention suggested that generals should remain behind, giving orders from the safety of the rear, but this wasn't the way she intended to wage war against the vampires. In her army the generals were the most powerful pieces on the board. She couldn't afford to lose them, of course, but they'd also be very hard to take down. She'd run calculations in her mind and decided the risks involved in exposing the two warlocks and herself would be more than matched by the advantage it would confer on her troops.

Focused on defeating the three of them, the vamps and their werewolf pets would have their flanks exposed to the rest of her army. If worse came to worst and the warlocks found themselves in a bind, they would always have the option of teleporting back to the rear of the battle in a blink of an eye to regroup.

She'd also decided to attack at noon because most vampires would be sleeping, and the compound's defense would be left to their slaves and enthralled wolves.

As the car approached the front gate of Vulpe's domain, it slowed to a crawl before stopping in front of the wrought-iron portal. She was in the passenger seat while the two other warlocks sat behind her. The driver was an expendable witch whose name she didn't bother remembering.

Demetra gave a quick glance at her fellow warlocks. They were as cool as she was. She saw no fear in their eyes as a werewolf approached the car to enquire about the nature of their visit. The driver lowered the window and before the wolf could say a single word, Demetra sent a shock wave that drilled a perfectly circular hole in the place where his heart has been. The wolf fell to the ground, lifeless, and the driver floored the accelerator.

The reinforced bumper of the car hammered the wrought iron with just enough force to bring the portal down, but their car was toast now, no longer usable. A detail of no consequence; they hadn't planned on using it for their escape.

The warlocks and the witch jumped out of the car, immediately engaging the three remaining werewolves in charge of guarding the portal. A dozen more beasts were running toward them, some of them already in their wolf form. The warlocks wasted no time dealing with the threat, dispatching wolf after wolf, though more kept pouring from every corner of the domain. But soon Vulpe's wolves found themselves engaged in battles by Demetra's witches and sorcerers who, all around her, were climbing over the domain's wall faster than the wolves could repel them. And this was only the part of the grounds visible from the front gate... The vast domain was mostly hidden by the surrounding woods and the massive, fortified castle standing in its center, but she knew that a similar scene was playing out across the entire grounds.

By now the alarm had been given, and she expected vampires to show up any minute. That was going to make things more interesting, especially when the elders would join the fray.

As their own forces emerged from every direction to engage the enemy, the warlocks soon ran out of enemies to fight and moved with intent towards the drawbridge blocking the castle's entrance.

Although the warlocks could easily teleport within the walls of the castle, the rest of their army couldn't do the same. Therefore, the wooden drawbridge currently resting in a vertical position against the castle's wall needed to be destroyed; there was no way around it.

The task took more effort than Demetra had anticipated, but eventually the drawbridge was blasted to smithereens. And then she realized her mistake... How were they going to cross the moat without a bridge? The twenty-foot gap presented little problem to her wolves, and most sorcerers could teleport over such a short distance, but the witches couldn't...

She considered how to solve her conundrum a second or two before deciding that the witches would be left outside the castle to make sure no vampire escaped. Between the three warlocks, the wolves and the sorcerers, they had plenty of firepower already.

The first vampires were appearing in the courtyard, and she watched them take position on the other side of the moat while issuing orders to her own troops.

The three warlocks and six sorcerers were the first ones to teleport to the other side of the moat, just as a deluge of bullets poured from the vamps' weapons. But Demetra's commandos had a second advantage on their enemy and they rematerialized into the courtyard without suffering a single casualty. The rest of the troops followed in their tracks a second later.

Several of the sorcerers fell under the bullets as did nearly half of the wolves as they jumped the moat, but enough survived to provide the reinforcement Demetra needed to take the courtyard and enter the castle.

Inside the castle, the battle raged, with spells flying in one direction and bullets in the other. Vampires not only possessed enormous physical strength, they also knew their way around firearms. The force fields the warlocks had erected around themselves rendered the projectiles harmless, but the rest of their troops didn't benefit from this trick. Nonetheless, the three warlocks were more than enough to tilt the balance in their army's favor, and it wasn't long before Demetra found herself in the same reception hall she'd visited a few months earlier during her attempt to steal the Eye of the Phoenix. The room was deserted, though. She'd hoped to find the elders there, ready to make their last stand, but she'd been wrong. She sent the other warlocks and the wolves still alive to search the other rooms, but after fifteen minutes of fruitless search, Vulpe and the rest of the elders had yet to be found.

Lucy and Irini had been in Irini's room, talking about their respective love lives—or lack thereof—when the sound of the portal being brought down by a car had reached their ears. It had taken the two daywalkers a half minute to understand what was happening and raise the alarm. The compound had trained for situations such as this one, and the vamps' response time was exemplary. Within three minutes every vampire had been awakened and was ready for battle.

It became clear fairly fast, however, that the battle couldn't be won; the opposing force was too overwhelming.

"You must leave, my liege," Irini had said to Vulpe. "You dying here would serve no purpose. You must take shelter. If we leave now, we'll have lost this battle, but if we stay we will lose the war."

Vulpe had eventually realized the wisdom in Irini's arguments and agreed to escape. Things hadn't gone quite as planned, however. Many of the escape routes prepared well in advance had been blocked by the invaders and reaching the evacuation tunnel had proved tricky. Most vamps had been unable to reach the hidden doors to the subterranean systems leading out of the castle.

In the end, Irini, Lucy and a dozen or so elders had managed to fight their way to the highest tower and had jumped the sixty-foot vertical drop leading to the other side of the moat. None of them would have been able to jump back up, but the landing posed no problem to the vampires who took off running as soon as they found solid ground under their feet.

The witches patrolling the grounds quickly fell on them, though. A few members of the group collapsed under their number, but the majority managed to escape, scattering in all directions.

When Lucy and Irini stopped running thirty minutes later, they were a good forty miles from the castle. Cristos was the only one still with them.

Chapter 15

The director found the warden in front of the mountain lions' cell, lost in thought. "Good morning, Wes."

Her voice startled him, and he quickly spun around. "Ma'am, I wasn't expecting to see you today. To what do we owe the honor of your visit?"

The director smiled a humorless smile, though the look on the warden's face was priceless. "If you find yourself in my shoes one day, you will appreciate the value of an unannounced visit. If you want to know exactly how an operation is running, don't advertise that you're coming to inspect it."

The warden nodded understandingly. "And how is your inspection going, Ma'am?"

"I'm fairly pleased with what I've seen so far. I've yet to find anything majorly wrong."

"That's good," said Wes, looking a bit too happy with himself.

She'd named him warden of the detention center from the day the facility had opened, and he'd never given her any reason to second guess her choice. She'd caught him torturing prisoners on camera on more than one occasion, of course, but he didn't know that. And truth be told, she didn't give a shit about the warden's mean streak... as long as he refrained from causing permanent damage to her pets. And given his wards' healing powers, there was very little he could do to cause permanent damage. The man was smart enough to know when to stop anyway. Smart and deprived of any sense of morality... The result was a ruthless leader who got things done in record time. A man according to her own heart.

"Have you received news from our team out in Montana?" she asked.

Wes hadn't worked in the field for some time and never as a DSA agent, but the director knew he liked to keep in touch with field operatives. Probably because they were the ones filling up his jail with interesting specimens.

"The men are in position, but they don't know how long they'll have to wait. It could be a while before the mark takes the bait."

"Do you know how many men were sent?" She'd been absorbed with other matters and hadn't kept tabs on the operation since she'd ordered it.

"An overwhelming force, ma'am. They followed your orders… Eleven men and six wolves. That will be more than enough."

The director wasn't convinced, but she hoped so.

"I just hope he'll show up," said Wes.

"I'm confident he will." She couldn't tell him where her confidence came from, but she had reasons to believe the mark would indeed show up, even if it took him a little time.

Using the wolves as weapons was a brilliant idea. Strong and reliable—as long as they were equipped with the mind control devices—they were also relatively easy to find.

So far only a handful of shifters had been weaponized, but soon the time would come to raise an entire army of werebeings. For this army to be efficient it would need proper training, however, and such training couldn't take place here at the detention center. The facility lacked both the space and the equipment necessary. Soon the prisoners would be transferred to a proper training camp. A place lost in the middle of the Ozark Mountains where their weaponization could be carried out on a large scale.

"You don't think eleven men and six wolves is a bit overkill to catch a single mark, Ma'am?" asked Wes.

"Maybe so, but this particular mark is worth the resources. We absolutely must add him to our collection. He could be the spearhead of our army." Although Biörn was indeed a formidable fighter, the true reason for capturing him had nothing to do with his fighting skills, but this wasn't something the director intended to share with Wes Thortan.

Chapter 16

Michael was sitting in a corner of the coffee shop facing the street, sipping on a cup of tea, when a BMW with darkly tinted windows parked along the curb on the opposite side of the street. He was surprised to see three vampires exiting the car a moment later. He hadn't expected Cristos to tag along.

Michael had been about to head to Jason Parrish's location when he'd received Irini's call. The little she'd shared over the phone had convinced him to postpone his plans, and he'd spent his day waiting on the vampires' arrival for a complete debrief. Irini hadn't mentioned anything about Cristos being with them, however. At least Michael now understood why the meeting had been set to thirty minutes after dusk… so that Cristos could come along without having to worry about turning into charcoal.

Although Michael had grown fond of Irini over the months since they'd been reunited—and had never felt the slightest bit of animosity towards poor Lucy—he was far from being a fan of bloodsuckers in general and Cristos definitely qualified as such in his book.

Lucy and Irini were technically hybrids and not full-fledged vampires. Lucy was a vamp-werewolf hybrid, while Irini was a vamp-werebear combination. As such, the two women weren't dependent on human blood for survival and could eat normal food. Lucy's diet remained exclusively carnivorous, but Irini had inherited a bear's omnivorous tastes and could live on pretty much anything. She strongly favored sweet delicacies containing massive amounts of berries, though.

Lucy saw Michael through the window and led the way into the shop. She smiled at him from the door, but he could tell it was forced. The three vampires fanned around his table and took their seats. The greetings were brief and Michael jumped straight to the point.

"What happened exactly, Irini?"

"Our compound was attacked. That's what happened. The dark mage's forces began the assault around noon, the time of day we're the most vulnerable."

"What about your werewolves, what were they doing?"

"They were at their posts, but they were no match for the overwhelming forces the dark mage sent against us. We had little time to count our enemies, but all in all, I'd say we were probably dealing with close to seventy attackers."

"The warlock woman was in the party, I presume? Probably leading the onslaught like last time?" Except that last time Michael and Ezekiel had been present to help the vamps...

"I didn't see her, but it's more than likely they had warlocks with them. They wouldn't have breached our defenses so quickly otherwise."

"They even had werewolves with them this time!" chimed in Lucy.

This last point gave Michael pause. The dark mage was recruiting shifters now? The situation was getting worse by the day. While their enemies were growing stronger and more numerous, the good guys' numbers didn't seem to increase much. It was true the elves had agreed to join forces with the wizards, but the faes had rejected Ezekiel's alliance and, knowing their kind's treacherous nature, Michael suspected it wouldn't take much arm-twisting for the faes to join the enemy. Assuming they hadn't already... "So your werewolves were quickly overwhelmed. And then what happened?"

"By the time they got inside the castle, all the vampires were awake and ready to fight, but once again we were overwhelmed by their numbers. We put up a good fight, but, in the end, we were forced to retreat. A dozen or so elders escaped with us, but we were forced to disperse and we have no idea where the others are or if they're even still alive," answered Irini.

"What about Vulpe?"

"Vulpe was one of them and so was his wife Milena."

"What about his brother?"

"I don't know if anyone took the time to free him from his cell."

Michael wasn't surprised. Vulpe's brother had failed in his coup to overthrow the leader of the Eastern Covenant a few months earlier and had been sentenced to a century of imprisonment. It was doubtful anyone would have thought about freeing the traitor in the mayhem of the battle.

"I'm sure Vulpe is alive," said Cristos. "Our normal lines of communication have been broken, but we have emergency protocols in place and we'll be able to reestablish contact shortly."

"How did you get here?" asked Michael.

"We had to charter a plane," answered Lucy.

"We couldn't run the risk of going to our normal airfield to use the covenant's plane," explained Irini. "For one thing, it's Vulpe's plane and he may need it. Plus we didn't think it was a good idea to go where the enemy may be waiting for us. So we drove to an airport three hundred miles from the compound and spent a fortune on a charter plane that arrived in Salt Lake City a few hours ago."

Michael nodded but Irini wasn't done talking. "Cristos couldn't get out of the airport during the day so Lucy and I went to retrieve one of the covenant's vehicles which was parked at a nearby safehouse. We then picked him up inside the underground parking lot."

As far as Michael knew, the fact that Irini and Lucy were daywalkers had so far been a well-kept secret, but apparently Cristos was now in the know. "Do you have any idea why they attacked your covenant?"

"The female warlock tried to recruit the Eastern Covenant a few days ago and was turned down by Vulpe. Apparently, the dark mage didn't take the refusal kindly. He probably wanted to send a message to others thinking of turning him down: 'Join me or die'," said Irini.

That made sense and was perfectly aligned with what Ezekiel had predicted. This was a war, no doubt about it, and neutrality wasn't an option. You either fought on the dark mage's side or against him, there was no middle ground. Once again Michael thought about the faes and knew that sooner or later his side would have to fight them.

"So you came here to hide?" he said.

Irini and Cristos looked almost insulted and Lucy appeared amused.

"To hide?! Who do you think we are?" asked Irini. "We came here to fight. We know the wizards have been recruiting heavily and that you and the elves are fighting on their side. We came here to help!"

"How do you know about the elves?" asked Michael.

Lucy suddenly looked away, and Michael knew everything there was to know. "Your sister, I presume?" he said, looking at the young woman.

Lucy didn't even blush, possibly because vampires couldn't blush... "I don't want Olivia to get in trouble. She probably didn't know she wasn't supposed to tell."

Michael sighed heavily. He was fond of Olivia and Lucy but the two sisters drove him nuts half of the time. "Well, whether you came to fight with us or not, I can't get you inside the elvish city. Dariel would never go for that, especially not after what happened with Dragos."

Michael saw Cristos flinch at the name of the elder he'd slain, but the vamp said nothing.

"We can stay in a motel out of town," said Lucy. "I know a few."

The others agreed.

"Then it's settled. I have an old friend to go and visit now," said Michael. He was thinking of Jason Parrish. According to Ezekiel the man was still hiding in the same part of the Gallatin Forest. He'd been there two days already and Michael had no idea what he was up to. He was apparently alone which made no sense. Had he been fired? Was he hiding from his DSA friends?

The night was young and since the vamps didn't have better things to do, it was decided they'd accompany Michael into the woods and find out what Jason was up to.

Chapter 17

The elves moved through the woods without a sound, not a leaf cracking under their light feet. Leka and the thirteen men and women accompanying him advanced in a spread-out formation. A steadily moving front, nearly five hundred feet wide, which thoroughly combed the forest as it advanced. Anyone present in the section of woods crossed by the elves would have had no chance to hide without being spotted by their expert eyes.

They encountered no threat, however, and reached the rendezvous point at the edge of the woods a full half hour ahead of schedule. This had been Leka's intent; it was better for the escort to show up early than late.

The elves remained under the canopy, however. And the few hikers passing on the trail a few feet away never knew they were there.

The delegation from the Frozen Kingdom arrived forty minutes later in four SUVs. A half dozen elves from the steppes of Siberia got out of the cars alongside Maya. The princess was holding a small package tightly in her fist. Soft, pliable parchment paper was wrapped around the object that couldn't be more than two inches in diameter.

"Good day, Leka," said Maya as the elf stepped out of the woods to greet her.

"How was your trip, my lady?"

"The trip was long, but nothing to report. Here, this is your responsibility now," she said, handing him the package.

He accepted the gift reluctantly and placed it inside one of his tunic's inner pockets.

"Will you be accompanying us, my lady?" he asked, although he knew full well this was the plan. She nodded and they soon started heading back towards *I-Naur-Tal*.

The tunics worn by the Siberian elves weren't identical to those of the Burning Kingdom but they blended almost equally well with the surrounding woods and soon the forest absorbed the armed contingent. The silent wave rolled up the mountainside towards the elvish city where both Maya and Leka had grown up, albeit in different quarters of the castle. Leka had never admitted it to anyone, but he'd always had a soft spot for Maya, with her golden curls and angelic features. He knew full well not to be deceived by the woman's appearance, however. Maya was anything but angelic. In the past she'd nearly sacrificed her own father to acquire more power. But time had passed since, and Dariel was well on his way to forgiving his daughter. It probably wouldn't be long before she was allowed to return to the Burning Kingdom for good.

The formation for the return journey was different from the one Leka's men had adopted on their way down. This time six of his men and all of the Siberian elves surrounded Leka and Maya while the remaining elves scouted the woods ahead of them. The approach was sound but suffered one major limitation: it assumed any potential enemy would be ahead of them and didn't account for an attack coming from the back, which is why they were caught by surprise when three mountain lions and a few werewolves fell upon the group a third of the way up the mountain.

The elves reacted in an instant and four of the wolves were caught by their arrows before they could close the distance, but the faster and more agile mountain lions managed to dodge the elves' projectiles. And the bullets now raining on them from the canopy above their heads didn't help their aim. The projectile shredded most of the elves to pieces before they could even locate the shooters hidden in the trees.

Maya, Leka and three of his men made a run for it while the surviving elves shot their arrows into the canopy. But their assailants had the higher-ground advantage, and although a few of the attackers fell under the marksmen's arrows, in the end the guns and mountain lions got the better of the elves.

Leka, Maya and their escorts were running at a speed no human could have matched but the mountain lions were closing the distance nonetheless.

One of Leka's men stopped, spun around, and dropped to one knee, aiming for a second before his arrow cut through the air and perforated the skull of one of the lions. Werebeings were hard to kill but elvish arrows weren't garden-variety weapons; the crystal that formed the arrowhead was lethal to praeternaturals and this one wouldn't be getting back up.

The two remaining lions got wiser and started running under the cover of the trees to avoid meeting the same fate as their slain brother. Meanwhile, the five surviving elves continued their ascent towards *I-*

Naur-Tal, knowing full well that even at this pace they wouldn't reach the city for another hour.

The eleven werewolves that fell upon them an instant later seemed to have appeared out of nowhere. A couple of the wolves died under the elves' arrows, but the beasts were soon too close for bows to be of any use.

Unwilling to go down without a fight, the elves pulled out their swords and daggers. But they were outnumbered more than two to one and soon Maya and Leka were the only survivors of the group while the other side still counted a mountain lion and five werewolves. Things weren't looking good.

The two elves were fighting back to back with the energy of those about to die when Leka told Maya, "It's time for you to leave, my lady."

He then turned towards her and placed his hands with crossed fingers in front of Maya's left foot. The princess immediately got the message and stepped onto his hands as he projected his hands upwards. With Leka's jumpstart and her own athletic skills, Maya was able to clear the wall of their opponents and landed on a tree trunk seven or eight feet off the ground. She quickly scaled the remainder of the tree and disappeared into the canopy, to Leka's great relief.

They'll be hard pressed to find her there, he thought, as werewolf claws shredded his torso. He brought his sword down on the beast's neck at the same instant the remaining lion's fangs locked down on his throat. Within a second the surviving beasts were all on the elf. As he felt life evading him and his blood pouring onto the forest floor, Leka reflected that it would have been better if Maya had kept the artifact instead of giving it to him after all.

Chapter 18

Michael and his three undead companions were getting close to Jason Parrish's hiding spot. Or at least the place indicated by Ezekiel who could see through the man's eyes—a miracle Michael still had a hard time comprehending. But Michael didn't have a direct line to the wizard, especially in woods with no cell connection, and it was possible Parrish had since abandoned the makeshift camp he'd built for himself within the Gallatin Forest.

The man's behavior made little sense to Michael who wondered if his old boss had lost it for good. Maybe three months of captivity had been more than he could bear.

They were a mere fifteen minutes away now. The vamps could have even closed the distance in five, but Michael was a bit slower, and they had to adapt to his pace.

He still felt awkward walking side by side with Cristos, the Eastern Covenant's head of security, but so far Cristos hadn't been a problem.

Irini and Lucy seemed to trust him enough to bring him along, and that probably meant something.

The two women were chatting in low voices, and Michael was about to suggest they stopped in case Jason Parrish was out and about searching for his next meal, when a gust of wind brought a scent to his nostrils. A scent he hadn't expected. In addition to carrying Jason's odor, the wind was charged with those belonging to at least a half dozen humans, possibly more. That couldn't be good. Ezekiel had been adamant that Jason was alone in his camp, so where did these men come from?

More concerning still was the werewolf stench that wrapped around the humans' smell. He perceived at least four or five distinct werewolves, which suggested Jason Parrish was being babysat by an army of equal parts werewolves and humans. That wasn't at all the intel he'd gotten from Ezekiel. But Ezekiel only saw through Jason's eyes and heard through his ears. If the DSA's men were hidden around the camp, Ez would have no way of knowing. "Wait!" Michael whispered to his companions, and they all turned towards him.

"What is it?" asked Lucy in a low voice.

"I think this is a trap."

"A trap?" repeated Irini questioningly.

"Yes, Parrish isn't alone. He's got a small army with him, I can smell them." No one thought to question the statement. His bear's nose was above suspicion.

"Can we take them?" asked Irini.

"Probably, especially if we have surprise on our side. The problem is we have no idea what we're running into. My nose is much better than a werewolf's, but the wolves still have noses… If they haven't detected my presence yet, they soon will. Same thing for the two of you." He nodded towards Irini and Cristos. As elders, the two vampires had a strong scent characteristic of their species.

"But they won't detect me," said Lucy with a grin.

She'd only been a vampire for nine months or so, and she hardly had any scent at all.

"I could go scout the situation for you guys," she offered.

Michael and Irini looked at each other for a moment, trying to decide whether that was a good idea or not. If Lucy were to get caught, she would be on her own for a while before the rest of them figured it out and finally came to her rescue.

"Don't worry about me, I'm a big girl. I can do this. It will be fun."

Cristos didn't seem particularly worried about sending Lucy on a recon mission, and Irini appeared confident her pupil could take care of herself, so Michael finally agreed to the young woman's offer.

They'd been waiting patiently for Lucy's return for fifteen minutes when they heard a sound behind them. The two vampires spun around ready to tear the enemy to pieces, but Michael raised an appeasing hand. Their visitor was a wandering grizzly in search of a snack. Michael gave the bear a look and the animal decided to go explore another part of the forest. It didn't move with any particular hurry, though. Appearance needed to be maintained; the bear was leaving, yes, but of its own accord.

Lucy returned twenty minutes later.

"You were right, Michael," she said in a low voice. "It's definitely a trap. I observed the situation from the treetops. Your DSA friends are all over the place. I counted at least ten of them, and they came with a small contingent of werewolves too. Six, I believe."

"What are they doing?" asked Michael.

"Nothing. They're surrounding Jason's camp, spread out over a twenty-yard radius, hidden in the thicket."

"What's Jason doing?"

"He isn't doing anything. Just sitting there, staring at his fire."

Michael thought about the situation for a moment. What were they to do? He'd allowed Jason to escape so that the man could lead them to the detention center hidden in the Nevada desert. Now Michael had a chance at catching a full contingent of Jason's friends for questioning… He mentally ran some calculations and decided the odds were good. He had three vampires, including two elders, to deal with seven humans and five werewolves. In addition, Lucy was part werebear and Irini was part werewolf which made them significantly stronger than your average vampire. They also had the element of surprise on their side…

There was just one thing that bugged him: how could the DSA have known Michael would find Jason Parrish in his hidden camp?

Chapter 19

Ezekiel couldn't recall how long it had been since he'd last visited Cairo. Two or three centuries at least; he couldn't even remember the circumstances of his last trip.

In the distance the three large pyramids of Giza pointed their summits towards the cloudless sky of the Egyptian desert. Few people realized how close the pyramids actually were to Cairo, a stone's throw really.

The wizard remembered them as they'd been when he was a kid. They'd only been a couple hundred years old by the time he was born in the slave quarters of the nearby pharaoh's palace. The palace was long gone, but the pyramids endured. They were showing signs of aging, of course, but for monuments that had stood for over 5,000 years, they looked great. They knew how to build back then…

The pyramid of Cheops was Ezekiel's destination, but he didn't intend to approach the oldest of the Seven Wonders of the Ancient World using the tourist route. He had no reason to visit the inside of the pyramid. What interested him lay underneath the gigantic structure.

He walked unhurriedly along greater Cairo's narrow streets, and for once he wasn't wearing his usual gray cloak and pointy hat. Wrapped in colorful clothes that blended perfectly with the rest of the population, he resembled an elderly Egyptian man. He still had his staff with him, but it had been disguised as a walking stick.

The store looked different than it had during his last visit but stood in the exact same spot. It'd been there for a really, really long time. The nature of the store's merchandise had changed numerous times over the centuries, though. Today the small establishment—barely a hundred square feet—sold cell phone accessories, cigarettes, post cards, and souvenirs.

The store was void of customers and the wizard ignored the mass-produced papyrus and other miniature pyramids, going straight up to the woman standing behind the counter. After exchanging a few words with the young lady in a language long forgotten, Ezekiel disappeared inside a back room separated from the shop by drapes of colorful wooden beads.

He pronounced a few incantations while tracing a glyph on the backroom's dirt floor with the tip of his walking stick, and soon the ground opened in front of him to reveal a stone staircase. The passage was barely wide enough for him to get through. A man the size of Michael would have never been able to pass the obstacle that constituted the narrow stairway.

The wizard descended the eighty-three steps all the way down to a corridor no wider than the stairway itself. He blew on his cane and the handle started glowing like a lantern. He could have used more costly spells to see in the dark, but this one got the job done and didn't deplete his magical energy.

He walked along the stone-lined hallway for about fifteen minutes before finding himself in front of a massive door composed of stone blocks perfectly cut into parallelepipedal shapes nearly two feet in length and a foot and a half in height. He knew from experience that the blocks composing the door were also a full foot wide. Fortunately, he wouldn't have to break through the portal with sheer force.

He chanted a few words and soon the door slid open in front of him, revealing an antechamber with a desk and a man sitting behind it. The room was smaller than the shop had been and, aside from an impressive quantity of scrolls laid out on the shelf behind the desk, the place was void of any other furnishing or source of distraction.

"Ezekiel," said the man. "It's been a long time."

"It has indeed, Anteros. Two, three centuries?"

"I'd say at least four! Time flies when you're having fun," Anteros replied, winking at Ezekiel. "I assume you want in?" Ezekiel nodded and Anteros stood up from his uncomfortable looking chair and came to stand beside the wizard. The two men then chanted in unison, open palms stretched towards one of the walls, and soon a shimmering door appeared within the stonework.

Ezekiel thanked his comrade with a nod and passed through the magical portal that led into what wizards referred to as the Cheops Library, one of the oldest libraries in the world, as old as the pyramids themselves. It wasn't a public library, of course; the depository contained a large fraction of the magical literature written over the past 10,000 years. Row after row of bookshelves, nearly twelve-foot high, could be found in the vast chamber that sat hidden under the foundation of the pyramid of Cheops. A half dozen librarians, all wizards of the Third Circle, could be seen circulating through the aisles in search of specific volumes. Some of them had their arms full of books to be reshelved.

Ezekiel wasn't exactly sure what he was looking for. All he had was a name: Amariel. And since he'd last seen Amariel in Cairo, he had thought that the Cheops Library would be a good starting point for his search.

He walked towards the head librarian, a woman who looked to be in her twenties but had looked that way for the past millennium, and enquired about the location of the section on Amariel.

"What are you looking for precisely?" she asked, her curiosity clearly piqued.

"I'm not sure. Maybe something she would have written herself, or a volume about her life. Or even a book detailing the magical inventions she contributed to."

She thought for a moment before accompanying him to one of the corners of the room. There, she pointed at a shelf where two dozen volumes of potential interest to Ezekiel were collecting dust. He thanked her and grabbed a couple of books before walking to a nearby table and sitting down on a bench that was much more comfortable than it looked. He opened the first volume and started reading. This was going to be a long day.

Ezekiel had been relentlessly reading for over three hours when one of the librarians approached him.

"Would you like some refreshment, Ancient One?" he asked.

Ezekiel looked up to find a man he hadn't met before. The man was dressed in Egyptian garments, just like everyone else in the library. "I'm alright, thank you."

"Is there any way I can be of assistance? If you tell me what you're looking for, I may be able to help you locate the information."

"I appreciate the offer, my young friend, but I honestly don't know what I'm looking for. It's one of those things where I'll know only when I find it."

The man smiled politely but didn't seem to understand. "Well, if you change your mind, I'll be around. Don't hesitate to come and get me.

This is my job."

Ezekiel thanked him and the other wizard returned to aligning books on a nearby shelf.

A few hours went by before Ezekiel opened a volume called *Legendary Lure and Amulets*. The first few pages were dedicated to a debate on the definition of an amulet which, according to the author, was supposed to be a lesser artifact. A trinket somebody carried with them which conferred some type of magical power improvement. The first few chapters dealt with various amulets Ezekiel had never heard about, but it wasn't until he reached the middle of the book that something finally caught his interest.

The chapter entitled 'Amariel's Amulet' was extremely brief and uninformative, however. According to the author, Amariel had devised an all-powerful amulet. One more powerful than the four great artifacts themselves. A statement which, among other things, seemed to contradict the author's own definition of amulet.

Ezekiel raised an eyebrow. Was there any truth in this statement? The four great artifacts the text was referring to were no doubt the Eye of the Phoenix, Amariel's Cloak, the Soul Catcher and the Healing Stone. Had Amariel truly made another artifact as powerful as those? More powerful, even, if this text was to be trusted.

He put the book down and looked up reflectively. As he did so, he noticed the younger librarian observing him. The man quickly got back to reshelving books, while purposefully avoiding looking in Ezekiel's direction. It could have been mere curiosity on the part of the younger wizard, but Ezekiel had an uneasy feeling about it.

Chapter 20

Cautiously approaching the enemy's position from a downwind direction, Michael watched Lucy walk into Jason's camp with the nonchalance of a hiker stumbling upon an exotic variety of mushroom. The young woman had been sent as a diversion, and Michael had no doubt she'd deliver an Oscar-worthy performance.

"Hi there," she said to Jason who was sitting on a fallen log looking bored out of his mind.

"Hi," he replied, suddenly snapping out of his reverie. "What are you doing here?"

"Just hiking with some friends, but I seem to have misplaced them," she chuckled.

"Well, you probably shouldn't stay around here. These woods aren't safe," he said, eying his surroundings uneasily.

He looked nervous, maybe even genuinely worried for Lucy's own safety. How touching... "I'll be alright," she said, passing in front of him and walking towards a large bolder behind which she knew a couple DSA agents were positioned.

"If you need to pee," he said, suddenly getting up to stop her, "I'd use a different spot if I were you. There's a snakes' nest behind that boulder."

Apparently he could think fast on his feet.

"That's alright, I'm not afraid of snakes."

As Lucy circled the boulder, Michael heard the shuffling of feet. The vampire soon found herself facing two men wearing black military fatigues and tactical gear, complete with night binoculars and infrared scope rifles.

She acted startled and hesitant before finally asking, "Are you guys hunters?"

"Yes," answered the man closest to her.

The men didn't appear the slightest bit nervous. At such a close distance, Lucy's magnetism had a calming effect on them.

Her eyes dove into those of the burliest of the two and, while his friend was mesmerized by her revealing cleavage, she enthralled him. She then ordered him to shoot his companion.

The smaller man watched in disbelief as his friend pulled a sidearm from a hip holster and shoved the weapon deep into his gut before pulling the trigger. The gunshot gave the alarm and soon all hell broke loose.

While Lucy had been distracting the DSA commando, Michael, Irini and Cristos had spread out, each of them tasked with targeting a specific group of enemies.

Cristos and Irini fell from the canopy in a perfectly synchronized attack, each targeting a DSA agent, while Michael tackled a group of three werewolves.

The wolves worked well together. They fought as a pack and gave Michael an above-average fight, but in the end Michael was an eight-hundred-pound bear and, despite a few bite marks that would soon be forgotten, he walked out of the confrontation with minimal damage. The three wolves, on the other hand, lay slain on the forest floor, their heads well apart from their bodies.

Lucy had neutralized two more DSA agents and with the two taken down by Irini and Cristos, only three werewolves and five humans remained: six, if one counted Jason who'd retreated to the top of a ten-foot boulder away from the fray.

Jason's five colleagues stood, weapons at the ready, behind their wolves. Their body language betrayed no fear. These were well-trained soldiers. The wolves seemed to be patiently waiting for their masters' orders—something Michael found more than a bit unusual. Even enthralled werewolves couldn't be micromanaged and fought of their own volition. But these beasts were different; not only did they willingly fight alongside the DSA men, they also seemed to obey their every order.

Michael was about to give the signal for the onslaught, hoping that the vampires would remember to keep a couple of the enemies alive for questioning purpose, when one of the wolves bounced not in their direction but towards Jason's boulder. Within a second, the beast was on top of the rock. He pounced on Michael's old boss in a flash and closed his powerful jaws around his throat, tearing flesh and cartilage to pieces. Parrish tried to scream but the air never made it to his mouth. Instead, it escaped through his torn throat in a wet gargle.

The move had surprised Michael but not enough to distract him from the goal at hand. He gestured for Irini to take care of that particular wolf and fell upon the remaining enemies with Lucy to his left and Cristos to his right.

The staccato of machine guns suddenly tore through the silence of the night and Michael felt a dozen bullets pierce his bear's flesh. Painful as it was, it wasn't enough to slow him down. His bear met the first werewolf in the air as the animal pounced in an attempt to jump over him. Michael's claws tore a wide ravine in the wolf's underbelly, causing enough damage to put the wolf out of the fight for the next few minutes.

Michael then focused his attention on the only wolf left standing, but Cristos fell on the beast before Michael had a chance to close the distance.

Soon there were only two members of the DSA commando left alive. Surrounded by four enemies, they were waving their assault rifles in wide arcs. They did look nervous now. Irini disarmed both of them in a flash, but before Michael had a chance to approach any closer to restrain the prisoners, the two men collapsed to the ground within a second of each other. The bastards had once again chosen suicide over capture.

"Damned cyanide implants," muttered Michael after regaining his human form. Reflectively surveying the battleground, he shook his head in disbelief; the offensive had no doubt been a success. All their enemies were dead while Michael and the vamps had hardly any scars to show for it, but they had failed to learn the location of the detention center. Worse, with Jason Parrish dead, they would no longer be able to use his eyes to spy on the DSA.

"We need to clean up this mess. We can't leave all these bodies here for a hiker to find," said Michael, looking around for a spot where his bear could dig a series of not-so-shallow graves.

It took him nearly an hour to excavate enough dirt to cover the bodies. They were about to throw men and wolves into the pit when Michael noticed the diadems inserted at the base of every wolf's skull. Whatever these things were, he suspected they were somehow connected to the diadems some of the human members of the commando were still wearing on their foreheads. Were these devices responsible for the wolves' strange behavior?

He retrieved the diadems from both wolves and humans and handed them to Lucy who, unlike him, had pockets. He then retrieved the body of Jason Parrish from atop the boulder where he was still lying. Why had the wolf killed Jason Parrish? There was little doubt that the beast had received the order from one of the human handlers, but why did the DSA want Parrish dead?

They'd clearly used Jason as bait to attract Michael into this trap, but the man had nothing to do with the failure of the operation and hadn't deserved being executed by his own side. But Michael dismissed the thought as soon as it formed in his mind. This wasn't what had happened here.

If the DSA had used Jason as bait, it meant they were aware of the trace Jason was carrying. It was unlikely they knew Ezekiel was behind the stratagem, but they'd somehow figured out that Jason was somehow tainted.

How they'd figured it out was the million-dollar question. Because the evidence suggested they'd known exactly what type of spying they were dealing with. And if they'd known about the magical trace Ez had put on Jason, it implied the DSA knew not only about praeternaturals but about witchcraft and magic too....

This was too much to absorb at once. It made no sense. There had to be another explanation. These were men, not sorcerers. There had to be a different way of seeing it, there had to be another reason for killing Jason. Michael sure didn't have a clue what it could be, though.

Chapter 21

Tabitha was staring at a gas station standing alongside a bar and a couple houses built in the middle of the desert.

Only two days had passed since she and Ezekiel had discovered the clue left by Methuselah, but Tabitha hadn't wasted any time. While Ez had left Australia to investigate the clue further, she'd remained behind and had crisscrossed the country from Perth to Brisbane and Sydney to Darwin to question a number of wizards and witches, trying to unearth any clue pointing towards the dark mage's new hiding place.

The only concrete thing she'd found so far was a trail of dead witches. Four victims already, but she suspected that was only the tip of the iceberg.

Now she found herself in the outback once again, looking for an address given to her by a witch of dubious reputation. The address in question belonged to a sorcerer who, although unknown to Tabitha, had supposedly made a name for himself in the region.

There's no way I would have stumbled upon this place by chance, she thought, walking towards one of the two houses that had probably looked new seventy years earlier. Before she had a chance to knock on the front door, she heard a voice say "Come in." Apparently, the sorcerer had some skills—that, or he'd been watching her approach through the window.

She pushed the door open and found a man sitting in a rocking chair that looked as old as the house. He was reading the local paper in the middle of a cozy living room.

"How may I help you?" he said.

"I hear you may have some information for me."

"For you? I don't even know who you are, lady!"

Tabitha flashed him a set of pearl-white teeth that would have given butterflies to any straight teenage boy, but which had no impact on the sixty something sorcerer who folded his paper and threw it onto the table a few feet in front of him.

"I am Tabitha of the Second Circle." There was no pride in her voice, she was just stating who she was.

"I suspected as much." For the first time, the man eyed her from head to toe. "And why do you think I have information for you, wizard?"

"You have a reputation in this neck of the woods. A reputation for knowing things. The local magical community seems to hold you in high regard."

"I doubt that very much. The local practitioners usually have enough sense to stay away from me."

His tone wasn't threatening, but he thought a bit too highly of himself if he believed he could impress her.

"What are you looking for exactly?" he asked.

"I'm investigating a number of witches' disappearances."

"Some witches have gone missing?" he said, looking falsely surprised. "I don't know anything about that… Trust me when I say I deeply regret it, but I'm afraid I really can't help you with your inquiries."

"How unfortunate," said Tabitha, giving him a sad smile. "I would have expected a sorcerer of your stature to have heard about such things. Oh well, it's my luck, I guess." She started heading for the door before slowly turning around, a puzzled look on her face. "Unless of course you're not telling me the truth…"

The man gave her a wry smile. "It wouldn't be very smart to lie to a wizard of the Second Circle, would it? I haven't heard of disappearing witches, I assure you… But I may have heard something about a witch who escaped after being kidnapped. Would that type of information be of interest to you, wizard?"

Tabitha pulled up a chair and sat a few feet in front of him, legs crossed and hands placed in her lap. "This would definitely be of interest to me, sorcerer."

"And how much would you be willing to pay for such information?"

"What price do you have in mind?"

"My price doesn't have to be monetary in nature," he answered, eying the petite woman in a way that would have made her skin crawl had she not been who she was.

"Not going to happen," she simply stated. "Four gold coins and my eternal gratitude will have to be enough."

The sorcerer contemplated the answer a moment before nodding. He did look disappointed, though.

"Very well, I'll tell you where you can find that witch. She used to live in a nearby town, but after what happened to her, she decided to relocate to a more... shall we say remote location."

He got up and retrieved a blank envelope and a pen from a drawer. He jotted down a set of coordinates before folding the envelope in half.

"Do you have the exact coordinates of every witch and sorcerer in the country memorized?" asked Tabitha.

"Only the important ones," he answered, handing her the note.

She looked at it a second before folding it back and placing it in an inner pocket of her yellow sari. She paid the sorcerer and thanked him for his help before taking her leave.

As she closed the door, she wondered how trustworthy the man was. Her instinct told her not very... Fortunately, Ezekiel was currently pursuing his research in Asia. In case of need, it shouldn't take him too long to show up.

She took a last look at the coordinates and vanished into thin air under the bewildered eyes of the gas station's dog.

Chapter 22

The dark mage wasn't only incredibly powerful, he was also sixty-foot-tall. Beside him, Michael's bear looked like an angry Chihuahua whose incessant attacks were barely noticed by the giant. The mage lifted his foot and Michael narrowly escaped being crushed under the weight of his invincible enemy. The dark mage carried a staff the size of a large tree in his right hand, with which he repeatedly struck the ground with a low knocking sound familiar to the bear. The knocking finally tore Michael out of his dream and, still half asleep, he opened an eye to find Sheila sitting up in bed beside him.

"I think there's somebody at the door," she said.

It sure sounded like it. Michael checked his watch on the bedside table: three minutes past 7 AM. He was typically up by this time of the day, but he had come back from his battle with the DSA around three in the morning to find Sheila waiting for him. She'd wanted to know what had happened in the woods, and it had been nearly four by the time they'd finally gone to bed.

Michael got up and slipped into a pair of hiking pants and a shirt before answering the door. He found Lady Leana waiting on the other side. This was the first time the High Queen had paid them a visit since they'd started living among the elves, and Michael had the feeling it wasn't good news.

"Good morning, my lady," he said. "Please do come in."

The elvish queen looked paler than usual. She accepted the offer and walked into the cozy living room where Sheila, draped in a black silk robe, met them. The two women greeted each other, and Sheila offered to brew some tea or coffee, but the elf declined.

"I suspect you haven't heard the news... I wanted to be the first to tell you," she said in a somber voice that caught Michael's attention.

"What news, my lady?"

"As you may know, the healing stone was to arrive in *I-Naur-Tal* yesterday. Maya was bringing it over from the Frozen Kingdom."

Michael slowly nodded.

"Leka and his men went to meet them at the edge of the forest to escort the delegation back to *I-Naur-Tal,* but they never reached the city. They were ambushed by werecougars and snipers. We don't know where the snipers came from, but they were expert marksmen. Nearly the entire delegation was killed in the ambush and the stone was stolen."

Michael didn't dare ask the question burning his lips.

Lady Leana looked at him in the eyes before pronouncing the words he'd been dreading. "Leka didn't make it. He fell protecting Maya."

Michael felt a deep sorrow invading his soul. He'd known the elf for only three years, but they'd grown very close and he considered Leka as one of his closest friends. Soon the sorrow made way for anger, an anger he needed to quench before it spilled out into the open. This wasn't the time or the place to lose control of his beast.

"How many survivors were there? Who gave you the news?" he asked.

"There was only one survivor, Michael. Thanks to Leka's sacrifice, Maya was able to escape. She's the one who told us what happened."

Michael nodded, but in his mind wheels were spinning. Maya being the sole survivor seemed a little too convenient. This was the same Maya who a couple years earlier had tried to kill him, had betrayed her own kind and joined forces with a warlock. And now the princess had miraculously survived an attack that had cost the lives of Leka and all his men...

Chapter 23

Ezekiel paid for his ticket and went to wait in line in front of a small bus. The vehicle could seat about twenty passengers and had barred windows designed to protect the occupants from the wild beasts they would soon encounter. Ezekiel hadn't visited Mumbai in over a century and things had changed quite a bit since his last trip. For one thing, the Sanjay Gandhi National Park he was about to enter had not been there back then. At the time, the Kanheri Caves—a complex of hundreds of caves and shrines carved out of a basalt formation—had been freely accessible. The caves were now located within the park's borders, however, and Ezekiel elected to pay the entry fee like everyone else.

The door of the small bus opened, and after the rest of the visitors rushed inside, the wizard took the last remaining seat, beside a British woman who was about twice his size.

The doors closed and the vehicle took the short drive to the gates of the wildlife preserve. A second gate opened to let the bus through and closed behind it before another set of gates allowed access to the preserve. Ezekiel understood the purpose of the lock, which wasn't unlike those found in jails, but he wasn't nearly as excited as the rest of his companions to go and visit the lions and tigers kept within the preserve. He didn't have a choice, though; the Kanheri Caves were the last stop on the guided tour, and he needed to go through everything else to reach his destination.

After twenty minutes of driving around the preserve, the only animal they'd spotted was a lazy lion too fat to be interested in anything other than his current nap. This made Ezekiel smile. The lock securing the entrance to the animal sanctuary was looking more and more like a tourist scam.

They exited the preserve and drove to a small jungle trail where macaque monkeys idly awaited for a tourist to commit the mistake of setting down their backpack or purse, but the said tourists had been warned and the monkeys weren't able to steal anything from that particular batch of visitors.

Ninety minutes later, when the bus dropped the group in front of the caves with instructions to be back within the hour, Ezekiel followed a group of Korean tourists more adventurous than the rest deeper and deeper into the vast area harboring the caves.

The caves weren't natural underground formations, however. They had all been carved into the basaltic mountain wall and were more akin to a succession of alcoves, most of them entirely open to the elements. Some of them were decorated with massive Buddhist statues while others looked like bare holes carved out of the peach-colored rock.

Eventually the Korean tourists got tired of their hike and stopped to take a break while Ezekiel followed the path that was becoming increasingly tortuous and difficult to climb. He went on for an additional thirty minutes and, after making all the right turns, eventually found himself in front of a cave of about three hundred square feet. The space was roughly cubic in shape with a floor, a ceiling and three walls carved into the mountain.

Ezekiel took a good look at his surroundings before stepping into the open alcove and, satisfied he wasn't being observed, walking to the back corner where he drew a glyph in the air. A black portal appeared in the rock and he stepped quickly through it.

The Mumbai Library was even older than its Cairo counterpart, and it was quite possible the cave leading into it had been excavated into the rock long before Buddhist monks decided to turn the mountain into one of the highest concentrations of Buddhist temples in the world.

Just as he'd done in Cairo, Ezekiel identified himself to the attendant at the front desk before being allowed into the sanctuary of magical knowledge that was the library.

After spending a day and a half in the Cairo Library reading everything he could find on Amariel, the wizard was now convinced of the fifth artifact's existence. The amulet's true nature remained vague and elusive, however.

Amariel had apparently been a very prolific wizard. In addition to her mysterious, all-powerful amulet and the Cloak of Invincibility, the long-dead wizard had also discovered a score of lesser spells and sortileges, including the one allowing a wizard to *bottle up* their own aura, as Michael had so eloquently put it.

Ezekiel walked to a section reserved for volumes regarding magical artifacts and perused the shelves in search of a particular book.

During his visit to Cairo, he had discovered that the Cloak of Invincibility, which protected its bearer from any magical attack but also prevented him from using magic on others, had actually been the result of Amariel's desire to avoid detection.

She'd first started dabbling with aerial glyphs and incantation and had eventually come up with a spell able to propel her aura into an inanimate object. Since no magical artifact was required, any wizard skilled enough to execute the complex magic involved could therefore *bottle up* their own aura. But by doing so, they surrendered the power that made them wizards, which hadn't been Amariel's intent at all. She'd simply wanted to avoid detection, not become little more than a mere human in the process.

Amariel hadn't called it quits, though. Determined to find a way to avoid detection while retaining her powers, she'd continued her research until she'd finally created her famous cloak. Unfortunately, the artifact didn't behave quite the way its maker had intended. Instead of simply shielding the bearer from detection, it essentially shielded their aura from the rest of the magical field. It was still a significant improvement over the bottling idea, though.

Ezekiel wondered once again why Amariel had felt the need to avoid detection; why would one want to become invisible to others? He could come up with a few plausible explanations for such a desire, but once again, the flip side of the coin had to be taken into consideration.

He picked a volume from the shelf and brought it back to the reading table. He sat down in front of the open book and slowly stroked his beard as he started reading. For hours, he flipped through pages, barely aware of the passage of time, only getting up to crosscheck a reference or to retrieve a book from a shelf.

It took him all day, but eventually he found signs of what he'd been looking for all along, the fifth artifact. It wasn't referred to under this name and wasn't being called Amariel's Amulet either, but Ezekiel was convinced that this was the information he'd been seeking. Things were starting to make a lot more sense.

Chapter 24

The search and rescue team Wes had sent to the Gallatin Forest had returned and the news wasn't good. The director wouldn't be pleased. The warden stared at the phone sitting on his desk and took a deep breath. He dialed the director's number, and she answered on the third ring.

"Something went terribly wrong with the operation, Ma'am. The team I sent to investigate just returned and they found nothing other than Jason Parrish's body. There was no trace of our men or the wolves accompanying them."

"They're probably all dead by now." The director's tone was detached.

"I agree. The place had been scrubbed clean, but the team's UV light revealed a massive amount of residual proteins all around, a real bloodbath. We'll never see our men again."

"That's unfortunate," said the director, but she didn't sound particularly upset by the news, not even surprised as a matter of fact.

The warden couldn't understand the woman. They'd just lost eleven highly trained soldiers and six wolves, and she didn't appear to give a shit.

"What did you do with Parrish's body?" she asked.

"My men took care of it, Ma'am. Someone would have to dig very deep before they find it. What I can't understand is why whoever killed them would have gotten rid of all the bodies but left Jason's for anyone to find."

"I think the answer is obvious; they only took care of the bodies *they* killed."

Wes nodded but said nothing; he still didn't understand why the director had wanted Jason Parrish dead. Even if the ambush had gone as planned and Biörn had been captured, Parrish wasn't to survive the trip. The director's instructions had been clear.

Wes failed to understand the need for Parrish's death, but he had no qualm with the order. He knew tough decisions needed to be made when running this type of covert operation. Parrish had been a half decent spy and had proven useful in the past, but he'd been stupid enough to get caught and deserved his fate. His escape after three months of captivity didn't redeem his failure.

The director's voice pulled the warden out of his reflection. "I was actually going to call you, Wes. I've something to tell you."

"I'm listening, Ma'am."

"You're being promoted. You'll be overseeing a new training camp we just opened in the Ozarks."

Wes' heart skipped a beat. He had most definitely not expected that.

"You'll have full control over the facility and carte blanche to turn the prisoners into even more lethal weapons than they already are. Unlike the detention center that was just designed to hold them, the training camp in the Ozarks is where they will be turned into the most lethal weapons any army has ever possessed. And you'll be in charge of the program."

This was something Wes could live with. The monsters they'd been collecting for the past year were already tough, but they could get tougher. He knew which buttons to push and now that he had carte blanche, he wouldn't be shy about pressing them. A few of the monsters were bound not to survive the training, but as long as it served as a lesson to the others, their death wouldn't be in vain. Now he really wished they'd managed to capture Biörn…

Chapter 25

The sorcerer had called the witch's retreat remote, but that was an understatement. As far as Tabitha was concerned, this was the middle of nowhere. She'd arrived a few minutes earlier and had already circled the dilapidated house a few times, searching for any sign of a trap. She'd detected no magical energy other than the feeble signature of the witch inside the wooden home.

Tabitha knocked on the door, and it was opened by a man with suspicious eyes and a wary look on his face. The witch looked genuinely scared, which wasn't particularly surprising. If he'd indeed been captured by the dark mage and had managed to escape, he had good reasons to be terrified.

"What d'you want?" he asked.

"To talk to you."

"I don't talk to wizards."

"You'll talk to me." Tabitha's tone wasn't threatening, she was just stating a fact.

Knowing he had little choice in the matter, the witch let her in and closed the door behind her.

"I heard you ran into problems a few weeks ago," she said, standing in the middle of a pigsty the man probably called a kitchen.

"I don't know what you mean," said the man.

His answer surprised her. He didn't look like he was hiding anything, and she suspected he wasn't.

"You didn't have a recent run-in with warlocks?" she asked.

Suddenly he started looking uncomfortable. "Who told you that?"

"That's irrelevant. Just tell me what happened."

"Nothing! A warlock came to me, that's true, but that wasn't weeks ago. Only a few days."

"And what did this warlock want?"

"Nothing, I tell you. She came and then she was gone."

As Tabitha pondered the witch's answer, she suddenly sensed the arrival of a powerful entity. It wasn't powerful enough to be the dark mage, but plenty powerful nonetheless. It *was* a trap.

She searched the eyes of the witch and saw nothing but fear. She doubted he even knew what was going on. The witch was just bait, the warlock had visited him to place a charm on his house, one to be triggered by the arrival of a wizard. The fact the warlock had shown up so quickly meant Tabitha's visit had been expected.

"I suggest you stay in your house and don't come out if you want to live to tell the story," said Tabitha. She needed to get out of the house and confront her enemy.

She doubted the warlock was powerful enough to be a problem, but she remembered Methuselah's fate and sent Ezekiel a mental warning to let him know her location. Just in case she was about to bite into more than she could chew...

She then vanished in front of the witch's eyes. She materialized two hundred yards away, standing on the hot ground of the Australian outback. She immediately located the warlock, a woman with long brown hair and high cheekbones. Her full lips were highlighted by lipstick a dark shade of brown.

This was the first time Tabitha had encountered a female warlock. A girl fight... this was going to be fun! As the wizard prepared to cast her first spell, however, she sensed the arrival of two more powerful beings and suddenly found herself at the center of a triangle composed of three warlocks. Things had just gotten interesting.

Chapter 26

Michael sat cross-legged beside Sheila on the edge of the basin, watching the water's mesmerizing aerial ballet. Like everything else in the elvish city, the basin blended perfectly with its surroundings and looked like it had always been there. The pool's enchanted water continuously squirted from different places around the basin, the propelled fluid meeting in mid-air to form complex liquid structures. A simple pool of water enchanted to look like a sophisticated water fountain.

Daka and Olivia sat a few feet to Michael's right, while Nayati and Kimama sat, fascinated by the magic of the dancing water, to the right of Daka.

"I can't understand why they killed Jason," Sheila said suddenly.

This was also a question Michael had been pondering.

"He was one of their own guys," she continued. "The man had just managed to escape from three months of captivity, for God's sake! That makes absolutely no sense!"

She had a point. Few governmental organizations eliminated their own agents, but it was in line with the cyanide capsules their operatives wore hidden in dental implants. The DSA definitely wasn't mainstream law enforcement, which technically made sense considering the type of individuals they went after. All their operations were, by definition, covert. Civilians couldn't learn about the creatures the DSA were tracking down.

The idea of a governmental entity dealing with praeternatural threats had some value from a human standpoint... except that it was total hogwash!

A few exceptions—usually involving vampires—aside, the attacks of praeternaturals on humans were exceedingly rare. The DSA actually ran a bigger risk of revealing the true nature of the world to the unaware public by chasing after praeternaturals than by ignoring them.

"Jason was killed by a werewolf, right?" Olivia chimed in. "Maybe the DSA never intended to kill him? Maybe it was a mix-up with the wolf, a miscommunication."

Michael didn't buy the theory. It had been an execution, a premeditated murder. The wolf had been instructed to get rid of Parrish, he was sure of it. That, combined with the fact the whole thing had been a setup in the first place, only confirmed his suspicion. The DSA was aware of the trace Ezekiel had placed on Parrish. And this was a very scary thought. Not only did the government know about magic, they knew enough to realize that Jason had been bewitched. The idea didn't sit well with Michael.

He finally shared his conclusions with the group, and they all looked at him, puzzled.

"How would they know about magic?" asked Daka.

"Who knows? The same way they found out about praeternaturals, probably," said Michael. "I can't think of another explanation."

"If they were able to spot Ezekiel's trace on Jason, it means they have witches or sorcerers working for them. Maybe even wizards," said Sheila.

"I don't picture wizards working with the DSA, at least not of their own volition, but I could see them having witches on payroll," replied Michael. "And if they have magical beings on their staff, the threat they represent is a lot greater than we first thought."

He knew these questions needed to be answered. Luckily, he had plenty of time on his hands and not much else to do. The DSA problem was likely the only one he could address without getting killed. The dark mage mess was so far above his paygrade that he couldn't even contemplate being of any help with it. Fortunately, Ezekiel and his allies were working on that. Michael could therefore focus his energy on avenging Cameahwait and rescuing Daka's packmates from wherever the DSA had taken them.

The thought of Cameahwait's death brought Leka to his mind. An even greater loss, though Michael would never say so in front of Daka. Cameahwait had lived a full life and would have died of old age sooner rather than later, but Leka had been killed in his prime. He'd still had millennia to look forward to.

And Leka's death was yet another conundrum. The dark mage had known that the elvish artifact was being transferred and knew precisely where to attack... How could this be? There was only one explanation: someone had informed him of the transfer.

Michael was convinced that none of the elves of *I-Naur-Tal* would have betrayed the secret. For one thing, only the High Elves who'd sat at the council table with Ez and Tabitha had been in the know... So, where did the leak come from?

Michael himself had learned about the transfer by chance when Leka had come to inform Ezekiel in his presence that the council was about to start. Sheila, Olivia and Daka had also been present, of course, but he trusted all three with his life. On top of it, none of them would have had the means to transfer the information outside *I-Naur-Tal*'s walls anyway. How could any of them have gotten in touch with the dark mage?

And then an idea came to his mind: what about Jason? He'd been locked in his room, but they hadn't always been speaking in low voices. Could he have overheard their conversation? It was possible but not likely. On top of it, if Jason had indeed been the source of the leak, it would mean the Healing Stone had been stolen by the DSA and not the warlocks. But the DSA could never have defeated Leka's men. Not in a million years! Yet Michael couldn't drive the thought away.

From what he knew, the elves had been attacked by a contingent composed of werewolves, mountain lions and snipers hidden in the trees, which indeed fit well with DSA practices... Hadn't they brought werewolves along when they'd used Jason Parrish as bait to capture Michael?

The blood started boiling in his veins at the thought of these humans getting the better of Leka. They would have to pay dearly for this.

Michael had almost convinced himself of the DSA's involvement in Leka's assassination when a thought occurred to him. If Jason Parrish had indeed overheard the secret discussion and communicated the plan to the DSA, Ezekiel should have known about it. Ezekiel had seen through Jason's eyes, heard through his ears. But Ezekiel hadn't mentioned anything about it. Therefore, Jason couldn't be involved and neither could the DSA... He was back to square one. Who had leaked the information to the dark mage?

Michael was no longer watching the water fountain; his eyes were drifting over the elves passing by, one of them a cute blonde who reminded him of Maya. Maya... the only survivor of the attack, Maya who had betrayed her own father three years earlier. Maya...

Chapter 27

Wand in hand, Demetra watched the wizard standing two hundred feet in front of her. The woman wasn't much to look at. Maybe five-foot-tall, she wore a bright purple sari that complemented her chocolate skin. A jewel was embedded in her forehead, just above the nose. She held no wand or staff but Demetra didn't make the mistake of underestimating the enemy. The magical aura emanating from the woman was unmistakable; this was Tabitha of the Second Circle.

Demetra had never encountered the wizard before, but she knew her reputation. This was a serious foe and Demetra was grateful for her reinforcements. Three warlocks wouldn't be too much to deal with for this particular wizard.

The atmosphere reminded Demetra of a duel scene in a Western movie. The arid, nearly deserted landscape, the sparse vegetation, the dilapidated house in the background, the cloudless sky with its unforgiving sun… The only thing missing was Ennio Morricone's music.

A flick of her wrist sent a lightning bolt pouring out of Demetra's wand and rushing towards Tabitha. The two other warlocks copied her attack a fraction of a second later, but all three bolts disintegrated on the shield erected by the wizard.

Demetra hadn't even seen Tabitha move, but she'd managed to create a protective barrier around herself that would be hard to pierce. Hard, but not impossible. A purely defensive strategy was seldom a winning one and Demetra continued her offensive with a deluge of fire. Once again, her two copycats responded with similar attacks. Soon the wizard was lost from sight under the fire pouring atop her protective dome.

Tabitha's defensive bubble suddenly collapsed, and for a second Demetra thought their enemy had been vanquished. Wishful thinking… She spotted Tabitha a moment later, standing directly behind one of the other warlocks. Sensing her presence, the man spun around waving his wand, but the wizard projected her hand in a quick motion and a blue beam of light hit him straight in the solar plexus, projecting him forty feet away. A giant crater was clearly visible on the left side of his chest, where his heart used to be… They were down to two against one and Demetra didn't like the odds.

Her remaining companion surprised her by taking the initiative, and soon a storm of boulders the size of bowling balls fell from the sky directly above the wizard. But Tabitha effortlessly evaded the attack, deflecting the largest ones, pulverizing the others, all the while keeping Demetra busy dodging a score of fireballs.

Demetra knew she needed to end the fight quickly; she couldn't afford to lose her remaining ally. If the man went down, she'd have no choice but to flee the battle, and she doubted such response would please the master.

The boulder shower ceased and, while maintaining her attack on Demetra, the wizard shifted her focus to the other warlock. A series of lightning bolts dropped onto him straight from the sky in rapid succession, and although he avoided the first few, one of them finally reached him and he was carbonized on the spot.

Demetra saw this as her opportunity. With the wizard's focus elsewhere, she teleported directly behind Tabitha and sent a shock wave careening into her enemy. The wall of displaced air hit the wizard like a train, the force of the impact propelling her a hundred feet. Tabitha landed in a disarticulated pile that reminded Demetra of a puppet whose strings had been severed.

Demetra cautiously approached her enemy, who remained utterly motionless on the ground. And for good reason… every bone in Tabitha's body had been shattered by the impact, and blood was slowly seeping from the wizard's mouth.

Satisfied that life had deserted the wizard, Demetra closed the distance. One of her tasks was still to retrieve the missing magical artifact the master was seeking, and Tabitha would have made for a great protector of such an artifact. The warlock almost felt a pang of pity at the sight of the wizard's broken body as she bent down to search her pockets. Almost… but not quite.

Chapter 28

Ezekiel materialized in the arid landscape of the Australian outback and immediately scanned it in search of Tabitha. He'd received her request for help ten minutes earlier and had covered the distance from India to Australia in record time.

He found the first sign of trouble when his eyes fell upon a scorched body lying amid the low brush. He located Tabitha an instant later. She lay motionless on the ground, easily identifiable by her bright sari. He also immediately recognized the form bending over her. He'd fought that particular warlock before.

Not bothering with a warning, he planted his staff in the ground and a fault immediately opened under the warlock's feet. The sinkhole nearly swallowed the woman, but she managed to escape by teleporting twenty feet away.

She faced Ezekiel an instant before retaliating with a rain of fire. Ezekiel countered the attack with a tidal wave materialized out of nowhere. He then projected his left hand forward and a bright light the color of emeralds poured out of his palm and rushed towards the warlock, but she was already gone.

Ezekiel wasted no time looking for his opponent, but her aura had vanished. The coward had fled. He walked to Tabitha's body to confirm what he already knew. The hazelnut eyes of his friend and colleague were staring at the vacant sky, unblinking. No life was left in them. Ezekiel felt his heart constrict in his chest and swallowed hard before bending toward Tabitha. He hoped Demetra hadn't found what she was looking for a moment earlier. He searched the inner pocket of the sari and let out a sigh of relief when his fingers found the coveted object.

Chapter 29

Michael was brewing some tea in the small kitchenette of their elvish dwelling when Sheila slipped out of the bedroom wearing a silk robe that did little to cover her curves. She came to stand in front of him, pausing in a suggestive manner. He did his best to smile as she dragged him back to the bedroom where she started undressing him. He knew she was trying to take his mind off his problems, and he appreciated the gesture, but sex presented little appeal at the moment.

He was down to his boxers when she suddenly stepped back, looking at him with concern. "You really don't look like you're into it."

"Sorry. I guess I'm not…"

Sheila sighed and put her robe back on. She looked disappointed, but he could tell she was doing her best to hide it. "It's just that today…" He trailed off.

"I understand."

Before he could apologize further, they heard a knock on the door. Michael went to answer and found Ezekiel on the other side.

"May I come in?" asked the wizard.

Michael stepped aside, not bothering to answer the rhetorical question.

"Hi, Ez," said Sheila. "I was about to make coffee, would you like some?"

"That would be lovely, my dear."

"Are you hungry? I can make breakfast too."

"Nothing for me."

"How about you, Michael?"

"I'm not hungry either, thanks."

Sheila and Ezekiel turned stunned gazes towards him. Upon reflection Michael realized this was likely the first time they'd ever seen him turn down food, but today wasn't a normal day and food was the last thing on his mind. "How are things going, Ez?" he asked, just to say something.

"About as well as one would expect," answered the wizard somberly. "What about you?"

"The same," said Michael. "I assume you already know that Jason Parrish is dead."

Ezekiel nodded. "I figured as much when our *special bond* was severed. What happened?"

"He was killed by his own side, but I don't think it was an accident as much as an execution. The camp he'd built in the woods was a trap. They were using him as bait, but we caught them by surprise. They had werewolves with them, but we took care of that problem too… Look what the wolves and some of the men were wearing." Michael held out two diadems to Ezekiel who stared at them for a long time before finally picking one up.

The wizard looked at it closely, holding it at a distance as if it were radioactive.

"The blue ones were on the wolves and the reds on the men. I think that's how the DSA controls the praeternaturals they capture."

"I believe you're right," said the wizard.

"Those prongs look like they can retract, but fully extended they probably enter the wolf's scull," said Michael, pointing at the tiny but relatively thick needles at the base of the diadem.

He then told Ez his theory about DSA having witches on payroll while the wizard listened in silence.

"What do you think?" asked Michael, concluding his account.

"I think you're correct. The fact they used our spy as a bait suggests they knew he was bewitched, which also suggests they have magical folks working for them, or at least coerced into doing so," said Ezekiel, pocketing the diadem.

Michael watched him but made no comment. As Sheila brought a steaming cup of coffee to Ezekiel, Michael moved on to the sad matter that had brought his friend to the elvish city today. "I still can't figure out how the dark mage knew about the transfer of the Healing Stone. How did he know where to place his men to ambush Leka? I thought about it for a long time and I can only think of one person who could have betrayed the secret."

Ezekiel stared into Michael's eyes a moment before the ranger whispered, "Maya."

Ez closed his eyes, apparently considering the possibility. When he opened them an instant later, he looked incredibly tired. Michael had always known him masquerading as a seventy-something-year-old, but one who was full of life and vitality. Not today, though. Today Ez looked like he was nearing his end and was tired of this life.

"I suggest you keep that theory to yourself for now," said Ezekiel. "Especially today."

Michael nodded his agreement. "Of course, Jason Parrish could have overheard us, but you would have known if he'd passed on the information to anyone, wouldn't you?"

Ezekiel nodded, shredding the last doubts Michael had on the matter.

"Too bad," said Michael, "because it would have made a lot more sense."

"What do you mean?" asked Ez.

"I mean that Leka's party was ambushed by shifters and snipers. That sounds a lot more like a DSA operation than the work of warlocks to me. But if Jason didn't speak, there was no way for the DSA to know of the artifact's transfer or of its importance in the first place."

Ezekiel nodded pensively. "Vampires like firearms as well, Michael. And vampires enthrall werebeings to do their bidding, as you well know."

"How could vamps be involved? They had no more way to learn about the transfer than the DSA did."

"That I don't know," conceded Ezekiel, "but it would make a lot more sense to me if some vamps were helping the dark mage or had joined his side rather than the DSA trying to get their hands on the Healing Stone."

This was something Michael hadn't considered before, but it did indeed make sense. The Eastern Covenant had turned down the dark mage's alliance offer and had suffered direly for it. It was likely the same offer had been extended to the Western Covenant. And they might very well have accepted.

"Are you sure you're okay, Ez? You seem... tired," said Sheila, hesitating on the last word.

Michael suspected she meant ill, because that's exactly what Ezekiel looked to him.

"I've had better centuries, my dear... As a matter of fact, I have more bad news to tell you."

They both stared at him attentively.

"You're now looking at the only remaining wizard of the Second Circle left on this earth. Tabitha was killed yesterday."

Chapter 30

Wes Thortan had wasted no time. Within hours of his promotion, he'd been on a private jet on his way to his new assignment. He'd arrived at the training camp late in the evening and had spent the night in the quarters reserved for the camp's first in command. He'd woken up early and had introduced himself to both the staff and the prisoners in a gathering which had taken place shortly after sunrise. It was important that everyone knew who was in charge. Authority was key for the success of the enterprise, and succeed he would. He had the charisma and the mean streak required for the job. Tough men needed tough leaders, and the prisoners he was in charge of turning into perfectly honed killing machines were as tough as they got.

Three hundred shifters had already been transferred to the training camp, which was much larger than the detention facility in Nevada. Lost in the heart of the Ozark Mountains, the camp spanned two hundred acres in the heart of the forest. The vast wooded area was covered with thick trees and the various buildings had been spread out in a way aimed at minimizing detection from satellites. It would have taken a keen eye—or someone who knew exactly where to look—to identify the structures as a military compound.

After introducing himself to the men, the warden had requested a guided tour from his second in command.

"This part of the compound, Sir, is designed to train the wards to fight as a cohesive unit. They all have excellent fighting skills on their own, but they do not fight well together," explained the lieutenant.

Wes nodded his understanding. Among the training grounds they'd already covered, the warden favored the compound nicknamed the bullpen, where the beasts were trained to fight different types of praeternaturals. It was of course ludicrous to expect a werewolf to take down a werelion, but a pack of werewolves could easily take down a big cat and this was the type of training the bullpen was providing. This was particularly important because despite the many werecreatures they'd captured over the past year, there were still far more of them out there, enjoying unrestrained freedom.

Werecreatures had already been used on missions together with their handlers and, a couple of recent exceptions aside, had met with great success. Training the beasts to hunt down their peers made sense; they were a lot tougher to kill than human soldiers and required no expensive medical treatment. Thanks to their baffling healing rate, the monsters were ready to fight again minutes or hours after sustaining injuries that would have permanently disabled any human.

Wes and his lieutenant jumped onto a golf cart and drove a quarter mile to a small building painted the color of the surrounding woods.

"This is where we train the creatures to storm buildings in record time," explained the lieutenant.

But no one was training at the time and they didn't enter the building. They visited four more training grounds, including a camouflage facility where the prisoners were taught how to blend perfectly with their surroundings, before turning the golf cart around and heading back to the camp's headquarters. As they drove near the entrance a commotion caught the warden's attention.

"Stay where you are or we'll shoot you both!" he heard a voice shouting.

He ordered his driver to head towards the altercation. As the golf cart turned a corner, Wes spotted four men with assault rifles trained on a woman with a fluffy ball of fur at her feet. A cat perhaps? Upon closer inspection, the cat was actually a snow leopard cub of maybe two or three months. The woman looked to be in her mid-twenties. He wasn't certain of her ethnicity, but he'd guessed she was from somewhere in Central Asia. Mongolia, maybe. Not unattractive, as a matter of fact. In a feral sort of way... "What's going on here?" he asked.

"Her collar isn't working, sir," answered the guard in charge. "We're trying to put her back in her cell but she won't obey. We're going to have to shoot her if she doesn't submit right away."

Wes took a few steps past the guards and towards her. "So, you're a tough one, aren't you?" he said patronizingly.

"Be careful, Sir! They're really fast!" warned one of the guards.

"You're a big bad kitty, aren't you? But it doesn't matter… No matter how tough you are, I'm tougher. The sooner you realize that, the better off you'll be. Now, get into your cage."

The woman ignored the order and stepped in front of her cub who hissed angrily. Not a very impressive sound, coming from an oversized cat.

"Shoot her," ordered Wes.

And a moment later the woman was lying on the floor in a puddle of her own blood. The guards quickly replaced her collar with a new one and after shooting her a few more times dragged her into a cage designed to withstand the assaults of a charging elephant.

She came back to life a short while later looking haggard and disoriented. It was a few seconds before her eyes focused on the warden standing outside the cage. His foot was pressed on her cub's head.

"I told you I was tougher than you," he said with a cruel smile. "Now let me show you what happens to those who don't obey my orders."

The cub was trying to claw at him, but Wes had positioned himself in a way that rendered the animal's attempts futile. He pressed harder and harder on the cub's head, eventually placing all his weight on the small cranium. As the cub moaned in pain, his mother's scream of rage pierced the relative quietness of the woods.

Wes could see both anger and resignation in her eyes. Even without the collar around her neck she wouldn't have been able to break free of her cage. There was nothing she could do to save her cub.

He enjoyed the look on her face. Her hatred towards him made her even more attractive in his eyes.

He kicked the cub a few times with his free foot and heard a few ribs cracking under the impacts, his smile widening at the sound. For a moment, he debated whether or not to kill the cub in front of his mother but decided against it. He wanted her to think he had a heart. She'd be all the more surprised when he came back to visit her later that evening.

He hadn't decided yet what he was going to do to her then. Maybe he'd leave the collar around her neck and force himself on her, relishing her helplessness. Or maybe he'd use one of the diadems to control her mind. Have her satisfy his most perverted desires… The choice was difficult, but he was confident he'd have made up his mind by the time evening came.

Chapter 31

The body of Leka lay draped in a white veil on a transparent bed of crystal suspended three feet in the air. Nothing seemed to maintain the crystal platform off the ground; it simply levitated in front of Michael, Sheila, Ezekiel and the rest of their party.

The elves were mourning their fallen brother in an elvish fashion. They all hummed in unison and although no words were pronounced Michael could tell the humming had meaning. No one spoke from the beginning to the end of the service, but eventually the humming ended, and Lady Leana herself approached Leka's body. She placed her left palm a few inches over his heart and muttered an incantation. She retrieved her hand as blue flames erupted all over Leka's corpse and started consuming it slowly. The brazier quickly grew in size, the flames leaping three feet in the air.

Michael, who was standing no more than five yards from the body of his friend, could feel absolutely no heat radiating from the consuming fire. On the contrary, he even felt a tinge of cold percolating through his skin and seeping into his bones.

The flames were doing their destructive work reducing the flesh of the fallen elf, but there seemed to be no by-product of the fire. No ashes visible on the transparent bed. No smoke escaping from the brazier. It took about five minutes for the cold fire to complete its work, at the end of which the flames simply extinguished and the crystal bed lay empty and perfectly clean.

Without a word, the elves scattered in every direction, returning to their daily activities. Michael, Sheila and Ezekiel were heading back to their assigned dwelling with Olivia and the three skinwalkers in tow when Dariel caught up with them. "A word, Ezekiel." The High King spoke in an icy tone.

Ezekiel appeared surprised but nodded.

"Do you still think it was a good idea to transfer the Healing Stone from the Frozen Kingdom to *I-Naur-Tal*?" asked the elf. Michael was pretty certain the question was rhetorical.

"I grieve the loss of Leka, Dariel. I truly am sorry, but there was no way for me to know that the escort would be ambushed, Leka killed, and the artifact stolen."

"As you say, Ezekiel, there was no way of knowing that such things would happen because such things shouldn't have happened. Such things couldn't have happened if we hadn't been betrayed!"

The elves within earshot of the discussion had stopped what they were doing and were now observing, with a mixture of surprise and bewilderment, their leader lecturing the wizard they called the Ancient One.

"I agree, Dariel, it does look like we've been betrayed. The enemy was informed of the transfer. Unfortunately, we have no way of knowing who betrayed us."

That was when Michael noticed that one of the witnesses to the altercation was none other than Maya. Dariel's daughter stood with a couple of her friends by a water fountain, a stone's throw to the right of her father. Michael had seen her standing beside her mother at the funeral, looking genuinely bereaved, but he still didn't trust the princess any farther than he could throw her.

"I know that my elves haven't betrayed you," said Dariel. "And I also know we've had a lot of guests in our midst these past few months, guests who aren't above suspicion."

"One cannot accuse without evidence, High King Dariel. Do not let grief cloud your judgement, my friend, this accusation isn't worthy of you."

"*You* tell *me* what is worthy of me, Ezekiel? Well know this, the Burning Kingdom is no longer part of your alliance. We're stepping away from your little war. And you and your friends are no longer welcome in I-Naur-Tal." Dariel then turned towards Michael and the others. "You'll pack your bags immediately, I want you out of this city by nightfall!"

"This is unfair," said Ezekiel. "Michael and his friends are here because they've been persecuted by their own enemies. They have nothing to do with the dark mage."

"You can't be certain of that, Ezekiel. And from what I hear, they've been consorting with vampires of the Eastern Covenant. I can't have friends of vampires staying in our city. There must be some limits to what we'll tolerate as hosts."

"We thank you for your hospitality, High King Dariel," said Michael, trying his best to sound as if he meant it. "We're in your debt for the time you gave us, the food and the shelter. My friends and I won't outlast our welcome. We'll be gone within the hour."

As Michael grabbed Sheila's hand and headed back towards what had been their home for the past three months, he caught Maya staring at him. He didn't know how to interpret the look in her eyes.

Chapter 32

It was early afternoon when Irini heard Cristos' phone ring inside his room. They'd rented three adjacent rooms equipped with communication doors, which they kept open at all times. Irini occupied the central room between Lucy's and Cristos'.

"Should we pick up? Who could be calling him?" asked Lucy, showing up yawning in Irini's room. She, too, had been sleeping, but being a hybrid, her sleep was much lighter than that of her full-blooded comrade who was deep in slumber this time of day.

The question had merit. It was the first time Cristos' phone had rung since they'd fled Europe. They'd been without news from the Eastern

Covenant ever since the attack....

Irini nodded to Lucy, and they headed to Cristos' room.

His bedroom was the darkest one of them all. The drapes had been reinforced with cardboard duct taped directly onto the wall to prevent any natural light from getting through.

Irini grabbed the phone and saw Vulpe's name written on the screen. She immediately answered. "My liege, this is Irini. Where are you?"

"In Transylvania. We've been running for days. Is Cristos with you?"

"Yes, and Lucy, too. We're in the US."

"The three of you were believed to be dead, Irini. I didn't expect anyone to answer this call. I'm here with a half dozen elders, but there might be more scattered elsewhere."

"What will you have us do, my liege?"

"Nothing for now. Remain where you are but be prepared to act when I call you. I still need to evaluate our options and try to locate other survivors."

Irini acquiesced to the leader's request and he terminated the call.

"What did he say?" asked Lucy.

But before Irini could reply, Lucy's phone rang in her room, and she left to answer it.

"It's my sister!" yelled Lucy from her bedroom.

Irini joined her protégée as she was putting the phone in loudspeaker mode. "It's Michael, he's got something to tell us."

"Irini, Lucy, can you hear me?"

"Yes," they answered at the same time.

"We've been evicted from *I-Naur-Tal*. We're now on our way to Yellowstone."

"What happened? Why are the elves kicking you out?"

Michael summarized in a few words the circumstances of their unexpected departure.

"So, the elves are no longer fighting alongside the wizards?" asked Irini.

"At least the Burning Kingdom isn't," answered Michael. "Ezekiel has already departed to try and do some damage control, but he suspects the other High Kings and Queens will follow suit and withdraw their support."

Irini knew this was terrible news.

"I'm calling you," continued Michael, "because I'd like you, Lucy, and your... friend—"

"His name is Cristos," interrupted Irini.

"And Cristos," repeated Michael, "to join us in Yellowstone."

"What for?"

"Because I'd rather our forces not be dispersed. There's something not quite right about all this. I can't put my finger on it, but I don't like it and I know we'd be stronger together."

"Cristos cannot walk in broad daylight and he won't exactly blend in with the crowd if he wears his daysuit," replied Irini.

"I understand that. You guys can wait for nightfall to join us. I'll send you coordinates."

"And you don't think Jason Parrish's friends will look for you in Yellowstone?" asked Lucy.

That was a good point. Irini hadn't thought about that.

"They might look for us in Yellowstone, but they won't find us where we're going. I don't intend to go back to my cabin. It's going to be the backwoods for us for the foreseeable future. Cristos can wear his daysuit all he wants; he won't bump into anyone."

"Alright. We'll come and join you. Just send us the coordinates, we'll be there after sunset," said Irini before hanging up.

"Now that's going to be fun," said Lucy, an amused look on her face.

"What do you mean?"

"I mean that Michael isn't alone over there; he's got Sheila and Olivia with him. And if he's got Olivia, he's got Daka. And if he's got Daka, Daka's packmates are there too... We're going to have a nice gathering of skinwalkers and vampires... Do you catch my drift?"

She was right; this was a terrible idea.

"I don't understand why we have to go to Yellowstone, there's like a million places more comfortable we could meet at and plan for the next move," said Lucy.

"I suspect Michael has an ulterior motive in going there..."

"And what would that be?"

It was Irini's turn to smile. "You'll see... If my guess is correct, I don't want to spoil the surprise."

Chapter 33

For the second time in three days, Ezekiel found himself inside the ancient magical library located in the Buddhists' caves at the heart of Mumbai's Sanjay Gandhi National Park. He had a serious problem, and he wasn't certain of how best to address it.

In front of him on the table were a book and two of the diadems Michael had retrieved from the bodies of a werewolf and a DSA agent. There was something about them that really bugged the wizard. As he'd told Michael, they were indeed infused with magic, but this wasn't in itself the most concerning aspect. He simply couldn't understand what he was looking at. He suspected, however, that the answer to the riddle was hiding somewhere inside the massive volume he was perusing.

He'd stumbled upon something similar during his last visit two days earlier but hadn't bothered looking into it further at the time; his focus had exclusively been on the fifth artifact then.

He finally found the passage he'd been seeking, and this time he spent fifteen minutes carefully reading every single word of the three-page pamphlet. A pamphlet that plainly described, in bold red letters, the type of magic used to infuse the diadems.

The DSA was using magic foreign to Ezekiel. Magic described in a book that had been collecting dust on the shelf of a secret library for thousands of years. This confirmed the wizard's suspicions. The fact he'd stumbled upon the pamphlet while looking for information on the fifth artifact couldn't be a coincidence.

The situation was even more dire than he'd suspected. Drastic measures needed to be taken before they ran out of time. Ezekiel now understood the part he had to play in the twisted game. And there was only one thing left for him to do… sacrifice himself.

Chapter 34

This time around, no gang approached Demetra as she entered Rio's slum and headed towards the shack where the master had been staying for the past few days. Once again she was baffled by his choice of accommodation, when he could afford the most luxurious hotels on the planet. She doubted it was out of fear of being discovered by their enemies, though. The master had killed Methuselah, a wizard of the Second Circle, with the ease of a child squashing a bug.

As she neared her destination, Demetra noticed something odd. The vibrational signature of the master seemed weaker than usual. The dark mage's powers were such that Demetra clearly perceived the unmistakable signature wherever she stood on the planet, but over the past few days she hadn't been noticing it as much as usual. She'd assumed that she'd simply grown accustomed to it, but now that she was only a stone's throw away from the source of the power, she could definitely tell that it vibrated with a slightly weaker intensity than it had before.

As she approached the corrugated metal sheet that served as a door to the shack, it shimmered out of the way. Demetra found the master sitting, eyes closed, in a corner of the vast living room.

"How did it go?" he asked, eyes still shut.

"The Second Circle has lost another member. Ezekiel is now the sole survivor of his order."

The master nodded but betrayed no emotion.

"The two warlocks you provided for the mission didn't make it back, however. Tabitha killed them both before I could finish her off."

Again, the master nodded impassively and Demetra wondered what wheels were turning behind those closed eyes.

"Did you find what I asked you to collect?" he asked.

"No." Demetra suddenly felt very uncomfortable.

"Tabitha didn't have it?"

She hesitated a moment before answering but finally decided the truth was better than trying to deceive the master. "I didn't get a chance to check. Ezekiel appeared as I was about to search her body and I had to take my leave."

Thankfully he didn't ask further questions. Demetra was no match for Ezekiel, and they both knew it.

"I need the artifact, Demetra," said the master, capturing her gaze.

Why the master needed such an artifact, Demetra couldn't understand. The dark mage's powers were such that no wizard dead or alive could hope to match them, so why was the artifact so important?

"I'll bring you the artifact, Master, but I'll need more help if I'm to go after Ezekiel. I cannot do it alone and it would be far too inefficient to try going after him with an army of witches and sorcerers the way we stormed the Eastern Covenant."

"Obviously…"

The two remained silent a moment. Demetra's eyes were trained towards the window which gave onto snowy mountain peaks that didn't belong in Rio de Janeiro.

"You'll have your warlocks by tomorrow," said the master. "And then I must go on a trip. I'll be gone a few days. In my absence, you'll be the one in charge. You know what needs to be done. Do not disappoint me."

Chapter 35

It was nearing midnight in Yellowstone and Michael's little troop was assembled around a campfire deep inside the forest. Spring nights in this part of the world were still very fresh and the fire had been built as much for warmth as for cooking the rabbits Olivia and the skinwalkers had hunted down.

It would have taken very little psychology for an outsider to realize right away the tensions within the group. The three vampires sat on one side of the fire while the three skinwalkers sat on the other. Olivia sat halfway between the two groups, at equal distance from Daka and her sister Lucy, while Sheila and Michael sat opposite Olivia. Michael was starting to realize that bringing the vamps and the skinwalkers together wasn't the smartest idea he'd had this year.

Tensions had suddenly increased when Cristos had retrieved a blood pack from his gear and started drinking it through a straw. He was the only vampire within the group who required blood to survive and even though it was technically not his fault, Michael profoundly despised the act. And the skinwalkers' presence only served to amplify the obscenity of the situation. But Michael couldn't openly tell Cristos to go drink his blood elsewhere. He'd come with Lucy and Irini and was therefore part of the group, for better and for worse. And since everyone else was eating, why shouldn't he?

The three skinwalkers were staring him down with something akin to murder in their eyes while the vamp returned their gaze, amused and seemingly as concerned as a hunter facing a baby deer. Michael wasn't even certain why he'd asked the vampires to join them, but somehow, he had the feeling it was important. It was the same instinct that had pushed him to pick this particular part of the park to set up their camp, far from any road and difficult to access.

The camp's location made a surprise visit from the DSA highly unlikely in the first place, but if those jerks somehow managed to track them down nonetheless, the vampires' presence would help even the fight. The three vamps were tough, even for their race. Cristos and Irini were both elders of the Eastern Covenant, and as a hybrid, Lucy was far more powerful than a vampire her age should be.

The meal finished, the breathing members of the group started getting ready for bed. There were no tents involved, but they'd purchased mats and sleeping bags on their way down to the park.

Michael gave strict orders to keep the sleeping bags unzipped through the night. In case of an attack, they had to be able to jump out of them unencumbered at a moment's notice. He then kissed Sheila good night before lying down beside her. He heard the soft, regular breathing of the journalist a few minutes later; exhausted by the activities of the day, she'd quickly fallen into the arms of Morpheus.

Michael lay there, eyes wide open, for a few minutes before finally deciding to get back up. Maybe a short walk around the camp would help him find sleep.

Lucy and Irini had gone foraging for berries for breakfast and Michael found Cristos by himself practicing a combination of attacks with two knives. "Can we talk a moment?" asked Michael.

Cristos gave him a look that wasn't openly hostile but was far from friendly.

Michael took the vamp's silence as a yes. "I understand that the situation is unusual and difficult for everyone, Cristos. You're Lucy and Irini's guest and for that I welcome you within our group. But I want things to be crystal clear between us; if anything were to happen to any of the skinwalkers during your stay with us, I'll have your head. Is that understood?"

Cristos smiled before answering. "If anything happens, you'll be welcome to try…"

Michael cocked his head in goodbye before turning on his heels and walking away into the woods.

Truth be told, Cristos was presently far from the biggest of Michael's problems. He was confident the vamp would behave himself and hoped to God the skinwalkers would do the same. The situation between Ezekiel and Dariel concerned him far more, as did the High King's accusation. Was the elf correct in his assumption? Had someone within Michael's group leaked the information that had led to Leka's death? Such a thing was hard to fathom. Daka, Olivia, Sheila and Michael himself had been the only witnesses to the exchange between Ezekiel and Leka. And all of them were above suspicion in Michael's eyes. So, where had the leak come from?

Could Olivia have told Lucy about the transfer of the artifact, and could Lucy in turn have related the information to other vampires? Lucy had still been in Europe at the time and could potentially have spoken to anyone in the Eastern Covenant... What about Daka? Could he have mistakenly mentioned the transfer to his packmates? There was no way for Michael to know. He could of course question his friends, but there was no guarantee they would tell the truth. If one had indeed been indiscreet, they might not be willing to confess their fault.

Michael's mind went again to Maya. The elvish princess made for a far better traitor. For one thing, it wouldn't be the first time she'd betrayed her father's trust... Unfortunately, that also made her a perfect scapegoat. Despite the extent to which Michael wanted to believe that Maya was responsible for Leka's death, the weight in the pit of his stomach suggested it was wishful thinking on his part.

Chapter 36

It had been less than four days since Wes Thortan had assumed command of the Ozark training camp, but he was pleased to see that his wards already hated his guts with a passion. At the top of the list was the female cougar, the woman he'd dutifully visited every night since his arrival. It was amazing how cooperative a mother became once you took her child away and threatened to return him to her in pieces.

No matter how hard the DSA tried, they would never succeed in capturing every single freak on the planet, which was why teaching the captives to hunt not only their own kind but other freaks was key. And this was by far the part of the training the warden enjoyed the most. It appealed to his bloodlust and sadistic tendencies. Seeing the creatures tear each other apart, witnessing the blood oozing out of their wounds, was always the highlight of his day. And now he would bring a new dimension to the fights.

The idea had come to him two nights earlier while lying in bed after having satisfied his perverted compulsions with the cougar woman. What if he were to raise the stakes of those interspecies confrontations? What would make things a bit more fun for himself and provide a bit more incentive for the fighters to do their best? The answer had come to him almost instantly.

Thanks to the ample supply of free labor at his disposal, it had taken only two days to build his version of an arena. Truth being told, the giant cage didn't look much like an arena. But with its twenty-foot-tall walls and bars across the roof, it was entirely enclosed, and much like the circus of ancient Rome, the combatants inside had nowhere to run.

The cage had been erected at the center of a clearing. An area small enough to be difficult to identify from the sky or by satellite imagery, but large enough to give the fighters room to put on their best show.

Once given the order to fight by their handlers, the diadems would force the beasts to rip each other to pieces until only one of them survived. For the fights inside his cage would be to the death, a way to weed out the weak and punish the troublemakers. He needed to be careful not to abuse the idea, however. No matter how satisfying it would be for him, the director wouldn't be pleased if half of her troops were killed before they saw battle. He could get away with a few casualties here and there though... Even the best penitentiaries weren't immune to the occasional *accident*, and this was a training camp after all.

It hadn't taken him long to pick the first contender to partake in the cage's inauguration. An alpha werewolf had been giving the guards some trouble and had therefore earned his spot inside the cage. Wes had considered what kind of opponent should be placed in front of the wolf but since wolves were fairly low on the werecreatures' food chain, he was afraid that a bigger shifter would kill the beast too quickly, which would be no fun at all.

He needed a fair fight, a balanced confrontation that would prolong the suffering of both parties. The wolf's opponent also needed to be expendable in case the fight went the wrong way... Another werewolf would have been an obvious choice, of course, but Wes didn't like obvious. Werewolf against werewolf sounded like a very boring headline and he'd wanted the few guards he'd invite to the show to enjoy themselves. This was meant to be entertaining. That's when he'd remembered the pack of skinwalkers captured on a Shoshoni reservation. There were enough of them that if one or two were to disappear... it wouldn't be a dramatic loss. But these weren't werecreatures and were therefore much easier to kill. Having no idea about the skinwalkers' fighting skills, he'd randomly decided to line up three of them against the werewolf. Even if the skinwalkers were weaker, they were still wolves and fighting three against one should give them an edge against their quickly healing cousin.

Wes heard the sound of steps approaching and turned his head to see two guards emerging from the small trail they'd carved through the woods. They were shoving the werewolf forward in front of them.

The skinwalkers appeared, escorted by three guards, a moment later. The fight was about to start.

Each beast had been assigned its own handler. The diadems didn't behave like a video game controller though; the handler didn't have control over his toy's every move, but his own thoughts still overrode those of the creature he controlled. Micromanagement was impossible, but on a macro level the handler directed the battle. For the most part they left the beasts to their own devices, though. After all, who knew how a wolf should fight better than the wolf itself?

The werewolf entered the cage and was told to remain on one side of the arena while the three skinwalkers—two males and a female—entered through a gate located on the opposite side of the cage. They were all given the order to morph and Wes was shocked to see how quickly the skinwalkers could do so. While the werewolf had taken five or six seconds to complete his transformation, the skinwalkers had morphed in the blink of an eye.

Now that all fighters were in their animal form, the werewolf's physical superiority was painfully obvious. His beast was nearly twice as big as that of the largest skinwalker, and the warden wondered if three against one was going to be much of a challenge after all. Oh, well… it was too late to worry about it now.

He nodded to the handlers and the beasts were immediately ordered to begin the fight. The werewolf rushed the closest of his enemies, the attack reminding the warden of a bull charging a torero. The skinwalker saw him coming but there wasn't much room to run so he stood his ground.

The werewolf collided with his prey an instant later but the latter skillfully avoided the fangs of his much stronger cousin while his two packmates closed on their enemy in a perfectly synchronized motion. One sank its teeth into the beast's flank while the other went for the neck. But the werewolf simply seemed to ignore their attacks and continued going after the third skinwalker whom he finally pinned under his powerful paws, his claws piercing the flesh of the weaker wolf. An instant later his jaws were closing on the neck of his victim and tearing flesh and blood vessels with innate efficiency. As the blood spurted out of the skinwalker's neck, the werewolf appeared to finally take notice of the two other wolves clinging to his own neck.

The warden was enjoying every second of the spectacle. The blood bath was literally giving him a hard on. He watched with mesmerized pleasure as the werewolf started shaking the other two free from his neck before falling with renewed fury against the one trying to go for his belly.

Within thirty seconds, he'd killed a second skinwalker and was left facing a single opponent. Wes already knew how the fight would end. He could have stopped it to save the skinwalker's life, but he really didn't want to. It was far too much fun to watch.

Chapter 37

After only two days in Yellowstone, Michael was already starting to go crazy with boredom. Under normal circumstances, he enjoyed walking the park's forest and hiking its ridges, but this type of activity presented very little appeal at the moment. The fact he couldn't leave his comrades alone without having to worry about the skinwalkers and the vampires getting at each other's throats didn't help, either. On the other hand, even if they had been the best of friends it was safer the group remained together in case their respective enemies showed up.

While the skinwalkers, Sheila and himself were hiding from the DSA, the vampires were hiding from the dark mage. And although the DSA appeared to be a feeble threat in comparison to the incredibly powerful mage, Michael still held a greater grudge against the DSA. Those humans had killed his friends Bob and Cameahwait, and they'd kidnapped Daka's packmates.

With the exception of Cristos who was sleeping wrapped in a duvet a few yards away, everyone else was busy one way or another getting lunch ready.

Michael had just placed a small log on the fire when Ezekiel appeared out of nowhere. The wizard greeted everyone and, nodding towards the sleeping form of the vampire, asked, "What is that, Michael?"

"*That* is Cristos," answered Irini. "It's a package deal; where Lucy and I go, he goes." She didn't sound particularly friendly, but Ezekiel ignored the comment.

"What's going on, Ez? I wasn't expecting you back so soon and you look even more tired than the last time I saw you." What Michael meant to say was that Ezekiel looked like shit, but he'd opted for a more tactful approach.

"Who's this?" Nayati asked Daka in a voice that was not meant to be overheard.

"*This*, my young pup, is the last member of the Second Circle of wizardry left alive on Earth," replied the wizard.

For once Michael felt that Ez's melodrama wasn't overstated. He was indeed the last member of his order and Michael could only imagine what it felt like to lose friends you'd known for countless millennia.

"And to answer your question, Michael," continued the wizard, "I do feel tired. Utterly overwhelmed by the current situation. The alliances with the elves have all collapsed. The wizards are left alone to face the mage's growing army and I feel like I have a bullseye painted on my back. I spend my days watching over my shoulder, not knowing where the next attack will come from. In times like these, I truly wish I were someone else, old friend."

Michael was more than a little surprised by the wizard's reply. It didn't sound anything like Ezekiel. He'd never heard him sounding defeated, but here it was.

"There is one glimmer of hope, however," said Ez.

"What's that?" asked Michael.

"I can no longer feel the aura of the dark mage."

Michael looked at his friend questioningly. "What does that mean?"

"I don't know. It's as if he's just left the planet."

"Could he be gone?" asked Sheila.

"I suppose he could, but that would make no sense. Why would he leave now, so close to reaching his goal? I have sensed his aura diminishing in power over the last several days; not tremendously, but enough to notice. Then all of the sudden, two days ago, it just blinked out of existence. It has spiked back up once or twice since but only for a couple minutes before completely disappearing again."

"If he's gone, where do you think he went?" asked Michael.

"I don't have the faintest clue," said the wizard. "But I fully expect him to be back with a vengeance. Wherever he's gone I doubt it's good news for us."

Michael nodded somberly.

The wizard stayed to have lunch with them and was about to take his leave when he approached Michael and whispered in his ear. "If anything were to happen to me, Gwendolyn may have some answers for you." He then tapped on Michael's shoulder amicably and blinked out of existence.

Michael stood there wondering what Ezekiel had meant by that. It sounded like the wizard was truly fearing for his life and Michael didn't like it the slightest bit.

Chapter 38

Michael lay restless atop his sleeping bag. His mind kept going back to Ezekiel's comments and how scared the wizard had appeared to be. Ez had taken his leave nearly twelve hours earlier, but Michael couldn't erase his friend's sunken cheeks and haunted eyes from his memory. He'd looked like a hunted beast.

Michael and the vampires aside, everyone else was asleep. He'd taken Sheila on a short walk in the surrounding woods after dinner, but his heart had not been in it, and he was worried the journalist would start to hold her lack of interest in her against him.

He suddenly felt a presence to his right and smelled the air for danger but detected nothing. He sat up and searched the night, but nothing was moving in the shadows of the trees. Still, he couldn't help but follow his instinct. He needed to go check it out.

He got up and the three vampires who were chatting in low voices twenty yards away immediately turned towards him. He shook his head negatively and headed in the opposite direction. Lucy was by his side in a flash; he'd not even heard her come.

"What's going on, Michael?" she whispered. "Have you heard something?"

"It's probably nothing, go back to the others. If it turns out to be something, I'll let you know. In the meantime, it's better for the three of you to keep an eye on those who are sleeping."

Lucy nodded her agreement and was gone as quickly as she'd appeared.

The farther Michael walked into the woods the stronger the feeling of a presence became, but he still couldn't detect any scent. This was concerning. A bear's nose was the best in the animal kingdom, but the presence he was sensing smelled like nothing at all.

He wasn't one to be easily scared, but he had to admit that the situation was a bit ominous. His unease had nothing to do with the dark silent woods; he felt in his element here. But he best enjoyed his woods alone, and he had the distinct feeling he wasn't alone at the moment.

Fifty or so yards away Sheila, Olivia and the skinwalkers lay asleep under the watchful eyes of the vampires, but he didn't worry about them. He was the target of whatever was out there, he was sure of it… But if he went down, who would protect the others?

At the realization, he decided to head back towards the camp. He hadn't made three steps when the threat he'd been sensing materialized directly in front of him. Before Michael could utter a single word, he felt a wave invading his body from the inside, flooding his system. And then he collapsed to the ground.

Chapter 39

After a short but particularly fruitful trip to the US Rockies, Demetra was back at the Eastern Covenant's stronghold in the heart of Transylvania. While a mere week ago werewolves and vampires had been patrolling the very grounds she was pacing, now she encountered only witches and sorcerers. Vulpe's summer residence was officially vampire-free…

As Demetra entered the castle, she reflected their army was growing at a pace far exceeding her expectations. Over the past week, she'd even managed to bring a half dozen wizards of the Third Circle into their ranks. Two of them were here in Transylvania while four others were currently in southwestern France, in the Eastern Covenant's summer quarters. They weren't alone, of course; a fair number of troops had been sent to train alongside the wizards. To train, and to watch the domain in case the vamps tried to stage a return, something she strongly doubted would happen. Her army had slaughtered most of Vulpe's forces, and she'd be surprised if more than a couple dozen vamps had survived the onslaught.

As she entered the main reception hall, two warlocks tilted their heads towards her. Their salute was designed to greet an equal, but these two weren't her equals. They'd been mere sorcerers only yesterday. She still had no idea how the master could convert sorcerers into warlocks, but that's precisely what had happened.

Of all the warlocks who'd fought for the master so far, she and Lotar had been the only two genuine ones. All the others had been fabricated by the master. But although their powers were nearly as great as hers, they lacked the experience, a flaw that made them cocky and easy to kill. They were more than a match for wizards of the Fourth Circle and could probably defeat the majority of practitioners belonging to the Third

Circle, but they'd proven over and over that they were no match for someone like Ezekiel, even fighting two against one.

Demetra snapped her fingers and the two looked at her. She gestured impatiently and they finally got out of their seats and came to her.

"Show me what you've been up to these past twenty-four hours," she said. "I want to review the troops."

One of them nodded and extended an arm towards the door in an *after you* gesture. They exited the room and went straight to the inner courtyard where a group of sorcerers were practicing advanced battle spells under the guidance of one of their own. The spells were rudimentary but efficient and would cause some serious damage to any practitioner of lower levels. Demetra suspected a wizard of the Third Circle wouldn't fall under such rudimentary curses, but that's why the master had supplemented their forces with other attributes...

The dark mage had provided praeternatural creatures to complement their magical army, and Demetra was still thinking of the best way to use those new factions.

One thing was certain, the master kept her plenty busy... Her last assignment had distracted her from the task of identifying the exact location of the Soul Catcher, but it hadn't been time wasted. Ezekiel thought he could hide his little friends in the heart of Yellowstone, but the wizard had been direly mistaken. There was no hiding from the master... Soon the bear and his gang of misfits would have a major surprise. One they'd never see coming.

Chapter 40

A single empty car was parked in front of the convenience store, but the parking lot wasn't truly deserted. Standing at its edge, nearly absorbed by the foliage of an unkempt bush, a form lurked in the shadows, unmoving. Michael couldn't tell whether the eerie twilight was due to dusk or dawn, though.

He watched as a male shopper exited the convenience store and headed for the only vehicle on the lot, apparently unaware of the shadow following closely in his footsteps.

The shopper didn't look familiar, but the shadow did; with his pointy hat and gray cloak, Ezekiel was easily recognizable.

The wizard extended a hand towards the shopper's back, but before he could touch him, the man spun around and a flash exploded out of the Colt revolver gleaming in his hand.

The bullet entered the wizard's chest on his left side, and even if by a miracle it had missed the heart, the crater in the wizard's back left no doubt as to the damage caused by the hollow point ammunition.

The wizard fell lifeless to the ground, his face a mask of surprise. The shooter smiled at his victim before opening the trunk of his car and placing the lifeless body in it. This had been an ambush; the man had known all along that the wizard was waiting for him.

In the distance, Michael heard someone calling his name. "Michael... Michael... Wake up!"

Michael opened an eye and found Lucy bent over him, with Irini standing by her side, looking worried.

"What happened?" asked Lucy.

"I have no idea," he replied.

"Were you attacked?"

"No."

"Then what are you doing on the ground?"

Michael sat up, feeling groggy. "I don't know. I remember going for a walk."

"Yeah... you went to check out some noise you'd heard."

He tried to remember but it was hazy, his thoughts all muddled. He remembered the dream, he remembered seeing Ezekiel being murdered, but he had no recollection of falling asleep. "I must have been more tired than I thought," he said finally, not really believing the words himself.

The two vampires looked at each other in the way doctors do before announcing bad news to a patient.

"I don't think that's what happened, Michael. There's something fishy about this."

"Where are the others?" Michael suddenly asked urgently.

"They're still sleeping, Cristos is watching over them."

Michael didn't like the sound of that, but they were only a few feet away, after all.

"How long have I been gone?" he asked.

"Twenty minutes, maybe. When you didn't come back, we went to look for you, but it took us some time to find you," replied Irini. "Try and remember what happened, Michael. I have the feeling it's important."

"I'm trying," he replied, getting back on his feet and feeling a bit woozy. Lucy and Irini's concern was understandable; he, too, would like to know what he'd been doing sleeping on the forest floor. This was the first time such a thing had happened to him. He'd never blacked out before, but this was exactly how it felt, as if he'd just passed out. This was concerning but the dream he'd had was even more so. It had felt so real, as if Michael had been there, watching the scene with his own eyes, which was ridiculous of course...

Suddenly he felt the need to contact Ezekiel. He reached inside the pocket of his hiking pants and retrieved a disposable phone. Finding a signal in the backwoods of Yellowstone was always a challenge, but Michael hadn't picked their camping spot randomly. Two network bars appeared on the device's screen, and Michael immediately dialed Ezekiel's number. The call went to voicemail after five rings and Michael repeated the operation twice more before finally giving up. It wasn't unusual for the wizard to be out of reach, but this knowledge didn't reassure Michael in the least.

Chapter 41

Ezekiel watched the man enter what was likely the only store in a fifteen-mile radius, an isolated convenience store of the kind one rarely saw nowadays.

The man had parked his car on the nearest spot, but due to the landscaping in front of the store, it was still a good twenty yards to the front door.

The sun was slowly dropping, chasing the remaining light away from the parking lot, but Ezekiel had carefully planned his attack; draped in the shadows of a massive bush native to the region, he remained invisible. Had he wanted to, the wizard could have literally made himself invisible, but it was bad practice to waste precious magical energy unnecessarily.

He watched the man disappear into the store and waited for his return. He hoped no one else would show up. It was important nobody witness what was about to happen.

His thoughts soon drifted towards Michael. He felt bad about deceiving his friend, but the deception was necessary. Ezekiel hadn't told Michael everything he'd seen through Jason Parrish's eyes. Nor had he revealed everything he'd heard through the man's ears. It was this withheld information that had allowed him to find this particularly unsavory character he was now stalking. Ezekiel only had a theory at the moment, but that theory felt right. It was time to put it to the test, and this man was the key to that. The gamble was significant, but Ezekiel saw no other way. Not after what he'd learned in the hidden library of Mumbai.

He now understood the true nature of Amariel's Amulet, also known as the fifth artifact. One indeed more powerful than any other ever created by faes, elves or wizards. Ezekiel had discovered where the dark mage came from... He'd wanted to tell Michael. He almost had, as a matter of fact, but he'd changed his mind at the last minute. It was simply too dangerous. He couldn't take the chance.

Ezekiel saw the man walking out of the convenience store, but he carried no bag. Odd but not overly alarming. Maybe he'd bought some gum or a pack of cigarettes, assuming he smoked. Ezekiel knew nothing about the man or his habits.

The wizard started moving towards his victim, as silent as a cat. He quickly caught up with him and started waving a hand to cast a spell as the man was about to enter his vehicle. But the man spun around, catching the wizard by surprise. Ezekiel saw something in the man's hand, something his mind didn't have time to recognize before a flash of light exploded in front of him.

Chapter 42

Three days after his departure from *I-Naur-Tal*, Michael found himself standing in front of its portal. As usual, the elvish city was invisible behind the camouflaged force field, but Michael had lived within its walls for three months and knew full well how to get in.

He'd made the trip by himself this time; Sheila and the others had remained in Yellowstone. He'd been uneasy about his decision but moving their whole group through the park and all the way to the Gallatin Forest wasn't a good idea. A single person was less likely to attract attention than nine, especially given the eclectic nature of their group.

Michael had snuck out of the park around dawn after leaving strict instructions for his companions to remain hidden. He hoped that the vampires and skinwalkers would behave themselves, but he couldn't worry about these things at the moment. He had more urgent matters to address.

Purposefully hiking the woods of the Gallatin Forrest, Michael had wondered more than once if he was being followed, but he hadn't seen anything or anyone. He had no doubt that elvish eyes had followed his approach, but the elves hadn't shown themselves to him, and it wasn't their invisible presence that had him concerned anyway.

Whoever had ambushed Leka's convoy had known where to do it, and it was likely Leka's murderers also knew the location of the elvish city... Could *I-Naur-Tal* be under surveillance? It was possible but not likely, as the elves would be hard to fool. They had sentries posted at strategic locations throughout the woods surrounding their city; it would be very difficult for anyone to get close without being spotted.

He passed through the portal and found guards he knew well on the other side. To his surprise, they readily assented to his request, and he was escorted to the castle. After being kicked out of the city three days earlier he'd expected a little more resistance from the guards, but he'd been wrong.

Twenty minutes later, he was sitting alone inside some sort of boudoir, waiting for an audience with High King Dariel. It wasn't the first time Michael had found himself in such a position. He knew from experience that it was likely he'd have to wait a while, so he was pleasantly surprised when the room's large wooden doors swung open a moment later and Dariel walked into the room.

"Thank you for seeing me, my lord," said Michael, bowing in respect.

"Good morning, Michael." The elf's tone was cold but not openly hostile. "Why have you come?"

"I have come to ask for your help, my lord. I'm concerned about Ezekiel. I have been unable to reach him and I was wondering if you had any news of his whereabouts."

"I know not where the Ancient One is." Dariel was standing in front of the wide windows, his eyes fixed on a waterfall whose water ran in an upward direction from the gardens below. "I can only tell you that Ez was in the area yesterday. I could sense his presence."

Michael knew that by *the area,* the High King was referring to a location radiating several hundred miles around the elvish city. "He came to visit us in Yellowstone yesterday, my lord," he explained. "Are you saying that you no longer sense him?"

The elf turned around to face Michael and nodded. "That is correct."

"I have tried calling him dozens of times and left several messages on his phone, but I can't get through to him."

"Why are you worried? This isn't the first time Ezekiel has proved difficult to reach."

Michael debated whether or not he should mention the dream to the elf and finally decided that it couldn't hurt. The High King listened to him attentively, nodding from time to time.

"And you believe your dream may be a premonition?" he asked.

"I don't know what I believe, but I know in my gut that something is going on and I need to warn him. Do you have any idea of where he might be, any clue at all? I'm not asking for certainty, just a general direction where I could start my search."

The elf shook his head. "As you already know, Ezekiel and I aren't on the best of terms at the moment. He told me nothing about his intentions before leaving the city."

Michael was sure disappointment was plainly visible on his face. "Do you have a way to reach him? Other than by phone, I mean…" he said halfheartedly.

The elf looked away a moment before answering. "I do. Are you asking me to try and get in touch with him?"

"I'd greatly appreciate if you could."

Dariel closed his eyes and stood motionless a long moment before reopening them. "I can't find him, Michael. I am sorry. Wherever Ezekiel may be, I cannot reach him. There's nothing I can do for you at the moment. I'll try again later and let you know if I succeed."

"What does that mean?" asked Michael. "Has it happened before? Have you ever been unable to reach him in the past?"

Dariel seemed to contemplate the question a moment. "Not that I can recall, but as you know my magic and Ezekiel's aren't of the same nature. We aren't perfectly aligned and me not being able to reach him doesn't necessarily imply that something happened to him."

Michael appreciated Dariel's hopeful words but in his gut, he knew that's all they were… words. If Dariel himself couldn't reach Ezekiel, it couldn't be good news.

Michael took his leave shortly after and was exiting the castle when Maya caught up with him. He hadn't been this close to the princess in three years. The last time they had been this close, she'd tried to kill him. Her magic placed her in a league on par with Ezekiel. Michael would have had no way to survive her wrath had her father not intervened. But Dariel wasn't around at the moment and Michael felt very vulnerable.

"May we talk a moment, Michael?" she asked.

"Of course, Princess," he answered, trying to sound respectful even though respect was the last thing he felt towards the woman.

"I know you and I have some history, but I want you to know that I hold no grudge towards you. I was in the wrong and I want bygones to be bygones. My father has informed me that Ezekiel is missing, and I wanted you to know that I have nothing to do with it. If I can help you in any way, I will."

She was looking him straight in the eyes and Michael didn't know what to say or even to think. His heart told him to run as far away as possible from the woman, but was his bias clouding his judgement? He couldn't help but think that Maya sounded sincere.

Chapter 43

Demetra and her acolyte were watching the woman suspended upside down five feet off the ground against the wall. Her arms and legs were spread wide apart. Blood was seeping from a corner of her mouth, collecting in a small puddle on the dusty floor of the Patagonian apartment. Demetra looked at her victim dispassionately. This wasn't personal. She had nothing against the woman, a wizard of the Third Circle who'd displayed some skills.

Following a series of clues, they'd found her in a small Argentinian village. An easy task since the wizard hadn't been trying to hide.

Demetra had reasons to believe that the woman possessed precious information regarding the Soul Catcher's location, but the wizard had been able to keep her tongue tied... so far.

"Let me try," said the other warlock.

Demetra gave him a look that shut him up. She hadn't brought him over to help her with the woman. He was just there to serve as backup in case Ezekiel decided to show up.

"I'll ask you one last time... Where is the Soul Catcher?" said Demetra

"Let me repeat myself one last time," said the wizard in a cracking voice. "I have no idea."

Demetra was starting to suspect that the woman truly didn't know where the artifact was. She'd already withstood hours of torture and even though her body could heal, the mental toll on the wizard's psyche would be much harder to erase.

Demetra waved her wand and shards of ice the size of medieval daggers manifested from thin air and flew through the room to impale the woman's arms and legs. The wizard screamed in pain as more of her blood poured to the dirty ground. Her gaze was fixed on a point behind

Demetra who turned around to follow it. But there was nothing behind her, nothing but a window looking onto vast mountains that weren't unlike what Demetra had seen in Utah. It didn't look like she was going to get her hands on the artifact today... What a waste of time.

Demetra was glad the master wasn't around these days. She wouldn't have to report her lack of progress. One thing bothered her about her quest, however. The master had been adamant about getting his hands on the most powerful artifacts known to the magical world. All but one... Why hadn't she been asked to find the Healing Stone designed by the elves? The Soul Catcher and the Healing Stone were related, and if one worried about death, one should also worry about injuries. Why would you go after one and not the other? Demetra couldn't understand the rationale behind the master's requests, but she knew she wasn't privy to all the secrets. Unless... Unless the master had already found the Healing Stone... She was the master's second in command, yes, but she was still only a pawn in a game she did not fully understand.

Where was the master right now? She no longer felt the all-powerful aura. No matter where she went in the world, the signature was completely absent, as if the master had vanished from the face of the earth. But how? Demetra knew no magic able to do that. There was, to the best of her knowledge, no spell able to transport one to another spatial or temporal plane.

The wizard's screams pulled her out of her reverie, and she noticed flames dancing atop the woman's feet. She stared at the other warlock. She was growing increasingly annoyed with him. Who did he think he was to disobey her orders? She waved her wand in his direction and his own wand went flying out of his hand. He looked at her in surprise for a second before a shock wave collided with his body and he crashed against the closest wall. She then turned her attention to the still screaming wizard and, with a flick of the wrist, sent a beam of light toward the woman. The attack drilled a four-inch hole in the woman's chest, pulverizing her heart in the process.

Chapter 44

After his visit to *I-Naur-Tal*, Michael had returned to Yellowstone a little after two in the afternoon, but he hadn't gone straight to the hidden campsite where his companions awaited his return. Instead, he'd changed into his bear—a great disguise inside the park—and was taking the long way home, approaching the campground by making wide circles, each one a bit tighter than the one before, a spiral centered around the campsite.

The purpose of the exercise was to survey an area covering a two-mile radius around the camp. Although his bear's nose could have detected a scent that didn't belong in the forest from sixty miles away, it was always possible for someone to approach downwind, which would make detection based on scent impractical.

Convincing himself there were no enemies spying on them wasn't his only motivation, though; he also wanted to survey the wildlife around the camp. He was happy with what he'd found so far.

The task took him the entire afternoon and a good part of the evening; it was nearly 10 PM when he finally caught sight of the campfire flickering in the night. The others would be done with dinner by now, but he wasn't particularly hungry anyway. His bear had feasted on an abandoned moose carcass and had spent thirty minutes eating dessert in a blackberry patch afterward. It had been a while since Michael had let his beast indulge in these types of raw delicacies, and it felt good to reconnect with his furry alter ego.

He found everyone sitting around the fire. His companions appeared to be civil to each other, which was more than he'd hoped for.

"Michael," said Sheila as soon as he appeared. "We were starting to worry. You were gone all day! What did Dariel say, does he know where Ezekiel is?"

"He doesn't know. And he can't reach him either. He says it means nothing, but I'm not so sure. I have a really bad feeling about this."

Michael could see by the faces of his companions, illuminated by the dancing fire, that they shared his concerns.

"But Ez said the dark mage's aura has vanished, didn't he?" said Olivia. "And if the dark mage isn't around, who could defeat him?"

Michael had asked himself the same question during his day trek. The two vanishing at almost the same time couldn't be a coincidence. Had Ezekiel figured out where the master was hiding? Had he learned his secret and gone after him? Michael tried to imagine what a parallel spatiotemporal plane might look like, but his imagination wasn't that good. The idea sounded a bit too farfetched, even to a werebear.

"Come and sit with us," said Sheila, patting the floor next to her.

Michael obliged and went to sit by her side. She wrapped her two hands around one of his enormous paws and rested her head on his shoulder. They stayed like that for a long moment with no one speaking, all apparently mesmerized by the twirling fire.

When the conversation finally resumed it drifted towards future plans. Where would they go from here? How long were they going to stay hidden in Yellowstone? With the exception of Sheila, they were all praeternaturals; action was in their blood. Standing still and doing nothing wasn't something any of them was used to, and that included the journalist. But Michael was torn by indecision, oscillating between going to look for Ezekiel and keeping those closest to him safely hidden in the park.

After an hour and a half of debate, they were nowhere closer to agreement on a path forward.

"I'm sick of this already," said Lucy, gesturing towards the surrounding woods. "If I ha—"

Michael suddenly got up, the urgency of his movement interrupting her in midsentence.

"What is it, Michael?" whispered Irini.

But he just lifted a hand to request silence. He sniffed the air a couple of times before whispering in a low voice, "Vampires."

Cristos gave him an inquisitive look, but he ignored it.

"How many?" asked Daka.

"Many," replied Michael. "Silvia's with them."

Silvia was an elder of the Western Covenant trapped in a fourteen-year-old's body, despite having been around for centuries. There was no love lost between Michael and the woman. And he wasn't the only member of the group on her shit list either. A year earlier, Daka and his pack had dispatched Silvia's second in command alongside several of his men, and the elder was unlikely to have forgotten.

"How far away are they?" asked Irini, already preparing for battle. She'd opened a duffel bag Cristos had been carrying around and retrieved two assault rifles, which she handed to Cristos and Lucy.

The three vamps had apparently raided one of the Eastern Covenant's caches on their way to Yellowstone. The Covenant had a number of safehouses spread throughout the world where its members could rest or hide depending on the need. Each house was equipped with blood packs, weapons and vehicles.

The skinwalkers turned into their wolves in the blink of an eye and Olivia quickly followed suit.

Michael turned towards Irini. "Can you put Sheila in a safe place?"

He was looking upwards, and Irini got the message. She hugged Sheila and jumped to the lower branches of a massive Douglas fir. Within seconds, the journalist was sixty feet off the ground, hidden within the dense evergreen, and Irini was back down with the others.

Michael turned into his bear as his friends were already fanning out around the campsite. Soon the enemy would be upon them. There was only one thing left for Michael to do.

Chapter 45

Using his nose, Michael followed the progression of Silvia and her men; they were getting closer. When they finally reached the campground, his bear constituted the only obvious target. Crouching in the shadows, the wolves were nearly invisible and the three vamps were nowhere to be seen.

Silvia had brought sufficient reinforcements that he was unable to distinguish every individual scent. Though he'd expected many enemies, his heart sank as they closed in on him and he spotted at least twenty-five bloodsuckers with the woman.

Michael had survived battles against more vamps before, but Dragos' army had been composed of newly turned amateurs. Silvia's death squad played in a different league; she'd have only brought experienced warriors with her. Some of them with centuries of experience, if their stench was any indication.

He was glad to have some backup, but as was always the case, worry was also part of the equation. His reinforcements were also his friends and, Cristos aside, he couldn't stand the idea of losing a single one of them.

Michael saw a few of his enemies raising their assault rifles, but before they had a chance to pull the trigger, they were turned into Swiss cheese by a deluge of firepower coming from the trees, courtesy of Lucy and Cristos. He knew the bloodsuckers would eventually get back to their feet, but it'd take them a long time to recover from this type of damage. They were effectively down for the count.

Two down, twenty-three to go, he estimated as the night exploded into an all-out war. Vampires fighting vampires, wolves running for cover before turning around on their pursuers and falling upon them, all fangs out. As usual, Michael's bear couldn't rival a vampire's speed, but his resilience to pain and the sheer power of his beast more than made up for it.

Silvia's men quickly realized that firearms were of no use to them. At such close range, friendly-fire casualties were as likely as hitting the intended enemy. This was true for the three vamps fighting on Michael's side as well, but they'd come prepared as evidenced by the two short swords Irini was wielding with the dexterity of a gladiator in ancient Rome. But despite the havoc she caused among the ranks of the Western Covenant, the enemy kept coming.

From the corner of his eye, Michael saw two vampires fall upon Olivia, easily recognizable among the smaller Shoshone wolves. But before he had a chance to worry about her, Daka and one of his packmates dispatched one of her attackers. Left alone with a single opponent, Olivia did a decent job of mauling the bloodsucker, but the Western Covenant was resourceful, and quickly another vampire came to join the fight.

Michael made a rush for it and had almost closed the distance when three elders fell upon him all at once. Two more soon joined in and his bear collapsed under their weight. From the ground, he watched Olivia struggling against her two experienced enemies. He roared with rage, but then Lucy came to her sister's rescue. The vamp-wolf hybrid had spent nine months training under Irini—one of the Eastern Covenant's fiercest fighters—and the training had paid off. Using a short sword similar to the ones Irini was using, she chopped off the head of one of the vamps before plunging the blade into the heart of the other.

The sight boosted Michael's energy as he thrust his bear's front claws through the chest of the nearest bloodsucker, pinning him to the ground while his jaws chewed through his neck, but he still had four elders clawing and pummeling his sides and back...

From his vantage point he had a limited view of the battlefield, so had no idea how the fight was shaping up. He hadn't seen Daka and his packmates for some time, nor Cristos for that matter. All he knew was that the number of vampires he currently had on his back simply wasn't something he could manage alone, which was why he was very pleased when his nose announced that his cousins had finally showed up to the party.

Michael had spent the afternoon funneling the nearby grizzlies closer and closer to the campsite. A precaution in case of an attack. It had been time well spent... As a werebear, he could request the help of his purely animal cousins. A request the bears were unable to refuse. It was coded in their genes; the call of a praeternatural had to be answered.

He'd relied on this gift only a handful of times in his life, and in every instance his cousins had not only answered the call but had saved his life in the process. Today was no different. The bears started plucking the vamps off his back one by one until he could get back up and assist with the dismembering.

He already counted six grizzlies on the battleground, and although one on one a bear was no match for a vampire elder, their presence significantly rebalanced the forces by keeping the vamps busy and off Michael's back.

A quick survey of the battlefield revealed the grizzlies to be in the most urgent need of assistance, so he focused his destructive energy on the vampires harassing his furry friends. He quickly dispatched three bloodsuckers and was surprised to see the grizzlies starting to team up to help each other. He'd never seen that before.

Michael was moving towards Lucy and Olivia who were fending off four enemies when Silvia and one of her men blocked the way. He could see hatred in the woman's eyes. She lifted an automatic sidearm and unloaded a dozen bullets into his body. Michael felt the lead piercing his flesh and bones and escaping through his back. No matter how many times they fought each other, Silvia never seemed to learn her lesson. You don't go after a werebear with military-grade ammo designed to pierce armored vehicles or neutralize human targets, you use hunting ammo designed to cause maximum damage and internal bleeding. The bullets momentarily paralyzed Michael's left front paw but he still had more than enough strength left in his body to fall upon the elder and bring her down under his weight. He saw terror in her eyes before his claws chopped her head straight off.

Michael surveyed the battlefield. He counted twenty bodies on the ground, but he knew there had been more fighters. It was just that those killed by the skinwalkers had immediately turned to ashes. When slaying vampires, skinwalkers never needed to worry about body disposal.

The Western Covenant had lost its entire strike force.

Michael turned back into his human form. "Any casualties on our side?" he asked. He could already see that two grizzlies had perished in the fight, but no matter how sad it was, he was more concerned about the wellbeing of his friends.

"Cristos is dead," said Irini.

Even though her voice sounded neutral, Michael knew how big of a loss it was to her. To him Cristos had just been another bloodsucker, but he'd been part of Irini's entourage for the past three or four centuries. The two might not have been best friends, but his death would still be hard to swallow.

"Nayati's dead too," said Daka, and the pain in his voice was unmistakable, as were the tears of Kimama.

Michael hadn't been close to Nayati, but Daka's packmate had helped him on several occasions in the past. Now Michael would be forever in his debt.

He couldn't help but wonder how Silvia had known where they were. No matter how big of a grudge she'd held against him, he doubted this had been a personal vendetta. The fact the vamps had found them in the heart of Yellowstone suggested the Western Covenant had been sent there, or at the very least tipped off. But tipped off by whom? With the exception of the men and women standing around him, no one, not even Ezekiel, had known precisely where Michael had intended to set up camp. Could the dark mage have eyes everywhere? Could he be spying on them using the eyes of the animals of the woods? Michael had read of such things in fantasy books, but he had no idea if it applied to reality. Although Ezekiel had a few spies in the animal kingdom, Michael knew it wasn't the most reliable way of keeping tabs on your enemies.

The DSA, on the other hand, had shown an uncanny propensity at tracking down praeternaturals. They were also much more likely to come after them than the dark mage was. Why would the dark mage bother about something as insignificant as a werebear and a couple of his friends?

But assuming it was indeed the DSA who'd sent Silvia and her friends to them, that would imply the government was working with vampires... An equally unlikely scenario. The bloodsuckers would never willingly work with humans, and Michael had found none of those mind-control devices on the dead vamps.

It seemed like an alliance between the Western Covenant and the dark mage remained the most likely answer, especially after the warlocks had tried to recruit the Eastern Covenant.

Michael was pulled out of his reflection as an argument rose up between Lucy and Kimama, the latter blaming the former for what had happened. Insults were flying on both sides. Irini and Daka soon joined the debate, and Michael had to step between the two groups to prevent further escalation.

He knew the uneasy alliance between the skinwalkers and the vamps would never recover from tonight's events. It was time for everyone to go their separate ways.

Chapter 46

Michael parked his pickup truck in front of an apartment complex in a dire state of disrepair and yawned. With the exception of a two-hour nap in Arizona, he hadn't slept in nearly forty-eight hours.

After the Western Covenant's attack, they'd buried their dead in Yellowstone and split into three groups. Irini and Lucy had left for an unknown destination, while Olivia, Daka and Kimama had decided to head for an old Shoshone campground in the Bridger Mountains. Michael didn't know the camp's exact location, and he hadn't asked. The wolves would be safer if no one knew where to find them.

Remembering the last conversation he'd had with Ezekiel, Michael had decided to go visit Gwendolyn in Houston. Of course Sheila had tagged along for the ride and after twenty-six hours on the road, they'd arrived in Houston around lunchtime.

Michael had dropped Sheila off at a motel out of town and paid for the room in cash to avoid being tracked through his credit card. He'd then headed to the northeast part of the city where the wizard lived in a dodgy part of town.

He got out of his truck and the eyes of teenaged gangster-wannabes all turned towards the 6'4" giant. Michael waved at them in a friendly gesture. "Twenty bucks for whoever keeps an eye on my truck while I'm gone."

But nobody took him up on his offer, and he received only blank stares from the kids blocking the building's entrance. They didn't try to stop him from getting inside but made no effort to move out of his way either. He squeezed through the obnoxious teens and finally reached the door.

Two minutes later, he was inside the wizard's spotless apartment. The place was small but cozy and well maintained.

Michael remembered the first time he'd encountered the one-eyed redhead. It had been in a *peculiar* bar called Mirror Mirror where Gwendolyn had been sitting in front of a bottle of vodka.

He smelled no alcohol on her breath right now, however, and he was pleased to see she was still sober. Just as she'd been the last time they'd met, some months back.

He couldn't help but wonder why the woman lived in this part of town. Apparently, wizards of the Fourth Circle weren't paid much if she couldn't afford better. Or maybe it was just a cover, a wizard thing, or some type of assignment. What did he know about such things?

"Would you like something to drink, Michael? I can make some tea," she said, showing him into her sparsely furnished living room and indicating a well-worn but surprisingly comfortable couch.

"I'm okay, thank you. As I was saying on the phone, I haven't been able to reach Ez for a couple of days now and, based on the last interaction I had with him, I have reason to believe that something might have happened to him."

A scar starting on her forehead and ending well towards the bottom of her cheek had robbed Gwendolyn of one of her eyes; the dead orbit was now hidden below a dark eye patch that gave her a mysterious look.

"I've been trying to reach him, too, since we last talked, but I haven't been able to get through either. Wherever Ezekiel is hiding, he doesn't want to be found."

Michael liked this explanation better than the alternative and hoped she was correct.

"He mentioned that if anything were to happen to him, I should come and find you. Do you have any idea what that's about? Did he leave you any instructions?"

The wizard appeared baffled by Michael's statement.

"No, nothing like that."

"So, why did he send me here?"

The wizard slowly shook her head; clearly she had no idea.

"Do you know what he's been up to lately?" asked Michael.

She thought about it a moment before answering. "Mostly doing research, I think. Based on the last time we saw each other."

"When was that?"

"About a week or so ago. He suspected the existence of a hidden magical artifact of great power."

Michael remembered the crash course on magical artifacts Ez had given them a couple weeks earlier. "Are you talking about one of the four most powerful ones?"

"You know about the four? I'm impressed... but no. According to Ez, there could be a fifth one called Amariel's Amulet. Initially he thought it was just a rumor, but he found evidence it was real."

"Did he tell you where to find the amulet, and what it did?"

"No. I don't think he knew at the time. At least not the location of the artifact. I suspect he was starting to have an idea of what it actually did, but he didn't share his theory with me."

Michael nodded; Ezekiel could be a secretive old wizard when he wanted to be.

"And do you know where he was conducting his research?"

Gwendolyn smiled at the question. "I do, but someone like you won't be able to get in."

"Never mind about that. Just tell me where?"

"The last time I saw him, he was heading for Mumbai's magical library."

"Mumbai as in Bombay? India?"

"The one and only."

Whatever Michael had expected, this wasn't it. His trip to the library would take him a bit longer than he'd expected; India wasn't a car ride away.

As if reading his mind Gwendolyn added, "But even if I gave you the address, they would never let a non-wizard in. And assuming you somehow managed to get in, how would you know what to look for among the thousands of volumes?"

"What if you came with me?" asked Michael.

She shook her head. "They still wouldn't let you in."

"What if you came with me *and* we dropped Ezekiel's name to the doorman?"

She thought about it for a moment before answering. "It's still a really long shot."

"Long shots are all we have right now. Let's go!" he said, getting up from the couch and heading towards the door.

Chapter 47

It was a quarter to one when the warden finally emerged from his office located in the administrative building of the Ozark training camp.

"Morning, Warden," said one of the guards in charge of watching the building where he'd spent the whole morning.

The warden nodded, but didn't bother answering.

"How was that burger last night? Good, right? Must have been... You skipped lunch today, right?"

"It was very good. Enough grease to clog a good third of my arteries, but it was worth it," he replied relatively amiably. Wes had felt the need to get away from the woods for a few hours the night before and had driven to the nearest burger joint for a double cheeseburger, the receipt for which was still lying in his car cup holder.

He stuck his hands inside his pockets and came out with a full can of blueberry Red Bull and a phone charger whose cord was maintained tightly coiled by a twist tie.

"We can't find those inside the camp," said the guard, staring at the warden's bounty.

"Tell me about it!"

He'd returned to the camp past midnight, but he'd still been up and at his desk before sunrise. He had a lot of catching up to do; he couldn't appear behind the ball in front of his men.

The warden's second in command showed up a moment later, eager to please. "You asked to see me, Sir?" he said, saluting his superior officer.

"I think it's time for a surprise inspection of the facility," replied Wes.

Surprise immediately registered in his lieutenant's eyes. "A surprise inspection?"

"That's what I just said. Are you deaf?"

"No, Sir! Absolutely, Sir. Where would you like to start?"

"I'll let you decide the itinerary, but I'd like to inspect every inch of this camp."

"Yes, sir," said the lieutenant before leading the way.

They started with the shooting range where a dozen trainees—werewolves for the most part—were shooting with sniper rifles at targets located fifty yards away. A short distance for a sniper, but none of the trainees could hit the mark or even get close.

"These people are hopeless," he said, sounding disgusted.

"None of them have ever shot a sniper rifle, Sir. There is a learning curve. On the plus side they really don't need the rifles to be lethal."

"Way to state the obvious!"

The lieutenant took the remark in stride and suggested they move on to the hands-on combat zone where the prisoners fought each other in their human form.

The warden spent twenty minutes watching the prisoners slam into each other with an intensity that would have crushed human bones. He smiled the whole time, a beatific smile... His lieutenant didn't seem to approve of his enjoyment, however. From the corner of his eye, the warden could see his subaltern observing him. There was disgust in the man's eyes. Good! He could work with disgust.

They then moved on to the interspecies' fighting ground where the prisoners in their animal form fought species against species.

They finally concluded the tour two hours later with a review of the cell blocks. All prisoners spent their nights behind bars, but a section of the jail was specifically designed for *problematic individuals*. A term with a rather loose definition.

All it took to be deemed problematic was to do something Wes Thortan didn't like. Which in some instances meant nothing at all.

When the warden and his lieutenant reached the cage of the female snow leopard, the warden saw sheer hatred in the eyes of the woman. He was pretty certain that the bars between them were the only thing stopping her from ripping him to pieces. The bars and the collar around her neck... The thought actually sent a shiver through his spine.

"She's been behaving, Sir, maybe we can return her cub to her. He's been in isolation for four days and he needs his mother," said the lieutenant.

The warden's eyes found the woman's and he held her gaze. "Let's give it another couple of days. If she keeps behaving herself then I'll consider reuniting the family," he said, winking at her.

Chapter 48

Unlike Ezekiel, Gwendolyn couldn't teleport, not even over a short distance, but she was far from resourceless. Something Michael was grateful for, since she'd saved him from spending twenty hours crammed in an airplane seat. Instead, the two had reached Mumbai in under eight hours and the bulk of that time had been spent driving from Houston to New Orleans.

The reason for their road trip had been located inside a house lost on the edge of the French quarter. Michael had stood in silence a long moment in front of the object, wondering if the wizard was pulling his leg. What Gwendolyn was calling a *portal* presented a striking resemblance to a *door*... and not a fancy door either. A plain white communication door between the kitchen and the dining room.

The principle of the portal was simple: one stepped through it and exited in another location sometimes thousands of miles removed from the departure point.

A trivial operation for a wizard, but not so trivial for Michael, and Gwendolyn had to cast a spell upon him before he could use the portal with a reasonable amount of confidence to reach the other side in one piece. From New Orleans, they'd ended up in Barcelona. And after a thirty-minute stroll along the streets of the Spanish city, they'd stepped through another portal that had led them to Jerusalem. From Jerusalem they'd arrived in Shanghai and from there had reached Mumbai.

Michael had never been to the Sanjay Gandhi National Park before, and he'd wished he had more time to explore it, but this was a luxury that would have to wait. After a walk amidst the Buddhist caves that constituted one of the park's main attractions, Gwendolyn and Michael had found their way to the library's antechamber where Gwendolyn was chastised by a wizard of the Third Circle for bringing a non-wizard into such a sacred place.

"This goes against our rules and you know it full well. You leave me no choice but to report you, and there will be consequences," said the man.

"My friend isn't just any praeternatural, brother," replied Gwendolyn. "His name is Michael Biörn. He's close friends with Ezekiel of the Second Circle."

"And if Ezekiel of the Second Circle were here today, I'd tell him the same thing!" answered the wizard in a patronizing tone.

Michael doubted that very much, but he kept the remark to himself. "I don't understand much about the rules of your order," he said, "but I know that two wizards of the Second Circle have perished in the past few months and Ezekiel, the only one left, has gone missing. That's what brings us here. We're looking for him."

The revelation seemed to surprise the wizard.

"What is he talking about?" he asked, turning towards Gwendolyn.

"He's telling the truth. Tabitha and Methuselah have both been killed and Michael is helping Ezekiel in his fight against the dark forces."

"And what can a praeternatural like him do against the dark mage and his allies?"

"He can do more than you think, brother. Three years ago, he killed the rogue wizard Seraphin and saved Ezekiel's life in the process."

This time the attitude of the librarian did change. "I see," he said, looking at Michael with newfound respect. "And why does he need to get into this library?"

Gwendolyn briefly explained that they were following Ezekiel's trail without giving further detail as to what they were precisely looking for—a wise move. The wizard of the Third Circle pondered the matter a moment before finally backing down. "Very well, I will let your friend in, but understand that this is the one and only time the rule will be ignored."

They both thanked him and a moment later Michael found himself staring at more books than he'd ever seen in one place before. The magical library of Mumbai, carved deep into the rock, covered an area equivalent to two or three football fields. Thousands upon thousands of books were sorted first into aisles and then into rows with a logic that baffled Michael. Books couldn't be checked out of the library and it was therefore impossible to consult a register where they would have learned which books Ezekiel had been recently interested in.

Amariel's Amulet was the only concrete lead they had, but neither of them knew anything about it. In the end, it took Gwendolyn nearly eight hours to identify an aisle containing seemingly relevant material. She handed Michael a series of books, grabbed a few herself, and they walked towards a large table where she started reading.

Michael spoke numerous languages but, one or two exceptions aside, none of the books she gave him were written in one he could read. The majority of them weren't even printed in an alphabet he recognized. He sat down in front of one of the only books accessible to him and dutifully started reading, uncertain of what he was actually looking for. Every hour or so, he'd get up to stretch his legs, but Gwendolyn never lifted her nose from the pages. The woman was a reading machine.

They had been there twelve hours when a pang of hunger resonated inside Michael's empty stomach. He doubted he'd find a vending machine anywhere in the library but, unwilling to disturb the wizard still absorbed by her reading, he got up and started looking for something edible. After a thorough search of the premises, he finally reached the conclusion that wizards didn't worry about trivial matters such as food and water, for there were none to be found.

He wasn't eager to get back to his reading but felt compelled to do so since Gwendolyn showed no sign of tiring of her task. Respecting the silence of the massive room, Michael returned to their table, walking far more quietly than a man his size should be able to. He was surprised to find a man standing ten feet behind Gwendolyn. The wizard had his back to him, but it looked like he was trying to read over Gwendolyn's shoulder, with a curiosity Michael found unnerving.

Who was this man and why was he so interested in Gwendolyn's lectures? He was dressed like the other librarians Michael had encountered during his fruitless search for refreshments, but there was something odd about him. His curiosity somehow seemed more unwholesome than academic.

Michael decided to backtrack and approached the table from a different direction an instant later, this time facing the man. Upon seeing Michael, the librarian resumed his activities as if he hadn't been standing behind Gwendolyn for the past five minutes. Michael gave no indication of having noticed the man's strange behavior and sat back down at the table in front of Gwendolyn who looked up. "I think I found something of interest."

"What is it?" he asked.

"I think this passage is about Amariel's Amulet, even though that's not what they're calling it."

"You think this is what Ezekiel discovered, the secret he unraveled?" said Michael in a voice significantly higher than the whisper Gwendolyn had been using.

She gave him a reproachful look.

"Sorry, I got carried away... Hold on to your thoughts," he said, getting back up. "You can tell me all about it in a minute, I need to use the restroom." His voice was a bit lower but still loud enough to be heard by half the library.

Gwendolyn looked at him, bewildered. "But you just went!"

"No, I was looking for food and there is none. Now I really need to use the restroom. I'll be right back."

He got up and once again disappeared among the aisles of books, discreetly looking for the librarian who'd been spying on Gwendolyn. He didn't have to go very far; the man was still circling around their table, which meant he'd been within earshot a moment earlier...

As stealthily as possible, Michael followed the wizard who was now moving towards Gwendolyn's table with cautious, calculated steps. This wasn't the demeanor of someone with nothing to hide. Michael was twenty feet behind the spy when he saw him pull a wand from an inner pocket of his robe and point it at Gwendolyn's back.

Michael grabbed the first book he could get his hands on and hurled it at the man in the manner of a frisbee, but a frisbee weighing four pounds and thrown by a werebear. The book hit the spy squarely in the head and sent him straight to the ground. Before he could recover, Michael was upon him.

The spy hadn't lost his wand in the fall, however, and he waved it towards Gwendolyn just as Michael grabbed the man's head between his huge hands and broke his neck in one rapid twist.

"Time to go," said Michael urgently to Gwendolyn who was already on her feet. "Grab the book. You'll finish it later."

"We can't check out books from this library, Michael."

"Well, then, we'll steal it."

"We can't do that either! There are wards protecting this place; if we try to take a book out of these walls it will be destroyed."

Michael thought about it for a moment.

"Do you have your phone? Take pictures of the pages."

An instant later Gwendolyn was busy snapping pictures of the book's pages.

"What are you doing?" asked a librarian at their back before turning his attention to his dead colleague on the ground. An instant later the man's wand was out, and he was calling for help.

Chapter 49

The night club was loud and crowded, nothing unusual for this type of establishment or for this part of San Francisco, famous for its nightlife. Neither Lucy nor Irini had ever visited the club before, but they wasted no time admiring the spectacle of sweaty bodies undulating on the dance floor and moved purposefully towards a backroom where a private party was being held.

The private room was no bigger than a half tennis court but nearly fifty vampires stood shoulder to shoulder in it. Irini knew nearly all of them but Lucy would have been hard pressed to recognize more than a dozen of them.

They found Vulpe and his wife Milena holding court at the center of the room.

"My liege," said Irini, bowing slightly.

"It's good to see you again, Irini," said Vulpe "I'm even glad to see you, Lucy," he added, with a twisted rictus that was probably meant to be a smile.

"So these are all the survivors?"

Vulpe nodded. "Forty-eight in total. That's it."

Of the forty-eight Eastern Covenant survivors, only a handful had been present at the castle when the warlocks had attacked. The others had been out of town or on post at the Covenant's other castle, in France. But wherever they'd been, the vamps had all answered Vulpe's call to gather in San Francisco.

"You believe the Western Covenant has joined our enemy, don't you?" Vulpe asked Irini.

"It's the only logical explanation, my liege. I don't see how the Western Covenant would have been able to find us in Yellowstone without help from the warlocks."

Vulpe nodded; he'd obviously given the matter some thought. "I believe you're correct. That's why I have asked our forces to gather here in San Francisco."

San Francisco was the Western Covenant's home. Irini couldn't recall the last time both Covenants had been gathered within the same city. Probably because there had been no such occurrence in the four hundred years she'd been a vampire.

Historically, the Eastern Covenant had been the most powerful of the two, but the balance had shifted now that the warlocks had killed the majority of Vulpe's vampires, and Irini was afraid of their lord's intentions. Did he plan to storm the Western Covenant with an army of forty-eight? That would be suicide. "So what's the plan, my lord?" she asked finally.

"The plan is to go and visit our American cousins, of course. We're more than overdue for a family reunion."

Chapter 50

The pickup truck was approaching the Louisiana-Texas border. Behind the wheel, Michael was watching Gwendolyn from the corner of his eye. Sitting in the passenger seat, the wizard was absorbed in the book they'd finally managed to take out of the magical library.

When he'd found himself surrounded by a half dozen wizards after killing the librarian, Michael thought his time had finally come. Most of the wizards were of the Fourth Circle but a couple definitely belonged to the Third Circle, and Michael knew full well he had no chance against such adversaries, especially in a concerted attack. But Gwendolyn had come to his defense and demanded that the veracity of his story was put to the test. The librarians obliged, though they never lowered their wands. After casting a truth spell upon Michael, they were forced to recognize his *story* as the truth.

The spy he'd killed had apparently recently transferred from the Cairo Library and Michael was shocked to learn the man was a wizard of the Third Circle. If the traitor hadn't kept his focus on Gwendolyn but had turned his wand against him, Michael and Gwendolyn would both have died in that library.

The hours spent with the librarians following the incident were wasted in speculation as to the extent of the dead man's treachery. How long had he been working for the dark side? How long had he been spying on guests? Why had he gone after Gwendolyn? The answer to that last question was obvious to Michael and he wasn't shy about sharing his point of view with the bookish wizards. Gwendolyn was on the verge of an important discovery and the spy had been placed in the library to prevent such a thing from happening. It was unlikely he'd been waiting specifically for Gwendolyn and Michael, but he'd been watching over the book, ready to intervene if anyone was getting close to learning the secret hidden within its pages. What that secret was remained unclear, but after the attempt on Gwendolyn's life, Michael had no desire to stay in Mumbai a minute longer than necessary.

As expected, the librarians rejected their request to borrow the book, but Michael pointed out that there was no way to know for sure that only one spy had been planted there. The dark mage or his warlocks, informed of what had happened, could very well be on their way to the library at this very moment…

It had been a long shot and he was surprised when the head librarian finally saw things his way and agreed to the request. A moment later Michael and Gwendolyn were running through Mumbai's National Park in the direction of its exit. From there, they'd made it back to New Orleans in record time and were already more than halfway to Houston by the time Gwendolyn lifted her chin from the book with a wide smile on her face.

"I found it! I found what Ezekiel was after…" she said. "The fifth artifact!"

"What is it?" asked Michael with one eye on the road and the other on his companion.

"The fifth artifact is Amariel's greatest achievement. Quite possibly the greatest spell ever created by a wizard."

"Okay… but what is it?"

"It's a battery."

"A battery?" repeated Michael, not sure he'd heard correctly.

"Yes, a battery!"

"What sort of battery are we talking about exactly?"

"It's a battery for magical energy."

"Whatever that may mean…"

"What it means, Michael, is that every wizard, witch and sorcerer, every magical being, has magical capital. A reserve of energy, if you wish. The size of that reserve depends on the skill set of the wizard. A wizard of the Third Circle will have much greater capital than a wizard of the Fourth Circle and much smaller capital than a wizard of the Second Circle, for instance."

Michael was following the demonstration up to that point.

"With greater energy come greater powers," she continued. "The more energy a wizard has, the more complex magic they have access to, the more powerful spell they can cast. Do you follow me?"

"So far…"

"So imagine if someone could artificially increase their magical capital by using a battery. A battery you can load by collecting the magical energy of others. A battery of unlimited capacity."

Michael parked the truck on the side of the road and turned his full attention to his passenger. "How would such a thing work?"

"Amariel invented a spell that drains energy from enemies defeated in battle and stores that energy in an amulet. Whoever wears the amulet can tap into that magic whenever they choose."

"Does it have to be a wizard?"

"No. A witch, a sorcerer, a warlock, anyone with magical powers."

"So, you're saying that a wizard of the Fourth Circle could steal the energy of a wizard of the Third Circle and cast spells at the same level as their more powerful peer?"

"They would have to defeat the more powerful wizard first, which is unlikely, but that's the gist of it, yes."

"And what if the owner of the amulet were able to defeat, say, four wizards of the Fourth Circle, or five, or ten... would they be able to accumulate enough energy to become as powerful as a wizard of the Third Circle?"

"I don't know how many they would have to defeat, but in principal, yes. And with enough Third Circle wizards defeated, they would be able to defeat a wizard of the Second Circle and so on. That's how the *math* works," she replied, putting air quotation marks around the word math.

Michael nodded, contemplating the answer. He still didn't understand how the fifth artifact fit into the dark mage's plan, but he was certain it was an important part of the puzzle. One that could even have explained how their enemy had become so powerful. But there was a problem with this theory. If the dark mage had used the amulet to increase his magical capital by defeating wizard after wizard, his rise in power would have been gradual. But according to Ezekiel, the dark mage had appeared out of nowhere one day, like flipping a switch...

"And you're certain Ezekiel knew about this?"

"Yeah. It made no sense to me at the time, but that last time I saw him he went on and on about batteries. I couldn't understand why at the time, but now I'm sure he was putting me on the right path in case of need."

That definitely sounded like Ezekiel.

"You're sure you have no idea where Ezekiel was heading the last time you saw him?"

"Absolutely none."

"Any idea where he was coming from?"

Gwendolyn looked taken aback by the question. She thought about it for a moment. "I believe he was coming back from that detention center where they keep the praeternaturals, but I wouldn't swear to it."

"What did you say?" said Michael, unable to hide his surprise.

"I said, I think he was coming back from that detention center... The one the DSA is running."

"Ezekiel knew where the center was?"

"Yeees... You didn't know that?" Gwendolyn looked genuinely surprised.

"No. He never told *me*! Do you have the address?"

"Yeah, he gave it to me. I really thought you knew. This is so strange..."

She recited the exact GPS coordinates from memory, and Michael wrote them down on a napkin before shoving it in his pocket. He couldn't believe it. How long had Ezekiel been sitting on the information? Why hadn't he told Michael about it when Daka's packmates were most likely held there? The wizard probably had a good reason to keep the secret to himself, but Michael didn't care. Now that he had the address, he intended to use it.

Chapter 51

The hotel room Michael and Sheila had rented in the suburbs of Houston wasn't luxurious by any definition, but it was clean and had everything they needed. Michael had been back in town for an hour only and had spent most of that time in bed with Sheila, celebrating their reunion...

The journalist was now taking a shower while he lay flat on his back, hands behind his head, staring at a ceiling in dire need of fresh paint.

What could have motivated Ezekiel's secrecy about the detention center? Had he really visited the place? The wizard had no reason to go there; the DSA was none of his business. It was Michael's problem. Ez had bigger fish to fry at the moment. The dark mage and his warlocks were already more than the wizard could handle.

Unless the two were somehow related. Michael hadn't considered this option before, but there was something to it. The Healing Stone had been stolen by a contingent composed of werewolves, armed men and at least three werecougars, assuming Maya could be trusted. Michael had associated the armed contingent with vampires at the time since the bloodsuckers liked heavy weaponry, but in retrospect werecougars didn't sound like vampire henchmen. One cougar with a few enthralled werewolves, maybe, but three of them was a bit much. The cats weren't easy to find, and it was unlikely the Western Covenant spent its time roaming mountain ranges looking for them... On the other hand, Michael had already encountered at least one werecougar controlled by the DSA.

He tried pushing the reasoning forward. If the DSA had indeed been behind the ambush that killed Leka, it implied the government not only knew where to intercept the convoy but also knew about the magical artifact the elves were escorting.

Michael and Ez had already figured out the DSA knew about magic and probably had some witches and sorcerers on payroll, but what if they had looked at it the wrong way from the beginning? What if the DSA had been just another branch of the dark mage's army? That would explain a lot... For one thing, it would explain why the diadems used to control their victims were infused with magic. And it would explain how they knew that Jason Parrish had been cursed to act as a spy. Maybe the DSA didn't rely on some second-grade witch but on the most powerful dark mage to ever walk this earth.

There was little hard evidence to support his theory, but the amount of circumstantial evidence was quickly growing and in some cases that was all you needed. Michael had the gut feeling he was finally on the right track, and he suspected Ezekiel had gotten there a lot faster than him this time around. Ezekiel had realized, or at least suspected, the relationship between the dark mage and the DSA.

Had Ezekiel gone to the detention center to investigate the connection? Did he think that was where the dark mage was hiding? If that were the case, the wizard had placed himself in extreme danger, and this time Michael would never be able to assist him... or would he?

Sheila got out of the shower and wrapped herself into a towel before grabbing a second one to dry her long black hair. She couldn't recall the last time she'd worn it this long. She usually maintained a neat bob with regular cuts, but it had been over four months since her last salon visit and she doubted she'd get a haircut anytime soon. Michael appeared to appreciate her long hair, so there was no urgency anyway.

No sounds were coming from the adjacent bedroom where her boyfriend was no doubt lost in thought. That's all Michael did these days. To his credit, he had serious problems to deal with. Problems that not only affected the hidden world to which he belonged but her world as well, the world of regular people.

For once, she felt utterly out of her depth. She'd been thinking about it for weeks and there was simply nothing she could do to help. She wasn't equipped to go after dark mages or warlocks. Her journalistic skills could have been useful to expose the DSA, but she couldn't do so without revealing the existence of praeternaturals to the world...

She felt gagged, hands tied... not a pleasant feeling. She spent her days reading, but mostly failed to be absorbed by her books. As a result, she was bored out of her mind. The only time her boredom receded was when her fear took over. Her fear of seeing the other side win the war, of seeing Michael getting hurt... or worse.

Her life had already been threatened on multiple occasions since they'd started dating. She'd been kidnapped and attacked... but despite all this she was more worried about his wellbeing than her own. Ironic since the man was virtually unkillable, while she was a mere human who bled from a paper cut.

She walked out of the bathroom to find Michael lying on the bed, staring at the ceiling.

"I know the exact location of the detention center in the Nevada desert," he said.

"How? How did you find out?"

"Gwendolyn gave it to me, and Ezekiel gave it to her. He had it for a while."

"And he didn't tell you? That doesn't sound like Ez," she said.

"No, it doesn't."

"Why do you think he kept the information from you?"

"Probably because he was afraid I would go there."

"And are you going to?"

"Yes. I'll head there first thing in the morning. I need to rescue Daka's packmates."

"Maybe you shouldn't, Michael. If Ezekiel didn't want you to go, maybe he had a good reason." She couldn't hide the worry in her voice.

"I don't have a choice, Sheila. Daka's packmates need me. They don't belong in there. The sooner I get them out, the better off they'll be."

Sheila couldn't argue with this point, but she was worried nonetheless. "And you plan on doing that all by yourself?"

He nodded. "I can't ask anyone to help. It's too dangerous. DSA are trained to deal with praeternatural threats, and I think I'll have a better chance of getting in and out if I go by myself. A one-man commando operation... I studied the terrain carefully and an approach from the south will give me the best chance of moving in undetected."

"And how do you plan to get inside without getting caught? You'll just knock on the door?"

"I don't know yet. I may be able to impersonate a guard... Don't worry. I don't plan on just rushing in, I'll take my time to prepare. But I need to be over there to recon the place."

She looked him in his eyes and took his hand. She loved him with all her heart but right now she had the feeling he wasn't telling her the whole truth.

Chapter 52

As their small group moved with purpose towards the main gate of the domain, Irini couldn't help but wonder if their plan was all that sound. She was accompanying Vulpe, Milena and three other elders on a protocol visit to the Western Covenant. A protocolary but unannounced visit... Their small delegation was designed to not raise too many eyebrows, and they hoped to get through the gates without any issue. The two covenants weren't at war, after all. In retrospect, it was likely Silvia and her men hadn't even known Irini, Lucy, and Cristos had been among the Yellowstone refugees when they'd attacked them. The real target had probably been Michael with whom Silvia had an ongoing vendetta.

Irini was glad Lucy wasn't part of the delegation. If things went south, her protégée wouldn't be on the front line. Of course, she'd still be part of the battle since the remainder of the Eastern Covenant survivors were hidden all around the compound, waiting for a sign from

Vulpe. At the least hint of danger, Irini would send a prewritten text to the others and they'd storm the Western Covenant's stronghold.

She truly hoped it wouldn't come to that, though. The Western Covenant had at least twice as many vampires on the premises as there were survivors of Vulpe's clan. And even if the Westerners were on average slightly younger and therefore less powerful than their Eastern Cousins, a one on two fight was never a good idea. And that wasn't even accounting for the enthralled werewolves they had on the premises.

Irini was surprised to see that the two men manning the domain's main gates were actually human. What a weird thing to do… Their blazers bulged with the weight of their sidearms, but the weapons weren't likely to deter any praeternatural or supernatural attacker.

"I'm here to see Grigore," said Vulpe to one of the men holding a clipboard.

"Is he expecting you?" asked the man, eyeing Vulpe's entourage. Although he didn't look afraid, it was clear he respected the size of the contingent.

"He isn't. Tell him Vulpe Zamfir is here to see him."

The guard hesitated a moment before gesturing to his companion who grabbed a radio from his belt and transmitted the information. The night was still young but Vulpe wasn't a patient man, and Irini was starting to wonder how much longer he'd be willing to wait when the man's radio crackled back to life.

"You can go in, Sir, but you need to go alone," said the man as he opened the portal.

Vulpe looked at him as if he were joking, and they all walked in, ignoring the two guards who stood there staring at each other, uncertain of what to do. Irini heard the man with the radio letting his friends in the manor know that the instructions hadn't been followed, but she was already too far away to hear the reply.

They were met at the manor's main entrance by two vampires armed with automatic weapons, but the guns simply dangled from their shoulder straps unthreateningly.

"My lord," said one of the men, nodding slightly. He didn't even comment on the fact Vulpe had come accompanied and he showed the visitors inside the house.

They went through a series of hallways and checkpoints, no doubt designed to impress visitors, before being admitted into a room the size of a tennis court—the Western Covenant's reception hall. Initially designed as a ballroom, the room had a fifteen-foot vaulted ceiling and no windows.

Irini had been here before on more than one occasion, and so had Vulpe and his wife. She particularly remembered the mural which occupied an entire wall and depicted a scene where vampires mounted on horses hunted humans on foot with the help of werewolves. For some reason, she'd always disliked the painting, even after she'd stopped valuing human lives.

"Welcome, Vulpe… Milena," said Grigore, nodding towards Vulpe's wife.

The leader of the Western Covenant had raven-black hair worn in a ponytail and a short-cropped beard. He looked to be in his mid-forties, but Irini knew better. He'd been kicked out of Transylvania by Vulpe himself and there was no love lost between the two leaders. A dozen vampires, mostly elders, were also present in the ballroom. No doubt a show of force.

"To what do we owe the pleasure of your visit, Vulpe?" Grigore made no effort to sound genuine.

Vasil, the covenant's second in command, stood slightly behind Grigore. He looked to be in his fifties, with prominent cheekbones and deep set eyes.

"We came to discuss an important matter," answered Vulpe, as he sat down in a vacant armchair in the middle of the room without waiting for an invitation.

Grigore gave him a look before sitting down himself. Milena came to stand behind her husband and placed her hands on his shoulders.

Matching her move, Andrea, the covenant's third in command, came to stand behind Grigore. She was watching the newcomers with obvious discomfort, nervously biting her brightly painted lips from time to time. The lipstick matched her hair that was worn in a complicated twist, no doubt an attempt to distract the eyes from her plain face.

"And what is this important matter?" asked Grigore.

"Three of my vampires were attacked a few days ago and by none other than your own."

Grigore's face registered surprise and discomfort at the same time. "I doubt this very much," he replied. "I have issued no such orders."

"Did you send Silvia and about thirty of your men to Yellowstone recently?" asked Vulpe.

Now Grigore no longer looked surprised, just upset. "I did, but not to fight vampires."

"Well, three members of my house happened to be among those Silvia tried to kill."

"I assure you I wasn't aware your men would be there. It is most unfortunate…" Grigore sounded almost sincere.

"By the way, you probably shouldn't wait for Silvia to return. She won't, and neither will any of her men."

A flash of anger appeared on Grigore's face and his pale skin took on a slightly darker, redder hue. The leader wasn't taking the news well. Not particularly surprising, given Silvia had been his own granddaughter.

"Is it war you're seeking, Vulpe?" said Grigore, nearly jumping out of his seat. "Do you think I know nothing about the attack you withstood? The Eastern Covenant is all but decimated. You made a mistake by coming here today."

Vulpe stared Grigore down in silence a moment before gently grabbing his wife's hand lying on his shoulder and kissing it.

"The Eastern Covenant isn't as dead as you seem to believe and a war between our two houses will cost you dearly. You've already lost Silvia. How many more elders are you willing to sacrifice? Make no mistake, you do not scare me, Grigore. Your men may get me eventually but not before I kill you."

Grigore was about to reply when Milena said, "You can always leave it to men to try and solve everything with violence." She sounded amused. "Vulpe, this argument isn't why we came here, is it?"

Vulpe looked at his wife and his features softened. "You're correct, my sweet. We came because we know about the alliance you made with the warlocks."

Grigore didn't answer but looked at his uninvited guest with the eyes of a cobra ready to strike.

"You seem to have a good relationship with the warlocks. Given that you're doing their bidding, I mean... As you know, our relationship with them is a bit more... complicated. The reason we're here is to ask a favor of you."

Irini suddenly became tense; what was Vulpe talking about? This wasn't part of the script they'd discussed.

"We'd like you to intercede in our favor with the warlocks. Tell them we made a mistake and are now ready to join them. They can count on the Eastern Covenant to fight the wizards."

Irini was speechless; she hadn't seen that one coming.

Chapter 53

Bright in the cloudless night sky, the moon cast an eerie twilight on Michael's surroundings. It had been nearly four months since he'd rescued Sheila in the Mojave desert, but it felt like yesterday. His current position was only a few miles from where the rescue mission had taken place, and the two locations looked virtually identical. Nothing in the landscape suggested the presence of a military facility. Nothing except for the airstrip and a couple of guards patrolling its surroundings.

Michael had approached the position from the south and encountered no patrols. He found this unusual. Military facilities were usually well guarded and he'd expected a secret one to be even more so... But aside from the two guards posted on either end of the airstrip, who looked bored out of their minds, he'd seen no one.

There were absolutely no buildings to be seen anywhere. Where was the detention center hiding? Most likely buried deep under his feet... If you want to hide something, burying it in the desert was a safe bet... But how was he supposed to get in? There was likely more than one entrance to the facility... he just needed to find one of them.

Cautious of his surroundings, Michael started another wide circle around the coordinates. This was his third, each one a bit tighter than the previous one. He made sure to stay low to the ground when crossing flat landscapes where he'd be visible from the airstrip, but for the most part he just moved carefully, smelling the air for signs of trouble. A few scents floating around reinforced his belief that there were more than just two guards, but the others were either underground or remarkably well hidden.

Suddenly he heard voices coming from his right and fell flat to the ground, holding his breath. The voices were a good distance away, but he took no chances. He crawled slowly towards them until he reached the edge of the cliff and looked down. The voices belonged to two men standing at the foot of the cliff, a good twenty feet below. Both held cigarettes whose tips glowed in the night. They were talking about sports, football he believed, though he couldn't be sure. He'd never cared for watching sports on TV. He got plenty of exercise in Yellowstone and had never thought of watching others playing a game as something entertaining. Where had these men come from? And then he saw it, about ten yards to their right, a rectangle slightly darker than the rest of the hill: a door.

Michael lay still until the men finished their smoke and returned inside the facility. He didn't catch the six-digit code they entered to unlock the door, but he suspected his muscles would suffice; they usually did. He didn't have much of a plan once inside the detention center other than finding what he'd come for, but sometimes improvisation was all one needed.

The men had disappeared inside the hill for about five minutes when Michael found himself standing in the spot they had occupied. That's when he noticed the cameras for the first time... and then the ground rocked with a series of small explosions. At least that's what it sounded like, but he felt no deflagration. Instead he found himself swallowed by a thick cloud of sand and dust that completely obstructed his sight. The sand cloud wasn't enough to impair his nose, though, and he knew immediately he was in trouble. The scents that had been faint a minute earlier were now strong and many.

As the dust started settling, he could see no less than a half dozen men dispersed in a half circle around him—a smart move since their position would avoid collateral damage in a crossfire. They'd simply sprung out of the ground.

As they started unloading their weapons, Michael felt the lead chewing through his bones and muscles. He'd fallen into a trap. Clearly they'd been waiting for him. But how had they known? The question remained unanswered as a bullet found its way through his brain and Michael collapsed to the ground.

Chapter 54

Demetra and the three other warlocks materialized into Lord Vaalt's dining room just as the high fae was finishing his lunch. She saw clear annoyance on his face but no surprise. She doubted they'd been expected, though, and she credited the fae's lack of reaction to his exemplary control over his emotions.

"Remind me to cast a spell against pest intrusion in the dining room," said Lord Vaalt to the fae on his right. "It would seem protecting my private quarters isn't enough, they'll come and pester us wherever we are."

There were only three high faes in the room, but Demetra knew that her party's sudden appearance was bound to attract more attention.

"Good afternoon, Lord Vaalt. My apologies for interrupting your meal. Before you get the wrong idea, I want you to know that we come in peace. You already allied with us and we simply came to request a token of your allegiance."

The fae remained silent, apparently waiting for Demetra to continue. She suspected he knew full well where she was going with this, however.

As expected, more faes started pouring into the dining room, most of them of the muscular type. A minotaur, two ogres, a troll and three more high faes strategically positioned themselves around the room, effectively surrounding the warlocks, and waited for any sign from their lord to jump into action. The muscle didn't worry Demetra, she could take care of the ogres, troll and minotaur herself without breaking a sweat. The high faes were the real danger... starting with Lord Vaalt whose powers easily equaled her own, but she had three other warlocks with her... They weren't particularly experienced, but she could still count on them for taking care of the riffraff while she focused on the truly dangerous members of the fae entourage. She hoped things wouldn't go that far, though. Vaalt knew he couldn't afford a war against the dark mage, and attacking Demetra and her companions would definitely qualify as an act of war.

"My master requests the missing fragment from the Eye of the Phoenix, Lord Vaalt, and I don't intend to leave without it. The sooner you provide what my master requires, the sooner you'll be free to return to your meal." Demetra tried to put as little emotion as possible into her demand; this was neither a threat nor a request. This was simply the order of the master to a subaltern. The fae needed to comply and that's all there was to it.

"The missing piece of the Eye of the Phoenix?" said the fae, his eyes going around the room as if he were surveying the forces at his disposal. "It's a fae artifact, it belongs with us. You already have two thirds of it and—"

"I believe you're mistaken about the purpose of my visit," she interrupted. "I'm not here to negotiate with you. I came to get the fragment. The matter requires no discussion."

The fae took a deep breath and slowly let it out. "Very well. I'll go fetch it for you."

"And I'll come with you," said Demetra.

"That won't be necessary."

"Oh, but I insist."

The fae didn't try to hide his exasperation as he got up from his chair and, replacing his napkin neatly folded beside his plate, left the room with purpose. Demetra immediately followed him to his living quarters, the three warlocks in tow.

As Vaalt entered his quarters, he stopped Demetra with a preemptive hand gesture. "I would be careful before stepping in, if I were you. I upgraded the room's defense after the first fragment was stolen from me. If you step over the threshold, I'm not sure your warlock magic will protect you."

Before Demetra could make a move or speak a word, he'd disappeared inside the room. He came back a moment later holding a yellowish piece of jewel shaped like a half moon and handed it to her.

She could feel the magic infused in the artifact but couldn't be totally certain she was indeed holding a piece of the Eye of the Phoenix.

"I assume this is the real thing?"

"It is indeed the third fragment. Faes aren't into deception," said Vaalt haughtily.

Demetra couldn't hide her smile. Faes were the definition of deception... but they were also physically incapable of lying, and if Vaalt told her it was the missing fragment, it had to be. "Thank you, Lord Vaalt. The master will no doubt be pleased by your willing collaboration."

She placed the jewel in an inner pocket of her tunic and added, "The master will be calling upon your forces in the not-too-distant future. Your response will have to be swift. Do we understand each other?"

"I hadn't realized you expected us to go into battle," said Lord Vaalt.

"What do you think a military alliance is about? Of course, we expect the faes to come into battle alongside our troops."

Demetra was about to signal to her companions that the meeting was over when she turned around to face Vaalt one last time. "I'd nearly forgotten, I'm also looking for the Soul Catcher. Any idea where I could find it?"

"The Soul Catcher is a wizard artifact. Why would I know where it is?" replied the fae.

"You didn't answer my question, Lord Vaalt. Any idea where it might be?" Demetra wasn't fooled by the fae's sidestepping.

"No, I don't know where it is at the moment."

"Do you know where it was last seen?"

"I haven't heard about this artifact in some years, but the last time it was mentioned to me, I was under the impression it was in the hands of the Second Circle."

This was the answer Demetra had been expecting, but not the one she'd been hoping for. The Second Circle was down to a single wizard, but Demetra had no idea where to find Ezekiel. She suspected he was busy recruiting fighters to join his cause, but the wizard was just wasting his time. His side was already so overpowered that they had no chance of surviving the upcoming battle.

This certitude wouldn't help her out of her predicament, though. Until she could get her hands on Ezekiel, she wouldn't be able to bring the Soul Catcher to the master… But she was bringing him the last Eye of the Phoenix fragment. He would now benefit from the powers and skill set of the most powerful high faes on the planet. That had to count for something.

Chapter 55

With the exception of three werewolves whose stench Michael could smell from his own cell on the opposite end of the hallway, the cell block was deserted. Since he'd fallen into the trap nearly twenty-four hours earlier, he'd seen only a handful of guards watching over the mostly empty prison.

He'd come back to life in the same spot he'd been shot but wearing an all too familiar collar around his neck. He didn't have to be reexplained the principle of the device that would sever his head with a high intensity torch were he to try to morph or lose his temper in any way. This wasn't his first time wearing one of these trinkets.

He'd been brought into the detention center under heavy guard, but his hope of finding Daka's packmates had quickly vanished. He'd also secretly hoped to bump into Ezekiel, but he'd been wrong on that count as well; the place was a ghost town.

The idea that Ezekiel would go undercover to infiltrate the detention center was pure speculation, of course, but Michael had known the wizard a long time and it made sense on some levels, especially if the dark mage and the DSA were indeed connected. For one, Ez loved nothing more than *playing dress-up*, as Michael put it. He'd seen him change into a variety of bodies ranging from a child all the way to Sheila herself in order to infiltrate their enemies over the years. And although the wizard wouldn't admit it, Michael was convinced that he thoroughly enjoyed the experience. The fact Ezekiel had apparently disappeared from the face of the earth also aligned with his theory. If the wizard had gone under cover, he wasn't likely to be easily reachable… Of course, it still didn't explain why Ezekiel hadn't said a word about it to him, and this sat uneasily with Michael.

He had no doubt Ez kept many secrets from him, but this particular one seemed unnecessary. Why wouldn't he want Michael to know where to find the place where Daka's friends had likely been imprisoned? Between the two of them they could have staged a viable rescue mission, unlike the half-assed one Michael had undertaken on his own. Unless Ez had known the detention center was empty… but even then, why had he kept the information from Michael?

Michael got up from the wooden bench where he'd been sitting and stretched his legs. He heard the sound of heavy metal doors sliding on their rails an instant later, quickly followed by numerous boots hitting the floor. His nose told him long before the soldiers appeared in front of his cell that these were the same men who had captured him.

They opened the two gates of the containment lock at once; he was the only prisoner in the cell, after all…

"Get out, it's time to go on a trip."

"Where are we going?" he said.

"You don't get to ask questions; you just follow orders. Now move your fat ass!" answered one of the guards with a display of bravado designed to mask the fear he felt at the predator's proximity.

But Michael wasn't fooled, the man stank of fear. They all did. That made him smile.

He followed the men and noticed that the werewolves were also being moved out of their cage. They were a good hundred feet ahead of him, but they all turned towards Michael in a synchronized movement, looking both concerned and ready for a fight. They had no idea what he was—werebears were supposedly extinct and few praeternaturals could identify his type on first encounter—but they knew they didn't like him. It was written in their genetic code… Werewolves and werebears were hereditary enemies. Thanks to their sheer numbers, the wolves had won the war centuries ago, but as the last survivor of his kind, Michael had been working on evening out the score ever since.

The prisoners boarded a military transport plane located at one end of the airstrip: a plane that hadn't been there a day earlier. The wolves were placed on one side and Michael on the other. In the middle stood a dozen heavily armed guards. The remotes controlling the beasts' collars were in their hands, ready for the first sign of trouble.

The fact they'd separated the bear from the wolves suggested the guards knew something about praeternaturals. That, or they weren't willing to take any chances. A fight between the four predators at a ten-thousand-feet altitude would likely spell disaster for all onboard.

As the plane took off, Michael couldn't help but think that showing up at the detention center had been a horrible idea. It hadn't been a total waste, however. At least now he knew who the spy was.

Chapter 56

The warehouse was located on the outskirts of Detroit and had been abandoned for at least half a century, if Demetra was to trust the building's state of disrepair. As she approached from the north, three of her sorcerers approached from the east, west and south respectively. This wasn't the sorcerer's first trip to the location but the wizard of the Third Circle who lived there hadn't been swayed by their arguments to join their ranks, which was why Demetra had decided to tag along for their second visit.

As she approached the building, she sensed the magical power within; this was indeed a strong wizard. Still significantly weaker than a wizard of the Second Circle, but also quite a bit stronger than your average wizard of the Third Circle. It wasn't surprising the sorcerers had failed in their initial mission.

The four of them entered the building in a coordinated attack and immediately found themselves flooded by a deluge of spells cast from every direction; clearly they'd been expected. It only took a second or two for Demetra to realize that they weren't facing one enemy but nearly a dozen of them. The spells weren't all of equal strength, and she suspected that the opposite force was composed of a mixture of Third and Fourth Circle wizards. This was already the third time her troops had encountered this kind of coordinated resistance; the trend was concerning.

Protected behind her shield off which the spells bounced harmlessly, Demetra saw two of her sorcerers fall dead to the ground under the assault of the wizards. She debated sticking around to take a couple of her enemies down but decided the risk wasn't worth it. She signaled to the remaining sorcerer to retreat, but a purple lightning bolt fried him before he had a chance to comply. Demetra felt anger rising into her blood as she snapped her fingers and vanished.

She rematerialized on the bank of a large lake located in Minnesota, the campground harboring the spearhead of the master's forces. The Transylvanian and French training grounds had been emptied and the troops had moved to Minnesota in preparation for the upcoming battle.

Before departing, the master had left her with instructions to convert or take down as many wizards as possible, an order Demetra had diligently executed. Lately it had become increasingly difficult to do so, however, and she suspected Ezekiel was to blame for it. The wizards were organizing, and her side would need to start hunting them down with more fire power, which presented a logistical challenge.

It would have taken at least twenty sorcerers to bring down the resistance they'd faced in Detroit, and since sorcerers couldn't teleport over great distances, it necessitated moving them by car, a slow and painful process. On top of that, she'd need to send twenty sorcerers to a location with no guarantee that they'd encounter more than one or two wizards. This was turning into a tactical nightmare.

She felt the surge in the magical energy field an instant before the master appeared in front of her. At first, she felt relief. Relief that she no longer had to call the shots and try to find a solution to the wizard problem. Then came fear that the master wouldn't be pleased with her progress, and that she'd end up paying the price of her failure.

"How have things been going in my absence?" asked the master.

Demetra spent five minutes summarizing the situation while the master listened in silence.

When she finally finished her summary, the master nodded once. "I'll take it from here. I have an assignment for you, Demetra, and you are to leave right away."

Chapter 57

Sheila was taking a walk in Memorial Park, Houston's response to Central Park in New York. If Michael knew where she was, he wouldn't be pleased with her. This was her own turf, and the DSA was likely to have it under surveillance in case she and Michael returned to town. Therefore, walking around public places in broad daylight wasn't a very smart idea, but she needed some fresh air; she was simply going nuts locked up in her hotel room.

She felt safe enough among the hundreds of joggers and sport enthusiasts surrounding her. Back in the day, she used to jog on the bike trails in the park's wooded area, but after she'd been attacked by thugs working for the Russian mob a few years earlier, she'd never found the courage to revisit her favorite area. It was a purely mental block, as Michael had long eradicated the threat, yet she couldn't bring herself to jog there anymore.

She was starting to worry about Michael. He'd been gone two days already, and this time she hadn't been able to sneak in with him on his trip. Not that she particularly wanted to go back to the detention center where she'd been locked up herself four months earlier, but the idea of Michael going there by himself didn't sit well with her.

The man was more than able to take care of himself—he'd proven it many times before—but things were different this time around. For the first time in his life, he was facing humans specialized in hunting praeternaturals. And he intended to go knock on their front door... She knew it wasn't exactly Michael's plan, but it amounted to the same thing.

She picked up her phone and dialed his number for the sixth time today, and for the sixth time it went straight to voicemail. Eyes glued to her screen, she collided with an incoming jogger who snarled with displeasure. Sheila answered with a profusion of apologies that the earbud-wearing jogger likely never heard as he kept running.

The inaction was really starting to get to her. She'd been forced to take a leave of absence and had no idea when she'd be able to return to her normal life. She hadn't showed her face at her newspaper's office in months for fear of being identified by a DSA spy. If the jerks had managed to track them down all the way to southern France, visiting her place of work was definitely not an option.

She'd been able to help Michael in the past on more than one occasion, but her investigative skills weren't paying off this time. She'd found precisely zero trace of the DSA anywhere. As far as the rest of the world was concerned, the department didn't exist.

Out of sheer boredom and with no expectations whatsoever, she'd even tried to find signs of the dark mage on the web. She'd spent two days drowning in a sea of fantasy and folklore websites where magic enthusiasts debated the existence and/or superior powers of fictional characters that made Michael and his friends look mundane in comparison.

Out of despair, she dialed Gwendolyn's number and this time the phone rang, but after the fifth ring the wizard's voicemail picked up. Sheila left a brief message asking Gwendolyn to call her back, but she harbored little hope the wizard would oblige.

Sheila was in agreement with Michael on at least one point: they'd been betrayed. Someone had been feeding information to their enemy. The problem was that they simply couldn't come up with any name that made sense. Aside from the elves and Ezekiel, there had been only four people who'd known about the Healing Stone being transferred: Michael, Olivia, Daka and herself… And even if Michael was correct in his assumption that Maya had once again betrayed her people, even if the princess had leaked the information to their enemies, she couldn't be the one responsible for what had happened in Yellowstone. No one outside the nine members of their group had known about their hiding place deep into the park's backcountry.

Sheila had never been very close to Lucy, and she knew just about nothing of Irini, Cristos and Daka's packmates. Could one of them have betrayed the group? It was possible, but the attack had claimed the lives of Cristos and Nayati, which suggested they hadn't been the traitors. This left Kimama, Lucy and Irini… She couldn't picture any of them as a spy, but if there was one thing she'd learned in the years she'd known Michael, it was that one should never trust in appearances.

Her phone rang and she saw Olivia's name on the screen. "Olivia! Has something happened to Michael?" was the first thing out of her mouth.

"I don't know… Why? He's not with you?"

"No."

"What's going on, Sheila? Where's Michael?" Apparently Olivia had heard the worry in her voice.

Sheila told the werewolf about her boyfriend's stupid idea to go rescue the skinwalkers by himself.

"How did he know where to go? Did he find out the detention center's location?"

"Gwendolyn gave him the address. Ezekiel had it all along, apparently."

"And he didn't give it to Michael?" Olivia sounded bewildered.

"No, Michael thinks he may have had a good reason for not doing so, but I have no idea what that may be."

Olivia remained silent for a moment before saying, "I need to talk to him and he's not answering his phone."

"Tell me about it! What's going on?"

"I got a call from Lucy."

"And?"

"Vulpe and the survivors of his covenant have joined forces with the dark mage."

"What do you mean?"

"I mean that both the Eastern and Western Covenants are now fighting alongside the dark mage."

"What about Irini and your sister?"

"They're part of Vulpe's house, they didn't get a choice in the matter. They've joined the enemy too."

Chapter 58

After a two-hour flight in an eastern direction the plane landed in a small, private airport that could have been anywhere from Iowa to Missouri as far as Michael was concerned. The surrounding fields and the flatness of the landscape provided no clue as to where they were. The guards ushered the three werewolves and Michael out of the plane and directly onto a troop carrier helicopter. The twin-engine Chinook was large enough to accommodate the prisoners and the guards.

Michael was surprised to find a woman already chained up at one end of the chopper's hold compartment when he got in.

As the chopper took off, the woman surveyed Michael and then the three werewolves. Her eyes were hard to read, but he was fairly sure he saw contempt in them. Clearly she was not impressed with her entourage.

She had short jet-black hair that suited her angular face. She was attractive in a don't-mess-with-me type of way. Her scent was familiar to Michael, but it took a minute to place it, simply because he'd never encountered any werewolverine before.

They'd been in the air an hour and a half, the last thirty minutes of which were spent flying over a densely forested area, when the chopper finally touched down in a clearing. This time Michael had a fairly good idea of where they were. The relief they'd flown over looked very much like the Ozark Mountains, a succession of oversized hills compared to the Rockies.

The prisoners were freed from their restraints one by one and pushed out of the chopper. Despite the collar worn by each prisoner, no fewer than fifteen guards escorted the newcomers through a narrow forest path where they couldn't walk more than two abreast.

They reached a small building a few minutes later and were led to what looked like a small classroom. Desks and chairs faced a large white board in front of which stood a man who introduced himself as the warden.

"Welcome to your new home," he said, with a smile that wasn't friendly in any way. "I hope you enjoyed your trip; we pride ourselves on the quality of our flight attendants."

The lame joke provoked chuckles from a couple of the guards.

"You will call me Warden, but you should think of me as your new daddy... I'm here to make real fighters out of you misfits. Did I say something funny, Missy?" said the man, suddenly turning towards the wolverine woman. But she simply smiled at him. The warden looked at the woman's handler whose fingers were already hovering over the remote control of her collar and nodded. An instant later she was brought to her knees by an electrical discharge that Michael heard cracking from where he stood ten feet away.

"Consider this a warning, Missy. The next time you show me disrespect it's the other button we'll be pressing."

Michael knew the other button would activate the collar's torches and sever the woman's head in seconds. He also fully believed it wasn't an idle threat; the warden was prepared to lose a few prisoners in order to make his point. Michael instantly despised the man.

The wolverine got back to her feet a moment later. The burn mark around her neck quickly disappeared but the smoldering look in her eyes indicated that she and Michael were on the same page about their *new daddy*.

Barely bigger than coyotes, wolverines were relatively small predators. But they were absolutely fearless and made up in aggressivity what they lacked in size. Michael had once witnessed a wolverine tree a black bear. Granted the bear had been fresh out of hibernation and probably not at its peak form, but still... He'd also witnessed a wolverine stealing a carcass from two wolves. Mostly fighting on its back, the oversized badger had relentlessly harassed the two wolves until they'd eventually given up and walked away from their kill, unable to deal with the pesky creature.

The woman, who had no doubt inherited some of her furry alter ego traits, would make an interesting ally. She was also significantly better than average looking, but that had nothing to do with Michael's analysis.

Yes, he noticed these things, but Sheila was the only woman he needed.

The warden had been talking for a good ten minutes when Michael snapped out of his reverie. He had no idea what the man had been saying and quite frankly, he didn't give a shit.

Chapter 59

As they prepared for the inevitable battle with the dark mage's forces, the wizards steadfastly practiced battle magic under the watchful eye of their leader. It was unlikely Nebraska had ever witnessed this amount of magical activity before, but the corn fields located in the prairies at the center of the state provided the discretion they needed. With the corn taller than men, their gathering was invisible from the nearby roads, and trying to locate them from the sky would have taken someone who knew where to look.

The leader observed three wizards ganging up against a fourth in order to test the power of her defensive shield. Every wizard was trained for battle magic—it came with the territory—but refreshers didn't hurt. The vast majority of wizards went years without engaging in a single conflict and you could easily get rusty. Battle magic training presented an inherent flaw, however. All spells cast had to be relatively harmless since killing your sparring partner would be rather counterproductive to the exercise.

Pleased to see the progress this particular group had made over the past few days, the leader moved on to the next, offering advice when necessary.

Under their mentor's leadership, the wizards were starting to organize and fight back, and their recent victories had invigorated their troops. Groups of wizards dispatched to go after known sorcerer lairs had met with success in most instances. Problematic witches had been dispatched left and right, and ambushes had been set to attract bigger fish.

Such a trap had nearly caught a warlock that very morning, but she'd managed to escape. She'd lost three skillful sorcerers in the engagement, though, so it still counted as a victory.

Lost in thought, the leader was nearly caught off guard by a Third Circle practitioner who came flying out of nowhere, propelled by a wind spell he'd been unable to block.

The *out of nowhere* analogy drove the leader's thoughts to the dark mage who'd reappeared after days of absence. All wizards had felt the dark practitioner's return in their core; the fluctuations his presence imposed on the magical field were impossible to miss. But they'd only lasted a few hours before vanishing again, and no one had any idea what that meant. Why was the dark mage's aura appearing and disappearing? What was he up to?

The warlocks had been busy recruiting and training as well, and the forces at their disposal were substantial enough to give the wizards pause. The dark mage not only had sorcerers and witches doing his biddings but warlocks, faes, vampires and even shifters.

The wizards still had a few tricks up their sleeves, of course, but their leader wasn't certain that would suffice. They would know soon enough, though. War was coming and there was no escaping it.

Chapter 60

More than a day had passed since Michael's arrival in the Ozarks camp, but he still hadn't seen any sign of the skinwalkers.

Life in the training camp gave the prisoners far more freedom than what they'd experienced in the Nevada detention center. They were allowed to roam freely from one training session to another under the watchful eyes of the guards and were for the most part only locked up at night. The reason the prisoners were given such freedom was due to the high-tech collars locked around their necks which would activate automatically were a prisoner to step outside the camp's boundaries.

Michael quickly realized that the collars used to control the prisoners inside the camp were of a different variety than those he'd seen before. Instead of responding to a single handler, the devices were activated by universal remotes. A guard could activate any collar by simply pointing his remote at his target and pressing the button.

The function of automatically activating the beheading torch upon morphing could also be disabled to allow the prisoners to change into their beasts for combat training. In these instances, the diameter of the collar extended on micro springs woven into its metallic fabric to accommodate the larger neck of its wearer.

The camp was also significantly larger than Michael had first expected. With only two thirty-minute breaks a day, it would take him a while to explore the entire facility. He was on such a break at the moment but needed to answer a call of nature so the camp's exploration would have to wait a minute or two.

As he approached the outdoor restroom a scent caught his attention: werewolves. Given that nearly three quarters of the prisoners were wolves, their stench was just about omnipresent, but these particular odors were distinctly familiar to Michael; they belonged to the wolves who'd travelled with him from Nevada. His nose also told him they weren't alone.

He heard the taunting voices before making visual contact, but this was a one-way conversation. He came around the building a moment later to find the three wolves cornering the female wolverine against a wide tree.

Michael had seen the woman a couple of times since they'd flown in on the same chopper, but she never showed any sign of wanting to talk.

On the contrary, she appeared reclusive and perpetually ill-tempered.

"You ain't so proud now, hey?" he heard one of them tell the wolverine.

"Fuck off," she replied, and it sounded like she meant it.

"The bitch has no sense of humor," said the wolf, the remark provoking laughter from his two companions.

In nature, a wolverine against three wolves would have been a tough fight on the best of days, but in this instance, with each wolf outweighing the woman by at least thirty percent in their human form, the fight was simply too unfair for Michael to not intervene. He briefly checked his surroundings for guards and, seeing none, walked towards the group. His footsteps caught the attention of the wolves who welcomed him with feral grins.

"I believe the lady asked you to fuck off," he said. "Do you plan on doing the smart thing and complying?"

The wolves' smiles widened.

"Look what the cat dragged in," said the leader of the trio, looking in turn at Michael and the woman.

It dawned on Michael that the three idiots probably had no clue what they were dealing with. It was unlikely they'd have encountered werewolverines in the past, and their noses were probably unable to identify the true nature of the woman.

"I don't think we're feeling like fucking off, asshole," replied the ringleader. "But fucking is still on the table," he added with a pointed look at the woman.

Michael was a man of few words, so he asked the only question that mattered. "You do realize you'll lose your head if you try to morph, right?"

"What does that have to do with anything?" asked the leader.

"Just a reminder..." he said as he punched the man in the face hard enough to snap his neck.

His two friends were on Michael in a split second. They were big guys, but he still had a hundred pounds on each and after driving his fist through the jaw of the first one, he was getting ready to hammer the other with an elbow to the head when he realized the wolverine was taking care of business for him. Michael watched with amusement as the woman repeatedly punched the remaining wolf in the kidneys and liver, her attacks too fast for the wolf to block. When the jerk finally folded in half, out of breath, a few seconds later, she brought him straight back up with a powerful knee to the face. Michael heard the man's nose crack from where he stood. Before the three wolves had time to recover from the beating, Michael nodded to the woman to follow him, and they quickly moved to a busier section of the camp.

The wolverine's name was Aurora, and she'd been captured while visiting friends in the Chicago area. She had no idea how the DSA had been onto her, but that was no big surprise; Michael had no idea how the DSA was onto anyone. Although now he had the conviction the DSA and the dark mage were working together towards a common goal.

"Where do you need to go next?" asked Michael.

"I'm supposed to be in training ground number five in ten minutes," said Aurora.

"Me too… Do you know where that is?"

She shook her head.

"Okay, let's find out. I think I saw a sign over there," he said, pointing north.

Five minutes later, they walked into a clearing where a man and a woman stood at the center of a circle composed of four wolves, a cougar, and a tiger. With Michael and Aurora that made for quite an eclectic group.

The man and the woman weren't shifters, but Michael suspected they weren't human either. Any remaining doubt was lifted when the two instructors introduced themselves as sorcerers. They wore no collars and appeared to be there of their own free will—more evidence supporting Michael's theory about a connection between the dark mage and the DSA.

"In this class you'll learn to fight against an opponent casting spells at you," said the female sorcerer.

Michael enquired why such a skill would be useful, but the sorcerers simply ignored the question and proceeded to split them into two groups of four. The werewolves were placed in one group and assigned to work with the male sorcerer, while Michael and the others landed with the female instructor.

They spent the next two hours dodging spells and trying to come up with a way of disarming the skilled practitioners, but their success rate was under thirty percent; the vast majority of the confrontations ended up with the sorcerers on top and the werebeings as bloody messes.

That night, Michael and Aurora sat together in the dining area, but few words were exchanged. The woman wasn't much of a talker and Michael being Michael, their table was by far the most silent in the dining hall. She finished her food which consisted of an abundance of meat of all kinds and pushed the tray aside.

"How did they get you?" she asked.

"You wouldn't believe it if I told you."

"Try me."

"These people have a detention center in the Nevada desert. I thought it would be a good idea to go and visit…"

"Are you telling me that you willingly gave yourself up to these nutcases?"

"I wouldn't quite put it that way, but I did willingly go to them."

"And what purpose was that supposed to serve?"

"I was looking for some friends of mine... skinwalkers. The DSA grabbed them a few days ago and I thought I'd find them there."

"But you didn't..."

"I didn't, and I haven't seen them here either, but I haven't had a chance to search the whole camp yet."

"I've heard nothing about skinwalkers." She looked at him a long moment before adding, "But I have heard of you."

"Of me?" He looked up, surprised. "Where?"

"Here, of course."

Which made sense... why would she have heard of him anywhere else? He wasn't exactly a celebrity.

"I've heard them referring to the bear... I'm assuming that's you?"

"As far as I know, I'm the one and only," he replied with a half-smile.

Chapter 61

The warden stood in front of the reinforced bars of the cell, mesmerized by the prisoner inside. Surprising the warden was no easy task, but in this instance, he was simply shocked to the core. Approximately seven-foot-tall and weighing well over three hundred pounds, the prisoner was a mountain of a man.

The warden's mobile rang with the distinctive tone assigned to the director, and he quickly answered the call. "Ma'am?"

"Did you receive our new guest?" asked the director without preamble.

"Yes, I'm looking at him as we speak."

"Show me," she said.

It took him a second to understand the meaning of the order. He wasted a bit more time fumbling with his phone, trying to figure out how to Facetime with the woman. Finally he succeeded and turned the phone towards the cage in the direction of the newcomer who was staring at him with murder in his eyes.

"He just arrived," Wes told the director. "And as you can see, we're keeping him in isolation. It turns out our new friend has a bit of a temper."

"I'm not particularly surprised," replied the director. "His kind isn't known to be social. Take good care of him, this will be the prize of our collection. He could give your Michael Biörn a run for his money."

The warden, who'd seen Biörn fighting on numerous occasions, wasn't convinced.

The warden headed toward the cell block's exit, with the director still on the line. "What are we going to do with him if he is unmanageable?" he asked once outside. "From the way he's behaved so far, there's a good chance the collar around his neck will kill him long before we manage to tame him."

"Don't worry about that. I'll handle him myself if necessary," replied the woman. "I'll be at the training camp tomorrow and will see for myself what we're dealing with."

This was the first time the warden had heard of a visit from the director. "Very well, Ma'am. Do you intend on staying long? Should I arrange for a room for your stay?"

"Yes, do that. I don't know how long I'll be staying, but a room may come in handy. Keep our friend in isolation until then. I don't want the other prisoners to find out about him before the big event."

Wes wasn't sure what that was supposed to mean.

Chapter 62

Michael saw the punch coming from a mile away and blocked it; the kick that followed was equally predictable and he simply stepped closer to the woman and pushed her off balance. Aurora landed on the ground but was back on her feet before he had a chance to offer her his hand. Around them other prisoners were engaged in similar hand-to-hand combat training.

Michael and the wolverine shared the same oversized cell, along with twenty other prisoners, and she'd come to find him the previous evening shortly before lights out. They'd spent a good chunk of the night trading information about their common enemy, but it had soon become obvious that she knew far less than he did about their captors. She'd been completely unaware of the threat until a DSA commando had grabbed her in Chicago. Michael having quite a bit more intel on the shady government outfit, he'd enlightened her on several points, including the diadem Aurora had seen some of the captives wearing around the camp. The use of the mind control device wasn't widespread, however, and Michael suspected the diadems were reserved for special occasions.

Controlling the speed and the impact, he threw a punch, and she was able to dodge it.

"Please don't insult me by holding back on me," she said.

"I wasn't," he lied, but the look on her face told him she wasn't buying his excuse.

She replied with a series of punches to the face that he blocked without breaking a sweat, and he countered with a knee strike to her abdomen. The blow would have knocked her off her feet had he not pulled back at the last second.

He was glad he'd intervened during her altercation with the wolves the day before, and he hoped for her sake that she had better fighting skills as a wolverine than she did as a human. He didn't know how old she was, but she sure hadn't been in many fights before, at least not on the winning end.

The bell rang and the guards ushered the prisoners towards the next training station where this time they were to fight in their animal form. Michael was paired with a lion while Aurora was put against a werewolf twice the size of her wolverine.

The lion kept Michael busy, but he couldn't help keeping an eye on Aurora's progress. Not giving the lion the respect he deserved was a mistake, however. A mistake he came to realize in the most painful manner when the cat jumped on his back and sank his fangs in at the junction between shoulder and neck. It took Michael all he had to get the feline off him, succeeding only by rolling to the ground and crushing him under his bear's massive weight. The lion scurried away, and they circled each other a moment.

In a flash, the cat pounced at the bear who received him with a colossal swipe of the paw that sent him tumbling to the ground in a bloody mess. Michael's four-inch claws had cut deep gashes across his adversary's face and neck, gouging the right eye in the process. But this was just training; the lion's eye would have time to heal.

At the sight of the bloodied lion, one of the guards decided it was time to stop the fight. Apparently their captors didn't want to damage their prized prisoners too badly.

The fight between Aurora and her opponent continued, however. She had managed to keep the werewolf at bay for the most part, but by sheer viciousness rather than skill.

Wolverines were notoriously difficult to spot in the wild and seeing them interact in their natural habitat was a rarity that few had had the chance to observe. But having been around over a thousand years, Michael had been given this opportunity on several occasions and one thing was certain: Aurora didn't look like she'd learned her fighting skills from her purely animal cousins.

The prisoners rotated through a few more sparring partners but with the exception of the first lion, none of his opponents gave Michael much of a workout. After two hours of practice, the prisoners were sent to the mess for their lunch.

Michael and Aurora were walking side by side to the building where the prisoners took all their meals when he caught a familiar scent, Daka's packmates. Following his nose, he soon found five skinwalkers huddled at one of the tables.

"Michael," said one of them. "What are you doing here?"

"I was looking for you guys. I was starting to think I'd never find you." Michael realized he didn't know any of the skinwalkers' names. They were just kids, not one of them over thirty.

Aurora came over a moment later and Michael introduced her to the group.

"Where are the others?" he asked. "There should be three more of you, right?"

The skinwalkers looked at each other, and Michael knew that these were the only ones left alive. "What happened?"

"There's an arena, a big cage where prisoners fight each other for the warden's pleasure," explained the only female of the group. "Our three packmates were thrown in the cage against a large werewolf. He killed all of them."

Michael's blood started boiling in his veins. "Would you be able to recognize the werewolf?"

"We didn't see the fight, but we know who it was."

Michael wondered if the werewolf had been wearing a mind control device or if he'd done the killing of his own volition. Michael had little love for the species, but if the werewolf had been forced to kill, it was a different story... "How long have you guys been here?" he asked.

"Just a few days."

"Have you visited the whole training camp?"

"Yeah," several of them replied at the same time.

"Any chance you thought of a way to get out of here?" Michael asked in a low voice.

They looked at each other and shook their heads.

"That's alright, we'll figure something out," he said, smiling at Aurora.

Their lunch was over, and the prisoners still had ten minutes left before the next training session when Aurora excused herself, and Michael was left alone with the five skinwalkers.

On their way to the afternoon's activities, their group crossed paths with the warden who was accompanied by two guards. The narrow forest trail forced Michael and the skinwalkers to walk right by the warden who smiled at them.

"Look who's here! I hear you guys all come from the same neck of the woods," said the warden. "You see... this is a great place! Bumping into old friends... Making new ones..."

Michael held the man directly responsible for the death of Daka's packmates, and he'd have broken his neck right then and there if it hadn't been for the remotes in the guards' hands. The warden had his usual glass ball handle cane with him and Michael promised himself that, collar or not, the man's slight limp would soon get a lot worse.

"I've noticed you spent a lot of time with our wolverine guest, hmm? How's that working for you?" the warden asked Michael with a wink. "According to your file you have a girlfriend. Isn't she the jealous type?"

His flippant tone made Michael's skin crawl.

"That's the problem with young people these days," continued the warden. "No loyalty to their partners. That's why all those marriages go to crap. But watch out for that wolverine youngster, she looks like she might be more trouble than she's worth."

He tapped Michael on the cheek a couple of times before taking his leave, whistling happily.

"That asshole needs to die," said one of the skinwalkers.

Michael looked at the kid who'd just spoken. "Don't you worry… he's already dead."

Chapter 63

The warden was surprised to see light under the door when he arrived at his office a few minutes before 6 AM. He walked in to find the director sitting in his chair behind the desk.

The woman gave him a cursory look. "Morning, Warden."

She wore an elegant black pant suit whose open jacket revealed a well-furnished cleavage under a cream silk blouse, and a gold necklace which carried a colorful pendant only partially hidden by the blouse.

"Good morning, Ma'am. I wasn't expecting you so early."

"That's alright. It gave me a chance to review your progress."

It was obvious she'd been going through his computer files. The PC was password-protected, but apparently that had not been much of a deterrent.

"Please have a seat." She pointed at a visitor's chair, while she remained comfortably installed in his swiveling leather armchair.

The warden sat down as she was saying, "I'm pleased. You've only been here a few days and I can already see progress. This facility will soon be training the most lethal units of our nation's armed forces."

The warden relaxed and smiled at the compliment, but the director wasn't done.

"Unfortunately, it would seem that your men will be seeing battle before their training is complete."

"What do you mean?" he asked.

"How much do you know about magic?"

He gave her a puzzled look. "Magic?"

"Yes, magic! You know… curses, witches, wizards… that sort of thing?"

"I've seen what our two instructors who call themselves sorcerers can do, but that's about it," he replied, confused.

"I see," she said, the tips of her fingers pressed together. She got up and took a few steps towards the window before turning towards him. "What if I tell you those sorcerers and werecreatures are only the tip of the iceberg?"

"I don't understand…"

"There's a whole kitchen sink of magical beings hidden in plain sight. Those shifters you train here are far from the top of the food chain."

His face registered surprise but he remained silent, attentive to the woman's every word.

"Sorcerers are real, obviously... But so are wizards, vampires and of course the faes... And I'm not talking about the cute little pixies one reads about in fairytales. I'm talking about ogres, minotaurs, trolls and the like."

The warden realized he must have looked absolutely perplexed right now, but it was a fitting expression given the nature of the revelation. "They're all... real?"

"That's correct. Oh, and elves too. I nearly forgot about those."

"Elves as in the Lord of the Rings?" he asked.

"Pretty close. Tolkien mostly got it right... surprisingly."

The director spent the next hour giving a crash course on praeternaturals and supernaturals to her subaltern who just stared at her, mouth open in bewilderment.

"You know those mind control diadems we use on the were creatures?" she concluded.

He knew exactly what she was talking about. "Yes."

"These marvels of technology actually have nothing to do with technology. It's magic that makes them work. You see, Warden, the operation you're running here is only one side of the equation. Taming the shifters and using them to the nation's advantage is an important endeavor, but an equally important one is to get the rest of the magical zoo under control."

The warden nodded in agreement.

"In the same way we're using shifters to hunt other shifters," she continued, "we've been recruiting magical folks to protect the nation from magical attacks."

"So, there are other camps like this one?"

"Yes! There are..." She smiled.

"Where?"

"That's irrelevant. But we have reasons to believe our recruiting hasn't gone unnoticed. Our enemies are onto us and our intel suggests they're getting ready to strike. If the information is confirmed, we'll need to send everything we have at them, including your trainees."

"How strong is this enemy?" He could hear his voice cracking.

"Let's just say we'll need all the fire power at our disposal to fight the wizards."

"Wizards?" repeated Wes with surprise. "Are these dark wizards?"

"Don't be deceived by names," said the director. "Sorcerers, warlocks, witches and wizards can all choose to fight on one side or the other. It just so happens that the majority of wizards stand against the nation's interest and need to be dealt with."

"How big of a threat do they represent?"

"A very serious one! Their leader is a powerful wizard who's organized them into a cohesive striking force."

"Are the odds in our favor?" asked the warden.

"Definitely," replied the director with a smile. "We've rallied enough factions to our cause that the wizards will be crushed like bugs. Nonetheless... if we could chop the head of their organization off before we meet them in battle, it would only make things easier."

Wes nodded pensively. "And do you know where to find this wizard?"

"Not exactly, but you happen to have a good friend of his among your prisoners."

Wes' smile widened. "You're talking about Biörn, aren't you?"

"Precisely."

"Do you want to question him?"

"No, that would be fruitless, it's very unlikely that the bear would know the whereabouts of his friend, but we can use him as bait. The two are close. Close enough that the wizard will likely show up if he senses Biörn is in trouble."

"And what kind of trouble do you have in mind?" The warden was grinning now.

"You've built a very nice cage. I suggest we put it to good use. We'll organize a fight between Biörn and the prisoner who arrived yesterday."

The warden beamed at the idea. "Now that's going to be a good fight..."

Chapter 64

Michael heard the sound of heavy bolts sliding on the other side of the wall an instant before the door of the cell swung open to reveal the loathed silhouette of the warden.

"I hope you slept well, because you're going to need all your strength today," announced the warden.

What kind of twisted training program had the sadistic asshole come up with this time? In the whole scheme of things it didn't really matter. Still, Michael was curious.

Aurora placed her hand on his cheek, a gentle caress he hadn't expected from the wolverine. "Whatever it is, you can do this," she said, her eyes sinking into his. She looked worried.

"We don't have all day. Your public awaits," said the warden, tapping an imaginary watch on his wrist.

Michael's eyes were trained on the opposite end of the cage where three guards were ushering in a mountain of a man. The giant was nearly seven-foot-tall, and that wasn't the troublesome part. The wind had covered the man's scent up to this point, but he was now close enough for Michael to smell it. And his scent was all wrong. It simply couldn't be... But when the mountain morphed into his beast an instant later, Michael realized he'd been mistaken this whole time.

For over a hundred and fifty years, he'd believed himself to be the sole survivor of his species, but the mountain standing on the other side of the fighting arena was here to prove him wrong. Easily nine-foot-tall and with off-white fur, the polar bear had a good hundred pounds on him. Just like Michael's bear wasn't a true grizzly, nor was his opponent a perfect polar bear, but only an expert would have been able to tell the difference.

The two adversaries wore identical diadems, their bases resting at the junction between the neck and the skull. Michael knew what it meant: they'd be compelled to obey their handlers' orders, compelled to fight each other, no matter what.

Michael didn't wait for the diadem to force his morphing. He couldn't afford to receive his estranged brother's attacks in his human form; he wouldn't last a minute.

Polar bears couldn't sprint as fast as grizzlies, but in a confined area the size of a tennis court it didn't matter; the white bear was on Michael a second before the grizzly completed his morphing. Michael felt his neck twist under the impact as his opponent's claws dug deep into his cheek and the underside of his massive head. Before he could react, the polar bear's other paw dealt an equally devastating blow to his throat, carving three deep gouges in the process.

The grizzly felt blood oozing from the open wound and, disoriented by the attack, decided to run to regroup. From the corner of his eye, Michael saw the warden cheering at his retreat. A woman Michael had never seen before bent towards the warden and whispered something in his ear. Michael hoped it would be the end of the fight, but he suspected this was wishful thinking.

The polar bear was now chasing him around the small enclosure. He had nowhere to run, but it didn't matter as long as he could outrun his kindred long enough to heal and come up with a plan. He was feeling no impulse from his diadem and suspected his handler was enjoying the show too much to bother.

Thankfully, the cuts on his throat closed up within a half-minute. As Michael felt the polar bear closing in on him, he feigned a movement to the right before veering to the left, tricking his adversary in the process. Carried by his momentum, the polar bear overtook Michael on his right. The grizzly then changed direction once more and, accelerating, rammed his eight hundred pounds into his opponent. The two bears rolled to the ground in a deluge of claws and fangs that sent blood spraying ten feet around them.

Michael couldn't recall battling a shifter who outweighed him before, and this fight was quickly proving to be the toughest one on one he'd ever fought. This was no surprise, however; polar bears were natural hunters, even more so than grizzlies. Unlike their brown cousins who only got twenty percent of their calories from meat, the polar bear were hypercarnivores and depended on hunting for all their meals.

Michael felt his opponent's jaws close on his shoulder, but he was able to headbutt him with enough strength to dislodge the beast before his teeth sank too deeply into the flesh. The polar bear roared in anger at the same instant Michael's teeth ripped the diadem off his opponent's neck and hurled it to the ground.

The polar bear reflexively swatted at him, leaving deep marks on Michael's left ear and cheek. The grizzly instantly responded with a two-handed shove into which he put all his body weight. The polar bear toppled to the ground under the impact. He got back on his feet in a flash, but his attitude had changed. He no longer displayed obvious signs of aggressivity; he still looked suspicious of Michael, though.

Michael had no desire to keep on fighting, but he knew he wouldn't be able to disobey his own diadem's impulse. When the impulse came, though, the command wasn't the one he'd expected. The impulse felt weak, for one thing, yet the order was clear: the fight was over. The two bears were apparently too valuable to be wasted on each other; their jailers had other plans.

The doors of their cell block had been sealed for the night and Michael was sitting beside Aurora in one corner of the large cage. His Arctic cousin was nowhere to be seen, probably kept in another cell block or even in isolation.

"Are you okay?" asked Aurora.

"I'm fine," replied Michael, who was anything but fine. They'd almost forced the two only remaining werebears on the planet to kill each other and this pissed him off more than anything else the DSA had done so far. These people needed to die.

"You don't *look* okay."

"I had a bit of a shock today; for a while I've been thinking I was the only werebear left alive."

"I see... And these assholes forced you to fight your cousin... If I could only get my hands around their necks."

Michael nodded in agreement.

Aurora stared at him in silence a moment. "I don't think the fight was just for these assholes' entertainment. I think they had an ulterior motive," she said finally.

"What kind of motive?"

"I think they were using you as bait, hoping for someone to show up to rescue you or something..."

"What are you talking about?"

"I overheard the warden and one of the guards talking this morning. The guard was asking why you were so valuable, and the warden replied because you were friends with a wizard of the Second Circle."

Michael didn't like the sound of that, but at least it answered one of the questions that had been bothering him. The reason the dark mage and his DSA allies had been hunting him down so relentlessly had nothing to do with him. They just wanted to get to Ezekiel through him.

"Do you really know a wizard of the Second Circle?" asked Aurora.

Michael nodded.

"And you think he's going to come rescue you? Because if he does, I wouldn't mind catching a ride out of here."

Michael shook his head. "I'm sorry, I don't think that's going to happen."

"Why not?" She sounded disappointed.

"Because I don't have the slightest clue where he is."

"I don't think these guys know that," replied Aurora, nodding towards no one in particular but clearly talking about the guards. "The warden seems to think you're instrumental in catching the wizard." She shook her head in disbelief. "Who the hell are these people who think they can go after a wizard of the Second Circle and not suffer the consequences?"

"I don't know who they are, but the reason they think they can is because they've done it before."

"Successfully?"

Michael nodded. Tabitha and Methuselah were gone, after all, and the DSA was just another arm of the dark mage's octopus.

Aurora shook her head. "These bastards all deserve to die. The warden, in particular, and in the most excruciating way possible."

Michael didn't reply. He was deep in thought.

"Any progress with your plan to get us out of here?" asked Aurora.

The truth was that he hadn't had much time to think of a plan. The training kept the prisoners busy, and they were exhausted by the time evening came. The situation had also changed unexpectedly over the past few hours, and Michael now had reasons to stick around a while longer. "Not yet," he responded noncommittally.

"That's alright," said Aurora. "The longer we stay here the more likely it is that an opportunity will present itself."

"An opportunity for what?"

"An opportunity to kill the warden," she said.

Michael had no doubt she meant it.

Chapter 65

The warden and the director had spent the remainder of the day conducting a review of the camp and it was late in the evening by the time they got back to the warden's office.

"That was disappointing," she said.

"I beg your pardon?" responded the warden, surprised. The woman had insisted on surveying every single one of the hundred and fifty odd captives, but she'd appeared satisfied with what she'd seen.

"I'm talking about the fight. About the fact our plan didn't work. The wizard never showed up."

"Maybe he never showed up because Biörn was never in real danger. After the first minute, he mostly had the upper hand. If his handler hadn't stopped him at the end, he probably would have killed his opponent."

"Maybe…" said the woman pensively. "Perhaps we should have him fight again, this time against a half dozen enemies."

"I don't see why we couldn't," said the warden, smiling.

The director's phone rang, and she immediately answered. "Yes? Very well. Wait for my instructions." She hung up and turned towards the warden. "I just got some good news. We've finally located the wizards' base. We don't have an exact headcount, but there are more of them than we expected. We'll definitely need every soldier at our disposal. How fast can your shifters get to Nebraska?"

"Nebraska? The wizards are in Nebraska?"

"So it would seem."

The warden thought about it for a minute. "If we wake them up now, they can be on choppers in an hour and at the airport in two. They'll be in Nebraska first thing in the morning."

The director considered the idea an instant before saying, "That won't be necessary. We still have more troops to rally. It will take some time. Just make sure you get them there by mid-afternoon tomorrow. I'll send you a precise location for the rendezvous soon."

"Who else will be joining the fight besides my freaks?"

"That's what I need to work on right now," said the director. "Now if you'll excuse me, I need to make some arrangements, and quickly."

She hurriedly exited the office before the warden could reply. Left alone, he contemplated the situation an instant before picking up the phone. There was no time to waste.

Chapter 66

Michael couldn't recall ever having been in central Nebraska before, and he doubted he'd come back to visit anytime soon. The scenery of corn fields extending as far as the eye could see was a bit too flat for his liking.

The choppers had dropped the shifter army a few miles from the wizards' position late in the afternoon. Divided into three battalions, the hodgepodge of shifters had then waited for the cover of darkness before traveling the remaining distance by foot. The first two combat groups counted only werewolves within their ranks, about sixty in each group. The third one, which was just shy of forty fighters, included every other shifter the DSA had been able to get their hands on over the past year.

Michael and Aurora were part of the third battalion's front line. A battalion led by no other than the warden himself who was bringing up the rear alongside the beasts' handlers.

The three battalions were slowly moving in a straight-line formation with a two-hundred-foot buffer between each group. At the formation's center, Michael and Aurora's battalion represented the praeternaturals' shock troops.

The shifters had morphed into their animals about a mile out from their objective and were therefore ready for battle. Their mission was to approach the wizards from a south-southwest direction and wait for the order to engage.

The cloudy sky and the absence of stars made for a night as dark as ink, but none of the werebeings seemed to notice. The handlers on the other hand all wore night vision goggles. Michael had his ideas on why they'd been waiting for nightfall before moving in on the wizards' position, and his suspicion was confirmed when a vampire smell reached his nostrils. With every step Michael took, the stench became more pronounced and it wasn't long before it overwhelmed his nose despite the presence of the werewolves whose scent couldn't be ignored. It looked like the shifters and the vamps were part of a concerted attack against the wizards. The six-foot-tall corn surrounding them prevented eye contact between the battalions, but Michael could tell they were converging and getting closer.

They were miles from the closest farm, which meant that despite the magnitude of the battle they were about to wage, it was unlikely to attract any civilian attention.

Supposedly the wizards had gathered around an abandoned barn, and Michael kept searching the horizon for the wooden construction whose roof should emerge in the distance given the flatness of the landscape.

Finally his eyes found the barn a few minutes before his battalion emerged into a section of field where the crop had been flattened over an area covering four or five football fields. Nearly three hundred wizards had assembled in a large circle in the middle of the squashed crop. They were facing outward, away from the circle's center where their leader stood on a dirt mound that offered a vantage viewpoint to what would soon become the battlefield. Michael couldn't distinguish the leader's features, but his nose told him all he needed to know. This was Tabitha. Apparently the woman was not as dead as he'd been led to believe.

When the vamp's battalion emerged from the north, Michael counted approximately two hundred bloodsuckers. The Western Covenant was larger than he'd suspected.

The air tasted of anticipation and fear, and he wondered what the DSA was waiting for. He was receiving no impulse to attack and given that none of his fellow shifters was making a move, it was clear their handlers were waiting for something. A smart move, for he strongly doubted Tabitha and her two hundred wizards would be defeated by a bunch of vampires and *remote-controlled* shifters. Their makeshift army would be torn to pieces before they could even reach the wizards' ranks.

They didn't have to wait long, however. Soon, rows upon rows of human-smelling fighters appeared to the east, on the opposite side of the battlefield. The fact they bore no weapons was a dead giveaway as to the nature of the particular battalion; these were magical folks, witches and sorcerers with probably a few warlocks thrown into the mix.

When the faes of Lord Vaalt showed up an instant later and blocked any potential retreat to the west, Michael reevaluated the situation with a more pessimistic outlook for the wizards. Tabitha's forces were now up against roughly two hundred vampires, a hundred and sixty shifters, one hundred and fifty faes of various types and nearly three hundred witches, sorcerers and warlocks. The wizards already had a hell of a fight on their hands, and the dark mage had yet to arrive…

The air around the wizards started crackling with static electricity and soon the same thing happened within the sorcerers' ranks. Michael wasn't sure whether the display of power had another purpose, but the static discharge lighting up the night with an eerie glow was sure intimidating.

The warden stood a mere twenty feet in front of Michael, close enough that his bear could have rushed and killed the man before the handler had a chance to stop Michael. But Michael had no intention of doing so.

An instant later, a woman could be seen standing beside the warden. Michael had no idea where she'd come from, but he recognized her scent immediately. She'd been among the audience that had watched him fight the polar bear… This was the woman the guards referred to as *the director*. She wore the same pant suit she had the day before.

She was talking to the warden and Michael took a few steps to eavesdrop on the conversation. Aurora's wolverine nudged him to get his attention. She was probably wondering what he was up to, but his bear was ill-equipped to communicate the information.

As a loud rumble rose from the battlefield—a combination of vampire hisses and the giant feet of ogres and other trolls thumping the ground—the director took off her jacket and folded it carefully before handing it to one of the guards to hold. As she did so the air suddenly felt saturated with power and the woman turned to the warden, her eyes blazing with an intensity visible even in the darkness of the night. She opened her mouth but before a word could come out of it, a salvo of colorful lighting erupted from the wizards' group and rushed towards her with lethal precision. But the woman simply waved her hand and the lightning bolts all collapsed on top of the protective bubble the dark mage had erected around herself—for the director was the dark mage, there was no longer any doubt about it.

That was when Michael noticed Aurora's wolverine sneaking up behind the warden. She quickly closed the distance and pounced on her enemy. She never reached her target, however. A second before connecting with the neck of her prey Michael's bear careened into the wolverine, sending Aurora to the ground. As the wolverine tumbled through the trampled corn, she turned into her human self in the blink of an eye. No werebeing could morph this fast, but this wasn't the most revealing thing about the rapid transformation. Her human form no longer looked anything like the Aurora Michael had met at the camp. On the other hand, she bore a disturbing resemblance to the warlock who'd escaped from Vaalt's castle with two fragments of the Eye of the Phoenix... Demetra!

Before Demetra could get back on her feet, Michael heard the sound of crushed glass, as if someone had stepped on a light bulb. But the sound had actually come from the crystal handle of the warden's cane whose shards now littered the ground.

At that moment Michael felt the first impulse from his diadem, but it was so weak it couldn't have forced a kitten to run away from a water hose.

A second later, the warden was upon him. The man laid a hand on his bear's head and, in doing so, sent him flying several hundred feet away from the dark mage and heracolyte before vanishing into thin air. Michael saw the warden reappear an instant later at Tabitha's side where he finally dropped his disguise. Michael wasn't even a bit surprised when the warden turned into the familiar shape of Ezekiel.

Chapter 67

Michael stood alone on the edge of the battlefield. Ezekiel's *gentle shove* had sent him well out of reach of the shifters' battalions. An attack from the dark mage and Demetra could have easily reached him, of course, but the two were too busy with the wizards to pay any attention to the lonesome werebear.

The battle was now raging between the two sides and it took the combined effort of Ezekiel, Tabitha and nearly fifty wizards of the Third Circle simply to contain the devastating attacks the dark mage threw at them. The two hundred or so remaining wizards—mostly of the Fourth Circle—were left to face more than three times their numbers of sorcerers, witches, faes, vampires and shifters of all kinds. Things weren't looking too good.

Michael received yet another impulse from his diadem ordering him to attack the wizards, but he had absolutely no difficulties ignoring the command.

The other shifters were now rushing the wizards. In the chaos of battle, Michael quickly reintegrated the converging shifter battalions and started taking care of business from within the enemy's ranks. He'd dispatched three werewolves and a black panther by the time he reached the wizards' ranks.

Thankfully, the wizards didn't target him but instead let him inside their protective circle. No doubt he had Ezekiel to thank for this small miracle.

Michael knew the mind-controlled shifters weren't responsible for their actions and he decided to focus his energy on enemies who were here of their own free will. Well aware of his limitations when it came to fighting magical folks, he was left with the option of going after the bloodsuckers or the faes. He chose the vamps.

As soon as a bloodsucker got close enough to the wizards' line, Michael charged and engaged the undead. The vamps were fast, but Michael had never been defeated in a one on one fight against their kind, and as soon as the undead teamed up against him, he invariably received help from the closest wizards.

More and more werecreatures were closing in on the wizards and Michael considered shifting his focus onto the werewolves, but then something unexpected happened. The night became illuminated by a green rain which fell onto the beasts' handlers who were controlling their pets from the edge of the battlefield. The handlers fell like flies under the iridescent droplets, and Michael realized that what he'd taken for rain was in fact a constant barrage of arrows. The green-tipped weapons, fired with unmatched accuracy, could only mean one thing: the elves had joined the battle, and they were on the wizards' side.

With their handlers dispatched, the shifters regained their free will and were either switching allegiance or running away from the battleground. The elves' intervention had been unexpected but lifesaving, as the wizards' ranks were thinning quickly. Nearly a hundred of Ezekiel's kindred had already perished under the assaults of their enemies.

While the sorcerers and witches, led by warlocks, were getting closer and more threatening by the minute, the dark mage seemed to possess endless resources. In addition to her own incredible powers, she wielded fae magic as naturally as Lord Vaalt himself—courtesy of the reassembled Eye of the Phoenix she wore around her neck. She alone was responsible for at least two dozen wizard casualties—all this while keeping Tabitha and Ezekiel in check. There was also a good chance the Healing Stone was stashed in one of the woman's pockets. So on top of everything else, she'd be healing within seconds from any non-lethal wound.

Michael was chewing his way through a vampire elder's neck when he caught a whiff of Irini's scent. A moment later it was Lucy's much more subtle odor that floated to his nostrils. Olivia's sister had to be very close indeed for him to detect her scent among the overwhelming stench of elders and werewolves.

Following his nose, he quickly found the young woman who was fighting back to back with Irini. Each woman was engaged in battle against a bloodsucker. Michael didn't recognize their opponents, but they no doubt belonged to the Western Covenant. Upon closer inspection,

Lucy and Irini weren't the only vampires fighting their own kind. Everywhere he looked, vamps were fighting vamps. Were these survivors of the Eastern Covenant? This was unexpected...

The elves and Irini's friends were keeping the faes and the Western Covenant plenty busy. Ezekiel and Tabitha still stood their ground, and soon the powerful high-born elves would be within range to cast their own spells... The battle was starting to look a lot more balanced.

For the first time Michael believed they had a chance at ending this, but then he realized the dark mage simply couldn't be defeated. No one could get close to her, and if her forces got to the point where victory was no longer possible, she'd simply vanish... And there was nothing anyone could do to stop her. She'd be gone for a while, just long enough to lick her wounds and rebuild an army, but she'd soon be back for another offensive. They'd never be rid of her... That was when he remembered the woman's jacket.

Chapter 68

The elves were quickly closing in on the dark mage who stood surrounded by her warlocks and other sorcerers. Busy battling on two fronts, the dark practitioners paid no attention to Michael as he surreptitiously deserted the wizards' ranks in search of a particular individual. Following his nose, the bear found the man he was looking for among the bodies of the fallen handlers, pinned to the ground by three elvish arrows and no longer breathing.

Michael stood staring at the battle raging at the center of the flattened field, four hundred feet north of his position. He'd regained his human form but wasn't entirely naked; a bear pelt was wrapped over his right shoulder and looped under his other arm like a caveman's garment. Not exactly what he'd expected, but it definitely proved his assertion had been correct.

He started running towards the battle but then thought better of it and slowed down his pace. Directly in front of him were the wizards' ranks. None of them were facing him, however. They'd broken their circle and had reassembled into smaller groups focused on three separate fronts: the vampires to the north, the warlocks to the east, and the faes to the west. For his plan to succeed, Michael needed to get around the enemies' ranks and approach from their backs.

The dark mage's position was easy to identify; it was where most of the crackling came from and was also the focus of the majority of the attacks. It took Michael nearly fifteen minutes to position himself. Once he did, he wasted no time moving towards his target. He walked unimpaired through the ranks of witches and sorcerers. The dark practitioners were far too busy fighting the wizards and their unexpected elvish allies to pay much attention to the caveman.

He was only twenty feet from the dark mage when Demetra, who was standing at her side, suddenly turned around and spotted him. She threw a spell in his direction, but nothing happened. Michael saw surprise registering on her face. The attack hadn't been of the visible kind, but her reaction clearly betrayed her intent. Her next attack was much less subtle, and Michael clearly saw the fireball rushing towards his head. He raised his hands protectively by sheer reflex, but the fiery projectile vanished as soon as it made contact with him. It hadn't caused the slightest discomfort to his bare skin.

The ranks had started to collapse on both sides of the conflict. Wizards, elves and dark practitioners were now fighting at close quarters all around Michael. He picked up the pace just as Demetra was reaching for the dark mage who stood only three feet to her right. The warlock's lips started moving and Michael saw the dark mage's head swivel towards her acolyte just as a bolt of green light fell upon Demetra, instantly turning her to stone. Michael didn't get much chance to admire the warlock's statue, however. A second bolt pulverized the work of art a split second later. He searched the battlefield, expecting to find Tabitha or Ezekiel on the other end of the devastating attack, but was shocked when his eyes fell upon Maya. The elvish princess had been the one who'd defeated Demetra. Maybe Maya *had* changed after all.

Bent on avenging her lieutenant's demise, the dark mage unleashed a deluge of firepower on the elf who was barely able to counter the attacks, let alone try to launch one of her own.

Michael required no further encouragement. He reached the dark mage who, sensing his presence, turned towards him and hit him with a shockwave that dissipated the instant it reached him. He saw incomprehension registering on the woman's face as he grabbed her head and twisted it three hundred and sixty degrees in a swift motion, breaking her neck in the process. By the time her eyes met his, there was no life left in them.

The faes had closed upon the wizards and were breaking their ranks by sheer force of muscles when the voice of Lord Vaalt resonated on the battlefield, booming as if he were using a bullhorn. Michael didn't understand the words spoken by the high fae, but the effect was instantaneous. The faes switched sides in an instant and turned against the witches and sorcerers. This completely changed the physiognomy of the battle.

While the surviving warlocks were kept busy by the high faes relentlessly assaulting them with magical attacks of all sorts, Michael unleashed his destructive energy on the surrounding witches and sorcerers who responded with an avalanche of spells. But Michael was wearing the Cloak of Amariel and the magical attacks bounced off him harmlessly. The cloak prevented him from turning into his beast but still allowed him to regenerate. Unable to use their magic against him, the sorcerers and witches proved very easy to kill indeed.

In the end, overwhelmed by the number of their enemies and turncoat-ex-allies, the remnants of the dark mage's army simply collapsed. A few of the more skillful ones managed to escape, but the vast majority of them met their end on the Nebraska battleground.

The dark mage was finally defeated but the price of victory had been very high, and Michael dreaded the final tally.

Chapter 69

Wes Thortan reached the Ozark training camp late in the afternoon and found it a ghost town. He'd been walking around the premises for a good five minutes and had yet to find a living soul. The guards, the prisoners and their handlers had all vanished. What the hell was going on?

He'd woken up earlier that morning sitting in front of a half-eaten breakfast in a diner nearly two hundred miles away, with no recollection of how he'd gotten there. The waitress who'd reluctantly answered his questions had done so all the while staring at him as if he'd freshly escaped from the local loony bin. From the bewildering conversation he'd learned that he'd not only partially eaten the food in front of him, but had been coming in for breakfast, lunch and dinner every day for the past week and a half.

He walked to his office and found it unlocked. It hadn't been ransacked and remained tidy and organized, but clearly someone had been going through his files. The director? Had she been looking for him? He'd been gone for nearly thirteen days, after all... His cane was nowhere to be found, however. What had happened to it?

The last thing he remembered prior to coming to his senses in that diner was walking out of the convenience store late at night. He'd sensed a presence behind him and had pivoted on one foot to face his stalker while pulling his gun out of his pocket. He remembered pressing the trigger, but not hearing the sound of the powder exploding in the weapon's chamber. Instead, he recalled a bright blinding light—and then nothing. Had the gun misfired? Had his stalker hit him on the head? That would probably explain the amnesia....

He walked to the building harboring the prisoners' cells and was relieved to find that this section of the compound wasn't entirely deserted. The five surviving skinwalkers were locked up inside their cell. They had a toddler with them, though. The warden immediately recognized the kid. It was the son of the snow leopard woman whose company he'd enjoyed night after night. What was he doing there? He should have been in his isolation pen, alone. He hadn't ordered the kid be moved. Who'd taken the initiative?

"What's going on here? Where's everybody? And what's that kid doing in your cell?" he asked the skinwalkers, but they all stared at him in silence.

He repeated the question angrily, kicking the cell's Plexiglas wall and already threatening the prisoners with reprisals if they didn't answer, but they simply stared at him. To add insult to injury they even smiled, openly mocking him.

He heard a loud whistle coming from behind him and spun around, nearly losing his balance in the process.

"Hello, Warden," said the child's mother. The woman who, only a few days ago, had been his to abuse. She stood a mere six feet away.

The warden's blood turned to ice when he realized she wore no collar around her neck. "Stay where you are! Don't approach me!" he said, pointing the gun he'd retrieved from his office at her. That was when he noticed the giant standing a few feet behind her: Michael Biörn.

As Michael started morphing into his bear, the warden instinctively unloaded his gun on the monster. By the time the woman closed the distance and grabbed him by the throat, his magazine was empty. His screams resonated throughout the empty camp as she tore him to pieces.

Epilogue

Michael hurried to grab the two remaining sandwiches from the tray just as Sheila bent down to retrieve it from the wicker table and carried it inside to the kitchen. Daka and Olivia had eaten their fill, as had Sheila, but Michael's hunger was just starting to recede.

They'd finally returned to Michael's cabin two days earlier after a four-month absence. The prolonged *vacation* had used up the whole thirteen weeks of paid time off Michael had accumulated over the years, and he'd been forced to take a leave of absence to cover the balance. He was glad to be back, though.

Ezekiel had assured him it was safe to return to the park. The DSA no longer existed, and all trace of the organization had been erased. The task had been relatively easy given that there were no DSA employees left alive and that the secret department had never actually been attached to the government in the first place... The director had convinced her employees she was leading a legitimate operation when in truth the department had never been sanctioned by anyone in Washington.

"I'd better head back to the reservation. I've delayed it long enough," said Daka, getting up from the wooden bench where he'd been sitting beside Olivia.

Olivia followed him to his car and kissed him goodbye just as Sheila exited the kitchen to collect empty plates.

"Let me help you," said Michael, grabbing plates and silverware and heading for the door. When the two of them came out of the cabin a moment later, they found Olivia back on her bench, but this time it was Ezekiel sitting beside her, a wide grin on his face.

Michael didn't bother asking where the wizard had come from. "Good to see you, Ez," he said, settling down on a wooden armchair in front of his guests.

"Hi, Ez," said Sheila, as she sat down on the armrest of Michael's seat.

"Good morning, children!" said the wizard merrily. "It's a pleasant surprise to see you here, Sheila. I thought you'd already be in Houston by now, eager to get back to work."

"You're not far off... I'm heading for the airport in a few minutes. Olivia's giving me a ride."

"Your ne'er-do-well of a boyfriend can't be bothered?" Ez stared reproachfully at Michael.

"I have to work this afternoon. The park's severely understaffed and, given that I just returned from a four-month break, taking the afternoon off seems a bit audacious, even for me," explained Michael.

"I'll give him a pass for this one time. I've seen his face enough lately, a bit of a break will do me some good," teased Sheila.

"What brings you here, Ez?" asked Michael.

"I thought you'd like to know that the four artifacts have been returned to their rightful owners," replied the wizard.

"The four? What about the fifth one? What happened to Amariel's Amulet?"

"After careful consideration Tabitha and I decided that such a powerful object didn't need to exist. Nothing good could come out of it. We destroyed it so it will never again create havoc."

"So it's gone for good? Like the dark mage?" Michael was surprised with the wizards' decision, but he saw the wisdom in it.

Ezekiel nodded. "Like the dark mage—or the *director*, if you prefer. She went by many names over the millennia but you may be surprised to know that she was no none other than Amariel herself."

"Didn't you tell us that Amariel had been killed by a warlock centuries ago?"

"Millenia ago, actually, but it would seem she faked her death..."

"When did you start suspecting she was the dark mage?" asked Michael.

"The mind-controlling diadems were what put me on the path. I found the description of the magic infusing them in an ancient book dedicated to her discoveries. It was her own magic. The coincidences were starting to be a bit too... much. My suspicions were confirmed when I finally met the *director* in the flesh. Amariel hadn't bothered concealing herself, she looked exactly the way she had when I used to know her, all those millennia ago."

"But *she* didn't recognize you at first, because at the time you were masquerading as the warden..." said Michael with a crooked smile.

"That's correct. When did you figure out that I was impersonating Wes Thortan?"

"Things started clicking into place when I ran into you with Daka's packmates at the camp and you called me a youngster. You're the only one to ever call me that, and it was already the second time the warden had... The first time could have been a coincidence, but twice was too fishy. You also subtly warned me about the wolverine woman that day, and that managed to convince me. I'd noticed that the woman didn't behave like your average shifter. Her fighting style and her reactions were off. After your veiled warning I started suspecting she was there to get information out of me. My suspicion was confirmed after the fight against the polar bear when she steered the conversation towards you, trying to find out about your whereabouts."

Ezekiel shook his head in amusement. "I was wondering if you'd get the hint. You can be slow sometimes..."

"Why couldn't you simply tell Michael who you were? Call him into your office and tell him the whole truth?" asked Olivia.

Michael and Ezekiel stared at each other uneasily for a split second, and it was Michael who finally answered. "Because he didn't know if he could trust me..."

"What?" exclaimed Olivia and Sheila simultaneously.

"Ezekiel suspected there might be a spy among us and he wasn't sure who it was. Jason Parrish had been the spy, of course, but he couldn't be certain of that. I could have been cursed to betray him, for instance... That's also why he told us that Tabitha was dead. It was disinformation in the hope one of us would reveal some tell-tale sign... Wasn't it, Ez?"

By the look on the two women's faces, it was obvious they considered the idea ludicrous, but Ez simply ignored the question. "What I'd like to know, Michael, is how you came up with the idea to put on the Cloak of Amariel during the battle. How did you even figure out that the Cloak was actually the director's jacket?"

Michael gave the wizard a broad smile. "You thought you were the only one who'd figured it out, didn't you?"

"Stop gloating and answer the question!"

"By the time I was captured at the detention center, I'd known for a while that the DSA and the dark mage were connected—"

"How?" interrupted Sheila.

"For one thing, the DSA set up a trap in the woods using Jason Parrish as bait to capture me. They knew he wasn't wearing a physical tracker of any kind, and yet they knew we'd be able to find him. It only makes sense if they had a way to know that Ezekiel had placed a magical tracker on Jason."

"And this tracker was pretty advanced magic, not something your garden-variety witch could accomplish," confirmed Ezekiel.

"This suggested the DSA was in cahoots with powerful practitioners," continued Michael. "The diadems were another indication, since they were infused with fancy magic. And there was also the willingness of DSA's operatives to commit suicide as soon as they were captured. I'd seen more than one killing themselves before I had a chance to ask them a single question. That's not normal behavior. Soldiers don't commit suicide that easily, but bewitched soldiers—"

"Fine! So you knew the DSA worked for the dark mage... How did that help you figure things out with the Cloak of Amariel?" interrupted the wizard.

"I'm getting to it... Thanks to that knowledge, I kept an eye open for the Cloak as soon as I got to the training camp. Just in case it turned up... I already knew it was an integral part of the equation and the reason the dark mage had been able to remain hidden for millennia while increasing her power—"

"What? How?" This time it was Olivia's turn to interrupt.

"Ezekiel had clearly mentioned that a dark mage couldn't be born as an adult, and yet we were definitely dealing with an adult; her hegemonic aspirations couldn't come from an infant. Therefore, there had to be an explanation... Taken individually, none of the major artifacts would allow such a miracle, but combined... the Cloak of Amariel and Amariel's Amulet would give the illusion of such a miracle."

Leaning back on his bench, Ezekiel was smiling approvingly. "That's right, but I'm not sure these ladies are following you, Michael."

"Using the Cloak, Amariel could insulate herself from the magical field," explained Michael. "And using the Amulet, she could defeat other practitioners and capture their power for herself. Ez had mentioned that there had always been variation in the magical field, some punctual spikes in intensity that would disappear after a few hours, and this going back as far as Ez could remember. I wager these spikes corresponded to Amariel removing the Cloak long enough to defeat another practitioner before putting it back on and once again disappearing from the magical field. Amariel was born a wizard of the Second Circle, but after faking her death, she spent millennia accumulating power through this process."

"That's correct," confirmed Ezekiel. "And recently, she even used the process in reverse... About nine months ago, she decided she'd accumulated enough power to finally reveal herself to the world and took the Cloak off for good... mostly."

"Mostly?" said Sheila.

"Yes, my child. You see all those warlocks springing out of nowhere were actually manufactured by Amariel herself. But since the Amulet acts like a battery, her vibrational signature would diminish every time she donated some of her power to a sorcerer to turn them into a warlock. Her signature was so strong that the drop caused by the transfer of power to one or two warlocks would have been hard to notice, but to a dozen... such a drop would have been noticeable, indeed. So to cover her tracks she'd put the Cloak back on for a few days, just long enough for us to forget exactly what her signature felt like, so that when she took it off and her vibrational fingerprint reappeared, it would be much harder for me or Tabitha to notice the difference." His demonstration over, the wizard turned back to Michael. "Please carry on…"

Michael got up to stretch his legs as he resumed his explanation. "All that to say, I was expecting Amariel's Cloak to be nearby the dark mage wherever he or she may be… Fast forward to the final battle. I'm standing a few feet behind the director and Ezekiel disguised as the warden when she decides to take off her jacket. The second she did so, she turned to Ezekiel with piercing eyes, and the wolverine instantly charges towards Ez. At that moment I realized the director was indeed the dark mage and that her jacket was no other than the Cloak of Amariel. As long as she wore it, she wasn't able to recognize Ezekiel since her magical powers were isolated from the rest of the world, but as soon as she took it off, she was able to see through Ezekiel's disguise and mentally communicated the information to the wolverine, also known as Demetra."

"Wait a minute…" said Sheila. "I get why Amariel couldn't recognize Ez with her Cloak on, but what about Demetra? Why didn't she recognize him earlier?"

"Because our friend is a trickster," replied Michael. "He did what he told me he would never ever do. He bottled up his own aura. That's why he seemed to have disappeared and not even the high-born elves could locate him."

"That's right, I did… I used the crystal handle of the warden's cane to store my aura. A receptacle that presented the advantage of always being close at hand and easily breakable in case of need… I broke it to recover my powers the second Amariel recognized me. I had hoped my trick would deceive her as well, but she was simply too powerful and saw right through it."

"Anyway, from that point on, it was obvious the director's jacket was the Cloak of Amariel and since she'd carelessly asked one of the DSA agents to hold onto it, it was fairly easy to retrieve in the heat of the battle. The Cloak can take any appearance, but I didn't have the skills to tailor it in any way. When I put it on, it simply picked up on my praeternatural nature and turned into a bear pelt."

"My big teddy bear is smarter than he looks," teased Sheila.

"If he were really smart, he wouldn't have let himself be captured by the DSA in the first place…" said the wizard.

"I didn't get captured just to rescue Daka's packmates, old gizzard! I was looking for you and getting captured was the easiest way to see if you were inside. I figured I'd always be able to break out of there if need be. I hadn't planned on being transferred to the training camp the very next day, though."

"So you thought I'd be at the DSA's detention center, did you?"

"You were at their training camp, weren't you? That's close enough…"

"And what led you to believe I'd be there?"

"You, of course. You'd told me to go find Gwendolyn if anything happened to you. And you'd told Gwendolyn where the detention center was located. What was I to believe?"

"I just leaked the information to Gwendolyn so you'd know where the skinwalkers were kept prisoner if anything happened to me. At the time I didn't know they'd be transferred as well. I implanted that dream in your mind so that you'd think I was dead and wouldn't go looking for me."

"You did that? So you were the one who attacked me that night?" Michael was flabbergasted by the revelation.

"I didn't *attack* you, I implanted a minor suggestion in your subconscious and placed a protection on you so that you'd be able to resist the diadem's impulse if need be."

"That's why the commands I received from the bloody thing were so easy to ignore…"

"You're welcome!"

"Well… I thought you wanted me at the center because you'd figured out the dark mage was behind the DSA and you'd gone there to ambush her in case she showed up."

"I did! But I hadn't planned on you figuring that out…"

"Gentlemen," said Sheila, "I'm sure you could go round and round all day with this, but I have a plane to catch."

"And I have a ride to give," added Olivia, standing up and grabbing her car keys from the wooden table beside the bench.

Goodbyes were exchanged and soon Michael and the wizard found themselves alone on the porch.

Ez stared at his friend a moment before asking, "She doesn't know, does she?"

"I don't know what you mean," lied Michael.

"You haven't told Sheila… I guess I can see why you wouldn't."

"I don't see the point. It wasn't her fault. She had no idea she was Amariel's spy."

"True. But how did you figure it out?" asked Ez, looking at Michael suspiciously.

"Dariel believed there was a spy among our group, and your behavior made it pretty clear you believed it too."

"What do you mean by that?"

"You were very careful with the information you gave us, almost reluctant… You even engaged in disinformation campaigns. For example, you told us not once but twice that you were the only remaining member of the Second Circle. The second time was when you introduced yourself to Nayati and Kimama. I thought it was an odd choice of words at the time. You usually introduce yourself as Ezekiel, wizard of the Second Circle… But in that instance you were trying to broadcast Tabitha's death to as many potential spies as possible because you didn't know who the spy really was. You couldn't even trust me with the truth—that Tabitha was alive and well because she'd carried the Soul Catcher in her pocket when she was attacked."

"You're just showing off now…"

Michael smiled. "Maybe a little… Bottom line is, we had a spy among us. Someone who, among other things, informed the dark mage that the Healing Stone was being transferred… After our undisclosed position was attacked by vampires in Yellowstone, there were only four suspects left on my list. Only four of us could have leaked both pieces of information: Daka, Sheila, Olivia and myself. I hadn't leaked the info and it seemed impossible one of the others would be a traitor, but then I remembered the curse you'd placed on Jason. The spell that allowed you to spy through his eyes and ears without him knowing a thing about it. That got me thinking. What if one of us was an unwilling spy? With this in mind, I considered which one of us four was the most likely suspect and Sheila was the obvious answer. She'd been in DSA custody after they arrested her at the airport when she got back from France four months ago. And since I knew the DSA and the dark mage were two faces of the same coin, it meant she very well could have been bewitched during her detention."

"Yes, I suspect that's when it happened," said the wizard, nodding slowly.

"To test my hypothesis, I told Sheila precisely how I intended to infiltrate the detention center but didn't mention a thing to anyone else. When the DSA goons fell on me as soon as I showed up at the center, it was obvious they'd been expecting me. My last remaining doubt vanished; Sheila was indeed the spy, even though she had no idea she was."

"I agree with you. There's no need for her to know that."

Michael walked to the edge of the porch and, peering at the horizon, said, "The big fallout between you and Dariel after Leka's funeral… it was staged, wasn't it?"

"It was. We simply wanted the spy to transfer the information to the dark mage."

"I can't believe I didn't realize it at the time." Michael was shaking his head in disbelief. "And Vulpe used a similar trick when he told the Western Covenant his forces were joining the dark mage."

"It sure looks that way. His vamps engaged their American cousins the minute the battle started."

Michael nodded and glanced at his watch. "Looks like it's time to get back to work… My shift starts in half an hour."

"Then I'll be on my way. Take care of yourself, old friend."

"I'll see you around, Ez."

The End

A word from the author

I hope you enjoyed this book, and I wanted to thank you for being one of my readers.

With over 300,000 books published in the US every year, new authors face an uphill battle when it comes to making their work visible to the public. So, if you enjoy my stories, I would greatly appreciate if you could help me get the word out.

If you believe Michael Biörn deserves to be discovered by a wider audience, please tell your friends about the books. This would make a real difference and help me publish more stories at a faster pace. Even a simple post on social media or liking my Michael Biörn Novels Facebook page would make a significant difference.

Of course, if you truly love these novels and decided to write a brief review for any of the books on Amazon, I'd be eternally grateful. Whatever you choose to do, thanks again for reading my stories; it means a lot to me.

Thanks,
Marc

Michael's back story

Download your free copy at:

http://bit.ly/MichaelBiornBackStory

Marc Daniel

After spending significant amounts of time in Ohio, France, and Montana, Marc is currently living in Houston with his wife, daughter and three dogs.

When he's not writing, cooking dinner or playing with his dogs, Marc enjoys woodworking, going to the theater and escaping the city to reconnect with nature.

Contact information:
marc@marcdaniel-books.com
www.marcdaniel-books.com
https://www.facebook.com/MichaelBiornNovels
@MarcDanielBooks

Printed in Great Britain
by Amazon